BODY SHOTS

A Contemporary Journal of New Short Fiction

PUBLISHERS
Alex Oleszewski
Cliff Hensley   Cori Hart

EDITING, TYPESETTING, LAYOUT and DESIGN
Cliff Hensley

COVER PHOTO
Heidi Lynn

Published annually in October, Body Shots is a publication of Subtle Body Press:

Alex Oleszewski | CEO
Cliff Hensley | Managing Director, Editor-in-Chief
Cori Hart | Creative Director, Senior Designer

VOLUME I, FALL 2024 EDITION, October 15, 2024

ISBN 979-8-9854370-4-1 (paperback)
ISBN 979-8-9854370-5-8 (ebook)

Library of Congress Cataloging-in-Publication Data available upon request.

Subtle Body Press, LLC
7901 4th St N STE 8671, St. Petersburg, FL, 33702
www.subtlebodypress.com

A letter from the Editor:

GENRE IS A CONSTRUCT.

GENRE DOES NOT EXIST.

Welcome to Body Shots,

Cliff Hensley

CONTENTS

NAMING RITES

Joe Nazare

Penthouse at Babel. A Common Anomaly. Aneurhythms. The Cthulhigans, Backwash Mimosas, and Panic Groom. Donner Party Favors and Curbing Cerberus. Muse Abuse.

If the scuttlebutt was gospel truth, then Baptwist had launched the careers of every last group.

Bands in a separate stratosphere status-wise from the Gimps. We were comparative neophytes, scrabbling at the base of the rock world and goggling up at its distant peaks. Every Thursday and third Saturday, we tunneled into Manhattan to perform at Ephemeral City down on the Bowery. We played mostly covers (everything from Nirvana and Green Day and Motorhead to Triumph and Sublime), with a handful of originals mixed in, including our set-closer: "Harder Than You Think," an anthem to unrequited lust stocked with enough double entendre to fill an entire AC/DC album.

The owner of Ephemeral City, Fat Lou (so-called for the bankroll in his pocket, not the flab on his belly), saw something in us. He liked our sound. Our stage presence. But hated our name, as he never hesitated to admit. I was slowly coming around to his view, realizing that an outdated Tarantino allusion would only carry us so far. We needed some cachet to cash in.

So my ears pricked up with the first mention of Baptwist, one night as we were packing up our gear. Fat Lou said the guy could work wonders in terms of giving a fledgling group a real boost. "A manager, you mean?" I asked.

"Nah, more like a designator."

But that's all Fat Lou shared before a phone call pulled him away. Intrigued, I proceeded to ask around the club and got mostly blank stares. There were random hits, though, people who'd heard of Baptwist and his alleged influence. Like "Memento" Maury Jacobs, E.C.'s resident bookkeeper. Geoff ("'Get off' without the T," he clarified whenever introducing himself) Gelb, events promoter. The barmaid Marian claimed that Baptwist had been the one to name Gothicmonger. "Or maybe it was Koppelgänger," she second-guessed herself.

Talcum X (as I'd affectionately dubbed the Nordic hulk who worked the door and always dressed in all black, from ballcap to jackboots) appeared the best versed in Baptwist lore. According to the milky militant, Baptwist's magic touch extended across the music industry. He'd denominated headbangers like Tinnitus Spite and Parental Horning; race rockers (Get with the Pogrom) as well as gangsta rappers (Prez Dispenser); punk groups such as Bane of Jane and their all-female answer, Girls Gone Riled; shock rockers (Leprotica, Gruetuity) and even a Vegas lounge act (Fastidious Sid and the Nitpickers).

There was a definite edge to most of the names accredited to Baptwist. Maybe he'd say that he was just catering to modern decadence. After all, ours was a generation where CCR stood for Carrie's Class Reunion, and the Bee Gees were Beer Goggle Gorgeous.

Most importantly, the man's coinages were *memorable*: they struck a chord and stuck with you. Something, it grew more and more obvious, "The Gimps" simply would never do. Seeking significant change, we bought into the Baptwismal mystique and began to haunt Fat Lou to hook us up. Perhaps just to shut us up, he said he'd see if he could arrange something the next time Baptwist was back in town.

Eventually, Fat Lou delivered. And so there we were that Sunday midday, standing in the hallway of a Bleecker Street walk-up, ready to be rebranded.

If I'm going to treat this as an actual narrative—and not just some diaristic scribble that my lighter might make a burnt offering of in the end—I guess I should formally introduce the Gimps. I was on bass, Pat played the guitar (we both shared vocal duties), and Tommy played the drums. They were cousins to each other, and almost like family to me since I had no relatives left alive that were inclined to connect with me. We'd been jamming together since high school. I'd just turned twenty-four, a part-time college student who yearned for eternal rock 'n' roll stardom.

Making a fist, I knuckled the metal-plated door of apartment 2B. My hand continued to thrum when I lowered it to my side. I tried to calm my nerves by downplaying the heralded labeler about to be encountered. C'mon, how intimidating could Baptwist really be? His own name made him sound like some Dickens castoff, like a figure from a Bible story told by Elmer Fudd.

My knock went unanswered for a good thirty seconds. At that point, Pat took a turn and the opportunity to recite, with a Green Jelly growl, "*Little pig, little pig, let me in.*"

Pat's bit drew the predictable response from his sidekick: a chuckle, cousin Tommy's characteristic form of expression. But it only brought a frown to my face. This was a potentially momentous day in the history of our band, and these two—who'd split a case of Rolling Rock before we headed out to the city—were treating the scheduled meeting as some lark.

At last, the door drew open and instantly confounded my expectations. I'd envisioned someone akin to Sammi Curr, not Riff Raff.

On my proudest day, I could claim to be of average height, but saw clearly now over the top of Baptwist's head, which was fringed by dishwater-blonde strands. His hair constituted the least of his thinning: the guy looked like Iggy Pop on a hunger strike. The arms poking from the sleeves of his Koffin T-shirt were a pair of broomsticks creped in skin.

Baptwist just stood there, fixing us with his sea-green eyes and craggy visage. The seconds accreted awkwardness, and I fought hard not to fidget.

But Pat was flush with liquid courage. "You gonna let us in or what?" he wanted to know.

Baptwist eyeballed Pat for several beats, then bared a mouthful of sallow pegs. "So you must be the lead Gimp," he rasped and turned from the doorway.

Great start we were off to here. Baptwist was going to think the three of us were the prime ingredients in an asshole casserole. Lips pursed, I glared "Be cool" at Pat and Tommy as I stepped inside ahead of them.

A pungent haze of cigarette smoke permeated the room, issuing with fog-machine ease. My watering eyes struggled to adjust to the gloom, to take in the furnishing of that shoebox of a studio space. The pieces on display would have made a Salvation Army store look like a Raymour and Flanagin. Next to a single, paint-flaking folding chair leaned a lopsided card table. Its centerpiece was a cairn of crushed butts, erected in a jar-lid ashtray.

With a jut of his cleft chin, Baptwist directed us to sit down on a futon shrouded in a stain-dappled sheet. An unfinished plywood shelf protruded from the wall behind the sofa-bed. It managed to bear the weight of a group of paperbacks, horizontally tiered in the absence of bookends: *Please Kill Me: The Uncensored Oral History of Punk, Southern Gods, Born to Run, Spider Kiss, The Armageddon Rag.* The first one I also owned a copy of and had read to shreds; the last two just made me think of my ex-girlfriend Krista.

"Yo, check it out." Pat picked up an easel-backed picture frame from the same shelf. It contained a reproduction of the cover of the Nippleslips' self-titled debut: the band members standing with black bars strategically superimposed chest-level on their loose-buttoned blouses and V-neck tops. The girls, who made the Pussycat Dolls look like a pack of ugly mutts, were a paparazzo's wet dream, and sexstruck admirers kept a constant lookout, hoping to catch a rosy glimpse of truth in advertising. Perhaps not coincidentally, the Nippleslips' current Peekaboom Tour had sold out nationwide.

The picture had a line of handwriting added to it: *Thanks B—We owe you **Big Time**!!!* The scrawl was signed "Ola," as in lead singer Ola Schoën, presumably.

Something other than envy bothered me about the picture. In this spartanly decorated apartment, it had all the conspicuousness of a prop. Still, I cringed when Pat, butterfingered numbnuts that he was, let the frame slip from his hand and crash face down on the shelf.

"Whoops." Pat uprighted the picture, resetting it in an approximation of its original position.

Baptwist, thankfully, ignored the faux pas. Having seated himself at the card table, he lifted a smoldering, gold-filtered cancer stick to his lips, then blew a grayish plume out the corner of his mouth. "That old greaseball over at Ephemeral City tells me you boys are hotter than a urophile for a christening," he said as we dropped down onto the futon.

How do you respond to a prompt like that? "Uh, yeah," I tried, "Fat Lou—Mr. Giulia—says you're the man to see. We've heard that you jumpstarted a lot of groups, like Metal's Mantle. Skifoosa Resort. Avenged Sevenfold."

"That last one wasn't me," Baptwist admitted, sounding truly rueful. Without taking his eyes from us, he picked up a black flair pen with his left hand and began inking words on the top page of a disheveled stack of sheets that had been torn from a legal pad. It was a neat, if vaguely unsettling, parlor trick.

"So how does this work exactly?" Nobody at the club had mapped out this get-together for us, and I felt a need to get some bearings.

"How it works is that I come up with what I deem to be a suitable name. Emphasis on the singular: this isn't Macy's dressing room where you can keep trying on items 'til you find something you like. You're offered one appellation, take it or leave it."

"And if we decide to take it, then what—platinum records and Grammys forever after?"

Baptwist answered with a question of his own. "You boys ever hear of Lemming Drop?" When we shook our heads, he waved his hand (the cigarette-gripping right) as if to say, "And there you have it."

"Don't go mistaking this," our gravel-voiced host elaborated, "for some Robert-Johnson-at-the-crossroads nonsense. We're talking marketing here, not the magical awarding of talent." As he spoke, he persisted with the automatic-writing routine. Somehow, he sensed when it was time to swipe the listing aside and uncover a clean sheet. "I make no guarantee of fame and fortune. All I do is try to optimize your chance of making a mark. Remember the prime theorem of pop culture: if enough people stop to sniff, it doesn't matter if it's monkey dung."

No promised key to the proverbial kingdom, then, just a handle to latch onto—for fans and perhaps the band as well. Glancing over my shoulder at that Nippleslips photo, I wondered if the real crux of Baptwist's verbal genius lay in the establishment of an identity for the christened group. An identity that in turn sparked further creation: the front man for the newly-declared Pox Americana decides to reimage himself as Peter Pandemic (and then compose a concept album called "National Anathema"); the initiates of Afflicionado fire off songs with inspired titles like "Outlet Maul," "Thrash Behavior," and "Hence Malevolence."

I kept probing for a catch, though. "And what do you get out of the deal?"

"There's a tithe, of course," Baptwist said.

Pat's brow furrowed. "A tithe?" he repeated. If he ever came across the word written down, his mumbling lips probably would have turned it into a homophone for "titty." I hate to say that my buddy wasn't very cultured, but for Pat, Homer was a Simpson, Beethoven a St. Bernard, and ballroom represented the advantage of boxers over briefs.

Baptwist succinctly defined his term. "I get a ten percent cut from the first record contract you sign."

"Okay," Pat said, but apparently still struggled to comprehend. "Shouldn't you be, like, filthy rich, then? And livin' in luxury…" He didn't mask his disdain as his eyes wandered across the man's apartment.

"Instead of a glorified crack den?" Baptwist finished for him. A smirk fishhooked his lips. "Not everybody feels a need to flaunt their possessions. Certain neighborhoods, it pays to lag behind the Joneses."

His focus on us unwavering, Baptwist continued to scratch words with his pen. I felt self-conscious as a patient watching his shrink jot down session notes.

A perceived flaw in Baptwist's business model also nagged at me. "But what about the Lemming Drops of the world? The groups who never get signed to a label?" I doubted that this Wicked Wit of the West Village merely worked on spec.

"Up front, everyone does pay a nominal fee, so to speak," Baptwist said. "As a gesture of commitment: a surrendering of something held precious."

"Like what?" I asked, wariness flaring as I pictured Baptwist's wallet stuffed with other people's organ donor cards.

"That I leave up to the candidates to decide. Over the years, I've been given pieces of jewelry. Favorite jackets. Family heirlooms. A woman once handed over the urn containing her dog's ashes." Baptwist flashed a conspiratorial leer. "Another guy parted with Polaroids of his wife—shots of her riding cowgirl way back when. Before she got saddled with gestational diabetes. An aspiring hair-metal band had me buzz each one of them peach-fuzzed as army draftees."

Snickering, Pat combed his fingers back through his flowing auburn mane. "Man, I ain't lettin' you touch a hair on this head."

"Much rather have me lavish attention on a different head, eh?"

The levity drained straightaway from Pat's face. "The hell d'you just say?"

"Oh, I'm sure you heard me, sweetheart." Baptwist made an "O" of his mouth and suggestively bulged his cheek with rapid pokes of his tongue.

Pat didn't rise to the bait; he launched himself at it like a blitzing middle linebacker on third-and-long. The inescapable sack sent Baptwist toppling backward, upending the rickety table in the process. Yellow sheets flew up, then fluttered to the floor like mammoth confetti.

A few seconds too late, I sprang from the futon myself. Pleading my berserker bandmate's name, I tried to pull him off his sudden adversary. All I could think was that if the teasing Baptwist had been testing us, the Gimps were failing miserably.

Pat's wailing arms continued to elude my grasp. I swung my head around. Spotted Tommy standing there staring at his feet as if embarrassed by his cousin's brutishness.

"Help me for chrissakes!" My cry snapped Tommy to attention. He darted forward, and together, we disentangled Pat, yanking him to his feet.

"*Goddamn freak.*" Pat punctuated the pronouncement with a wad of hocked phlegm. And still, his rage wasn't mitigated. He cocked back his left, Lugzencased foot and booted Baptwist—who'd just drawn himself up onto his hands and knees—across the jaw.

The smack of steel-toed leather against flesh was awful, but what followed sounded even worse: a pebbly rattling down onto the room's scarred hardwood. An anguished groan, my own, added to the discord.

"Let's get the hell outta here," I told Pat and Tommy, shoving both of them toward the door. I followed right on their clomping heels.

Before exiting, I ventured one last carnage-gauging look over my shoulder. Baptwist had been knocked onto his scrawny haunches by Pat's blow but now sat up cross-legged. He stared at the puddle in front of him, studying the scattering of tooth shards as if they were a set of mystic runes. His lips were peeled back from his pink-drool-oozing mouth, and for the life of me, I couldn't tell if he was grimacing—or grinning.

"Alright, man. Thanks." Pat tapped the end-call icon on his cell, then ballooned his cheeks in an extended exhale.

"Whatdidhesay?" I blurted, looming over his shoulder.

For three days straight, we'd been holed up in my basement apartment, saturating it with the vinegary stench of stress sweat. Gradually, we realized the police weren't going to ram through the door and haul us in for aggravated assault. But that still didn't mean we were home free.

"Talcum says he just got done hanging the flyers for our next show," Pat relayed, "and that Fat Lou's been cheery as can be all week."

This was incredible news, infinitely preferable to the scenario I'd been picturing: Fat Lou—apoplectic over the fiasco at Baptwist's—calling up his goombahs down in Little Italy and booking us a trip to the Meadowlands inside a Cadillac's trunk. The Gimps meet Jimmy Hoffa.

Pat ratta-tat-tatted the kitchen table with his palms. "Sounds to me, boys, like we're in the clear."

"Yeah, well, we're damned lucky, you hot-headed asshole," I said, taking the tennis ball that I'd been compulsively squeezing and now threw it at the back of my friend's precious-locked noggin.

The thwonk of the rebounding ball elicited a chuckle from across the room. Tommy sat indenting my green-suede sofa, flipping through an old *Rolling Stone*—the one with Passionista posed mostly unclothed on the cover.

"Think that's funny, hobbit-crotch?" But Pat, clearly awash in relief, couldn't keep a straight face himself.

I have to admit, I felt no less alleviated, albeit slightly chagrined by the recognition that the iron band cinched around my chest for the past seventysomething hours had been self-forged. I'd magnified the potential fallout from what went down in that smoke-bombed hovel. Just like I'd built up Baptwist into too big a figure. This was no industry insider; at best, only some eccentric wordsmith. And maybe a complete phony, ultimately. I started to wonder if the denizens of Ephemeral City had sent us out on the music-biz equivalent of a snipe hunt. The supposed career-boosting renaming could've been just a prank, an initiation ritual that had gotten a little out of hand. No true harm done in the end—except, of course, for the instant extraction of some unfortunate role-player's nicotine-tinged Chiclets.

The guy's dental bill could be coming out of our purse the next time Fat Lou reached into his pocket, but such a price to pay felt like a steep discount at that moment. Granted, I might've overreacted by dreading a double tap from a button man; still, the sense of having dodged a bullet was undeniable. Some serious life affirmation seemed in order. "Whatta you say we get out of this crypt and go get shitfaced?" I proposed to Pat and Tommy.

They didn't say nay, so we relocated to the Pleasure Chest, where we devoted ourselves to tipping back drinks and tipping strippers one strategically placed dollar at a time. In the middle of our fifth round, I sat drumming my foot on the rung of my barstool as Kid Rock's "So Hott" provided an appropriate soundtrack to the onstage gyrations. Yessir, I was feeling finer than French wine when a buzz-killing thought bubbled up from the dregs.

I realized the three of us were right back at square one. "Hey, you know," I told the other two Gimps bracketing me, "we still have to figure out a new name for the group."

Pat nodded, then added: "Yeah, I didn't want to bring it up when we thought our heads were on the chopping block. But I've got some ideas. Check it out." His swiping hand hung the name on an imaginary marquee: "'Eight Inch Putts.'"

"Sounds like a tribute band that doesn't measure up to Nine Inch Nails," I said.

Pat's thoughts kept chugging down the same track. "How about: 'Anacondoms.'" Barely had the concoction spilled from his mouth, though, when he appeared to grasp the ridiculousness of branding ourselves prophylactics. "Anhh," he vetoed his own proposal. Frowning, he took a swig of Coors Light and marked me with the bottleneck on the way down. "This kinda shit's supposed to be *your* strong suit."

True, I served as the group's lyricist. But composing songs—or culling titles from those verses—was a whole other ballgame than trying to seize upon the right signifier for the band itself. If it was that simple, I already would have supplanted "The Gimps." As Pat had just proven, some sophomoric pun or inane portmanteau wasn't going to cut it.

"Right," I grumbled. I spent the next few minutes in sullen introspection, oblivious to booming music and nude bosoms. Particular verbal skill was called for here; the chosen name had to have both precision and resonance. I reflected on the various laureates I was studying for my Intro to Poetry class at Rutgers-Newark, their penchant for finding the perfect words and ordering them for the greatest impact. As I sat pondering poetic genius, I drifted tangentially to a thought of the paper on Eliot I still needed to churn out by midterm. And then, sudden as a tsunami, it hit me, inspiration surging past inebriation.

"I got it!" I announced, straightening up from my slump. "We could call ourselves 'Adverse Libre.'" Reading the incomprehension splashed across my friends' faces, I quickly added: "You know, a twist on 'free verse,' with a nice hint of antagonism thrown in."

"Yeah," Pat said, "the legions of English majors who flock to Ephemeral City will love us."

His rebuff promptly empurpled my ego, and the sense of insult was compounded by the sound of Tommy's yucking appreciation. Pat's sarcasm was one thing, but damned if I was going to just sit there and be mocked by Harry Laconic, Jr. "I don't hear any brilliance spilling from your lips," I said, side-eying Tommy.

Knowing him like I did, I didn't expect much in the way of articulated response. That's why I was so surprised when Tommy said, "Actually, I might've come up with something."

My eyebrows arching, I swiveled around to face him. Pat spoke over my shoulder: "Hmph, can't wait to hear this."

Our joint scrutiny stalled Tommy, who sat momentarily mute. He swallowed, and his bobbing Adam's apple brought up the promised bon mot: "Trimordial."

Now *I* was the one who lacked the ability to speak. The name was oddly powerful, suggesting prominence and originality. Its accented prefix also made it a perfect fit for a three-man band. Tommy's seizing on such a clever handle was astonishing. "How the hell d'you come up with that?" I asked him at last.

His initial response was to drop his gaze. The bar's darkness made it hard to tell if his cheeks were crimsoning. "Last night I couldn't sleep," he muttered. "I was flipping through the channels on your TV and heard some mumbo jumbo about 'primordial ooze' on one of the science shows." His eyes sought mine. "Think it's a lousy name?"

I belched laughter. After all the nonsense we'd gone through, who knew that the solution to our name problem lay in nothing more esoteric than Tommy watching something other than sports or porn. "It's a *kick-ass name*." I practically had to shout my declaration as the Kiss classic "Heaven's on Fire" came raining down from the speakers. "Sounds like 'The Gimps' can finally be retired."

Turning to check Pat's reaction, I found him bobble-heading agreement. "Okay, c'mon," I said, gesturing for the cousins to lean in closer. We reached out and tiered our hands like huddled teammates.

One, two, three: "Trimordial!" we pronounced ourselves.

And the rest is mystery.

Who knows why we started to flourish: Coincidence? Natural progression? Placebo effect? Maybe calling ourselves gimps had unconsciously handicapped us, and now we sensed greater freedom, a broader possibility. Whatever the reason, the needle moved.

For starters, we were motivated to compose more songs of our own and stop being so reliant on covers. We also designed a band logo to splash on prospective merch: a muscle-roped arm thrusting a trident from roiling waters. This burst of creativity brought newfound confidence, and we decided to spread out into fresh venues (Trimordial never entered Ephemeral City). After a howling tune called "Hyde in Plain Sight" consistently drew the most favorable crowd response during our sets, we uploaded a performance video of the song to YouTube. It steadily accumulated views and likes and enthusiastic commentary.

The generated buzz helped get us college radio airplay and then an invite to Band Madness in Indianapolis, a month-long battle structured along the lines of the NCAA Tournament. We advanced three rounds before getting knocked out in the Elite 8 but ended up being the first ones approached backstage that late March night. Thick-bearded, burly, but affable, Alan Shantyman was a scout for Massive Aggressive, an indie label on the rapid upswing. Alan left with our demo and got right back to us three days later, saying that his bosses wanted to fly the band out to Los Angeles for a face-to-face. "Which means they're damned serious about signing you guys," he added.

A virtual whirlwind encircled us; we happily scrambled to pack for the trip. Lacking official representation, we secured (via videoconference) the services of a West Coast entertainment lawyer: the slickly dressed, clearly bullshit-intolerant Mick Cammon, who'd allow us to emerge with our anal cherries intact should any deal—handshake or Hancocked—be struck at the scheduled meeting.

The label set us up at the Westin Bonaventure. We busied ourselves with enjoying our stay but kept the debauchery relatively in check (if everything went well with Massive Aggressive the next morning, we'd party like Mötley Crüe at Mardi Gras). A Whip Hand song played from a docked iPod, but at a volume several levels below eardrum-lancing. Beer bottles modeled a tinted-glass fusillade atop the coffee table. I dragged away on a bomber joint, inhaling contentment.

To my left, Pat sat spending quality time with his latest "cocksure girl"—his designation for a certain type of female never hesitant to test the equipment. For all I know, he wasn't trying to be cute and thought that's what the adjective actually meant.

This one boasted a big silver tongue-stud—a Frankenstein neck-bolt repurposed. She had a pretty, heart-shaped face and looked like she was smuggling a couple of grade-D grapefruits under her pink halter top. Still, I would've preferred that Pat take the girl over to one of the suite's beds rather than have her demonstrate her skills at the foot of the leather sectional we all occupied.

Emission accomplished, Frankentongue drew back, and Pat hiked up his pants. He looked at me and nodded toward the girl, but uninterested in slurpy seconds, I waved off the offering. On the other side of me, Tommy was too preoccupied with his own score to pay anybody else any attention.

When the brunette moved to climb into Pat's lap, he immediately pushed her away. "Okay, babe," he told her, "I'll give you a call real soon." He'd just met her tonight, and they both knew he didn't have her number. "In the meantime, why don't you go gargle about a gallon of Listerine."

Huffing, the girl stood and stormed out of the suite, salting the air with obscenity as she went.

Grinning as if complimented, Pat levered out his seat's footrest. His cousin, meanwhile, leaned forward and nose-Dysoned the single line of coke he'd dusted across the coffee table. Springing up tall, he war-chanted: "Trimordial!" His extending arm jabbed three forked fingers skyward.

I laughed at his antics and took another hit of my joint. Giddy and giggly, Tommy bounced in his seat as if mounted on a Hippity Hop. "Hey. Hey guys. Wanna hear something funny?" He didn't wait for confirmation. "It wasn't no lame-ass nature show."

I could feel the smile on my face twist out of shape. Because terrible intuition (on some mental sublevel, had I always suspected?) clued me in on what my friend was about to admit. All at once, it seemed vital that the normally reticent Tommy just STOP TALKING.

Panic jacked up my heart rate. Made it feel as if I had an angry fist trying to pound through the drywall of my chest. Regular breathing revved toward hyperventilation in a nanosecond. My panting equivalent of *oh-shit-oh-shit* sounded wavecrash loud inside my head, but failed to drown out a quick electronic hiss.

I wrenched my gaze toward the doorway of our suite, desperate to verify that it was only Frankentongue returning to retrieve her purse or some other forgotten accessory. Of course, it wasn't the cocksure girl, or any other would-be groupie, crossing the threshold. It was a ghost from our not-distant-enough past, appearing in the scraggly flesh.

Over a Cheap Trick tee and blue jeans, Baptwist wore a black leather duster that flared cape-like behind him as he stalked straight toward us. His motorcycle boots couldn't have added more than a couple of inches to his height, yet the diminutive figure loomed dauntingly tall from my vantage point, and I couldn't help but note that neither of his bony hands grasped a keycard.

Hotel staff swiped him in, I tried to tell myself. Who knew the connections this guy had, how deeply he was tapped into the whole La La Land scene. Even more disconcerting than the fact that Baptwist had tracked us down at last was the thought that he had known where to find us all along and had simply lain in wait until the moment for vengeance turned syrupy sweet, here on the eve of Trimordial's big break.

As he stopped and stood over us, I could see that he sported a full set of chompers once more. Part of me wondered if the teeth had been re-grown rather than replaced; in either case, they were already discolored the yellow of a deodorant-stained undershirt. Baptwist's grin was large as a shark's, and just as deceiving. Any semblance of mirth was belied by the rest of his demeanor, which oozed contempt. The tacit denigration was unmistakable: *You goddamn Gimps.*

Logy from booze and orgasm, Pat just slouched there with heavy-lidded eyes, making no reaction whatsoever to the intrusion. To the other side of me, Tommy sat upright and vibrant, his coke- or fear-fueled tremors turning the sectional into a seeming locus of poltergeist activity. As for me, my bladder felt like a swollen water balloon about to burst.

Baptwist's stare bored into me, and the words began to reel down before my mind's eye, closing credits on 4X rewind.

Lazarus Just Lazy

Replenishing Druids

Coquette Mallet

Rehab Reject

Month of Mayhem

Everybody in Effigy

The Old Man and the Seizure

Shivving Kit

Cameltoe Cameo

It Takes a Pillage

Guano from Heaven

Adversatile

It was a silent litany of sex and drugs, death and violence, and general grotesquerie.

Roanoke Colonic

God Fodder, Too

Rental Floss

Strays in Vegas

Snot Rocket Science

Albatross Ascot

The Macabre Republic

Apostasy Creed

Kong of Bongs

Scofflaw School

Grimoire for Dummies

The verbal blitzkrieg continued. Helpless immobility trumped my desire to draw into a fetal curl.

Nightmare Ally

Inhuman Conditioned

Banshee Karaoke

The Foxhole Atheists
Meth Labyrinth
Neuroses Are Blue
Squalor Splendor
Rampage of Aquarius
Canonical Sexts
Grandeur Indictment
Resting Witch Face
Vegetative Statesmen
Lobster Boy Band
Scarlet-Letter Day

The names kept coming, an accelerating cascade, crashing to and piling up on the base of my consciousness like Tetris blocks. A single thought overlaid the rubble: When it came to sick puppies, this sonuvabitch was Cujo, and we had gone and rattled his chain.

Snuff Film Outtakes
Oedipal Arrangements
The Perp Walks
Atrophy Wife
Scat's in the Cradle
'Caust Effective
Derivative Sinner
Carrion Items
Catamites for Michael
Evening Noose
Least of Eden
Graverobber Barons
Trysts Beat Fists
Kick the Abbott
Hexarcana
Knievel Ways
Dearth Merchants

In for Infamy

Perversion Therapy

Vendetta Yen

Glory Road Rash

Site of Blood

And the last name to drop:

Trimordial

The mental contact broke joltingly. Unhesitating, Baptwist reached out, his long, splayed fingers reminding me of the facehugger in *Alien*. But it wasn't me about to be Hurt. Palming the front of Tommy's head instead, Baptwist casually stiff-armed him back into the sectional's cushions.

He withdrew his hand and held it up as if swearing an oath. The lines etched into his palm had filled in neatly, forming an intricate network of crimson tributaries.

"And darkness and decay," he intoned. I was too stoned—too petrified—to catch the Poe quote at that instant. Baptwist turned his head and pinned me with his green glare. It blazoned to peak animosity, a solar flare from a star that paradoxically sucked all warmth from the universe. Only utter desperation, that cringing instinct towards self-protection, enabled me to tear my eyes off him.

A peripheral rustling suggested that Baptwist was on the move, heading back whence he came. As I sat there gathering my devastated wits, Tommy sharpened into focus beside me. He lay in the same position in which Baptwist had left him. The bloodspring from his nostrils had already started to crust on his upper lip.

"Tommy!" A vaguely registered door slam coincided with my screech. Trimordial's drummer paid me no mind. He was too intent on staring a thousand yards past the space Baptwist had vacated.

The coroner ruled "drug overdose." By the time we buried Tommy, Pat almost had me believing it was true.

"You didn't see shit," he clarified for me mid-freakout on the morning after the incident. "There wasn't any boogeyman invading our hotel room." When I kept insisting on a murderous visitor, he gruffly countered: "Then how come you never mentioned anything to the cops?"

Baptwist's marrow-riming final look crystallized in my imagination.

"Because you saw jack-shit," Pat reiterated when I failed to voice an answer. Grim resolution sculpted his face. "Tommy OD'd. And we were both too wasted to even realize what was happening. End of story."

He sang that same dirge all week, as we flew back east and laid his cousin to rest. Pat was so adamant my own conviction steadily eroded. Maybe I *had* imagined Baptwist's reappearance. Maybe I'd sensed Tommy expiring there beside me in that suite and—brimming with stoner paranoia—had simply superimposed a nightmare on a really bad scene.

Pat's was no doubt the more rational explanation, and rationality held an incredible allure at that moment. So, the day after the funeral, I drove over to my bandmate's house to recant my horror report.

His mom had returned to work, I figured, but Pat would have nowhere to be but home. My jiggering of the doorbell, though, roused no response. Turning back down the front steps, I walked over to the driveway to check the garage. I could hear the low grumble of Pat's old Camaro as I approached, and instantly, my own body began to shimmy with trepidation. It took me several torturous seconds to steel myself, and then I pressed my face to one of the square glass panels lining the garage door.

The interior was storm-clouded with car exhaust.

All I could really make out at first was the pair of cherry-red taillights burning through the haze. The fumes failed to reach me on my side of the door, but I was choked with déjà vu, as the sight inside the garage reminded me of another foully-smogged room in a West Village apartment.

Staring into the swirling haze, I was able to glean further detail from the scene. A flannel-sleeved forearm angled out the driver's side window, with the palm twisted skyward and the fingers hooked into a claw. And my only thought upon discovery of the corpse was not that I'd lost a longtime friend—but that Trimordial had now been reduced to a solo act.

Sheer terror cattle-prodded me. Sent me running towards my car parked out front. I sped off like a getaway driver fueled with Red Bull, yet I couldn't distance myself from the questions proliferating in my head. Had Baptwist preceded me at Pat's house? Had I arrived too late—or nearly fatally early? Could that arrangement in the garage—the same spot where the Gimps had had their very first rehearsals—be all Pat's doing? Perhaps he'd simply fixed a carbon-monoxide cocktail to chase his own guilt. Because if Pat hadn't attacked Baptwist way back when, his cousin wouldn't have had the chance to peek at Baptwist's notes and take (in vain) one of his names. Tommy would've seen jack-shit.

But that one wayward glance carried us off, and way leads to way, and now I'm haunting a whole lot of roads less traveled. I left Pat's death and my former life behind me that day. Pointed my Eclipse south on the Turnpike and just kept going. Cliff-jumped right off the face of the earth, as far as anyone who'd ever known me was concerned.

Still, I didn't stay underground forever. Couldn't, really. Because I realized there was no outrunning unfinished business.

At some point, I resurfaced in a dive bar in Trenton, desperate for companionship and to feel the blast of live music. That's where I met Daryn, a strawberry-blonde bartender who gave a whole new meaning to fetching. Banter led to flirtation and, later that night, to pillow talk, during which she confessed to being an aspiring singer. So I told her about my own history (severely abridged version) in the biz. The next thing I knew, we were planning to start our own band.

And thirteen months after that, here we are. We play the Jersey Shore circuit, from the bars on the Point Pleasant boardwalk to the teen clubs way down in Wildwood. Modest venues all, and, honestly, as beneath us as Hades is the empyrean. Because this group brims with talent. Is already better than Trimordial ever was (or maybe had any right to be). Javier, a southpaw from North Plainfield, plays guitar like a Mexican Hendrix. Feely Dan has the Midas touch on the keyboard, never failing to produce gold notes. And Daryn doesn't just supply eye candy—as lead vocalist, she's even sweeter to the ear.

They're good kids, too, all three of them. But they keep pressing me—as the eldest and most experienced, I'm looked up to as the leader—to take the next step. Daryn, in particular, is always hounding me to book us better gigs. I temper her enthusiasm. Tell her that we have to work to perfect our act. And so the band plays on. And on and on.

What I wouldn't give to wipe away that pouty look Daryn gets any time I mouth platitudes about paying our dues. If I thought it safe to share fully, I'd let her know that we both crave the same level of success, that I'm tantalized by the near taste of the Big Time I had way back when in Los Angeles. And that my own past misfortune is the real reason we're still sharing billing with misfit outfits like Sharty Pants and Whiplash Mustache.

For all my status as de facto manager, I've always let the others dictate the type of music we compose and the specific songs we play. The only nonnegotiable when we first hooked up was that I'd be the one to christen the band. The trio looked jointly skeptical when I revealed what we'd be called, but no matter. They aren't the target audience; it isn't them I'm signaling whenever our name shows up on windshield flyers or in tiny ads in the backs of local papers. No, it's somebody else who I hope recognizes the gesture, and appreciates the sacrifice (lest he decide to make one of his own).

I pray there'll come a time when my penance is deemed complete, but until that fateful day Baptwist comes calling again, I'm prepared to persevere, to keep my group toiling in self-enforced obscurity:

Anonymust.

AN ECSTATIC CRY IS LIBERTY

Abhishek Sengupta

Abhishek Sengupta is imaginary. Mostly, people would want to believe he uses magical realism to write novels about world issues, even though he is stuck inside a window in Kolkata, India, but he knows none of it is true. He doesn't exist. Only his imaginary writing does and has appeared in some periodicals and anthologies around the globe, and won a few international prizes, including the Bristol Short Story Prize in 2023. If you're gifted, however, you may imagine him on Twitter/X @AbhishekSWrites.

ACT I

<u>Six Kitchen Knives</u>

If I told you I met Ipsha on the day the first fairy rained from the skies, you'd think it was either a conspiracy or a coincidence. But I'm speaking of a time when neither of those anomalies existed in Bishadnagar. The smiths, tailors, and carpenters in the kingdom hadn't yet learned (or had long forgotten) the art of crafting conspiracies and forging coincidences. More so because anomalies, in all forms and shapes, had been banned by the king. It was a time, rather, when Bishadnagar was true to its Bengali name: it was a veritable kingdom of gloom. If you were to assign any point of intersection between the beginnings of my wilful descent with Ipsha and the fairies' unwilful plummeting from the skies, you'd be better off choosing the gloom that enveloped the kingdom over everything else.

A jute trader like me wouldn't have met Ipsha had I not entangled myself in the ripple of her respiration. You mostly knew Ipsha was around when you heard her breathe. I didn't know that then. I didn't know that, on summer days, Ipsha's breathing was a dulcet melody that reminded you of a firebird flapping its wings, chasing away the dark rainclouds from the skies. When I heard it that time after I docked on the shores, I had little choice but to follow that melody into the Mahogany Jungle that surrounded Bishadnagar.

The wind that blows from the innards of the Mahogany Jungle can seize your arm, take you anywhere. But only if you let the jungle spread its roots in your conscious mind. Since I had allowed it, thanks to Ipsha, the jungle effortlessly pulled me into its phantasmagorical labyrinths.

Inside the jungle, the Mahogany Night lay waiting on a web it had spun between any two trees for a clueless drifter like me. Before I knew it, I had stepped into the dark and was utterly lost in its pitch-black viscosity. Thankfully, during one of my prior trips to Bishadnagar I had overheard someone sharing a catchphrase when discussing the Mahogany Jungle: Act quick when Night. The voice was wondrously worked up even for a tavern chat. "As soon as the Mahogany Night has swallowed you, show a presence of mind and a strong resolve to fight your way back into the morning. Find an escape, fast, because, gods forbid, if you stay in that Night for long, it'll spread around you like malaria. And before you know it, all exits will be flung so far afield from you that you'll never be able to cover as much ground as the ever-expanding Night does. You'd be trapped forever."

I fought right away. I fought as if the Mahogany Night was death personified. I threw my arms and legs until the motions felt like swimming. Yet my butterfly strokes didn't help. There was no actual sense of progress. A strange peace remained undisturbed about the dark, despite all my efforts to escape it.

I then realised desperation wouldn't do; I couldn't escape the Mahogany Night without grace. I switched to freestyle, my movements gentler and more fluid.

They say true progress cannot be quantified, yet you feel it inside your heart. Convinced I was inching closer to the exit, I pulled myself back into the morning at the opposite bank of the Night, beyond which the same labyrinthine jungle stretched.

Not that stepping into the morning effectuated a true escape, because I was still thoroughly drenched in Night even when I was out. The jungle was notorious for never letting any actual sunlight penetrate its being. So, the Night on my body never really dried off. Instead, as I pushed deeper into the jungle, relentlessly, still hypnotised, towards the origin of Ipsha's breathing, Night's sticky coating steadily accumulated more of Ipsha's melody on my skin until all my being was covered in Ipsha's tuneful vestiges. So I knew I was ready to meet Ipsha.

Was that a good thing, though? I knew the people of Bishadnagar feared Ipsha no less than they did the Mahogany Night.

To give you a basic idea of how Ipsha became a menace in the lives of the kingdom dwellers, I'll tell you a bit about Bishadnagar first and its all-encompassing gloom.

There were no snow-capped mountains around Bishadnagar. So, the saltwater river that flowed on the eastern fringes of the kingdom had been forced to begin from a hut in which the middle-aged woman named Haimanti stayed. In the past three centuries, ever since the Mahogany Night had voraciously swallowed her son, she had wept so religiously, day and night, that she hadn't found the time to age a day. No wonder, then, that the river that originated from her tears was named after her. The water of river Haimanti was at once the source of livelihood and gloom for its subjects. A morning dip in river Haimanti ensured you were shrouded in gloom for the rest of the day. And gloom, as even the children of Bishadnagar were forced to learn, was good both for your skin and your soul. The saltwater of gloom never evaporated no matter how sultry the day was, and if you regularly coated yourself in gloom, you stopped ageing. That way, you had already shrouded yourself in immortality, much to the gods' chagrin.

The gods had originally willed gloom to act as an exit doorway, as a means for population control. For example, in normal circumstances, if you were ever depressed and fell in love with gloom, you would've aged faster, crumbled into yourself, and had easy access to an early, wish-fulfilling death.

In Bishadnagar, that core property of gloom never really took off because the residents rarely fell in love with it. Here, gloom was a means to an end. A show of power. A way to throw your weight around. And a reason for long-standing conflicts between two generations of a family. Here, parents forced their sons and daughters to regularly bathe in the waters of river Haimanti so that they could remain children for the coming eternity, whereas the little ones were forever making excuses to skip their daily dips in gloom so they could become adults as soon as possible.

But even though the children of Bishadnagar never grew, their anger did, until it led to the events to which even the gods could no longer remain silent spectators.

It all began with a group of hundred-year-old children. Six of them, to be precise. Fed up with the daily coating of gloom on their bodies imposed by their parents, they decided to rebel one day. On a sultry afternoon, in the middle of the street, in front of everyone, in perfect coordination with each other, they slashed their own throats with six kitchen knives, each of the same make and design.

The grownups barely had time to react or stop screaming, because right then, all the living children of Bishadnagar, regardless of the age they were stuck in, heard the dulcet melody of Ipsha's breath inside their heads and found themselves demoniacally attracted to the Mahogany Jungle in the outskirts. And so severe was the pull of the so-called anomaly, they all poured down the streets and began marching towards the jungle in an almost hypnotic trance. A parade of ordered unity.

Had the parents not intervened in a timely manner and forced the children back into their respective homes, they would have all lost their children that day to the viscosity of the Mahogany Night even before they reached Ipsha. And even then, it took the living children over a month to recover from the terrible weakness the spell of anomaly had wrought on their souls.

It was then that the king had to ban anomaly, in all forms and shapes, from the kingdom of Bishadnagar. There was nothing more potentially harmful in Bishadnagar than anomalies, and if ever an untoward incident were to occur, the first thing the residents were instructed to ensure was that their entire family (especially the children) was inside their respective houses, and then bolt the door from inside, so that even if Ipsha called the children again in another spell of her dulcet melody, they couldn't leave. And all residents were advised to stay put in their houses, until the royal guards had cleared the streets of all anomalies, regardless of whether it was children or lovers who had committed suicide.

Yes, lovers.

You see, procreation was deemed illegal in Bishadnagar, immortality being so rampant that the population never dwindled. And since we're speaking of a time when there were no proven birth control measures, physical intimacy could get you sentenced to a life of immortality in a dark dungeon. Alone. You and your lover, in separate cells. The real punishment, however, was that even in prison, they'd bathe you daily in waters drawn from river Haimanti. Death was still an anomaly and, therefore, forbidden.

Instead of getting caught and spending an eternity exiled from love, the lovers often chose to hang themselves from a banyan tree. Whenever someone reported such a sight of dead lovers hanging together, the residents promptly carried out the task they did best: bolt themselves inside their homes and wait for the royal guards to clear the streets of the anomaly to gloom's rule.

In the end, this extreme subversion of gloom must have angered the gods enough that they decided to cast the fairies from the skies, making the conditions conducive for my decisive meeting with Ipsha.

The first sight of Ipsha is always overwhelming, no matter who you are or where you come from.

When I laid eyes on her in the hidden depths of the jungle, she was swaying sideways in a rather leisurely state, musing between an assemblage of mahogany trees, humming the flavours of her undulating breath. My feet froze. I could think nothing beyond her, and every iota of memory that defined my identity was lost. I was nobody, and I was just an everybody. Tearing my eyes away from her was difficult. I reminded myself that our definition of beauty is symmetry and the compressed mould of formless flesh named Ipsha was anything but attractive by those standards.

That, however, was only a poor attempt to convince myself. The truth was, Ipsha's allure was just as undeniable as it was inexplicable.

It is easy for a casual passerby to mistake Ipsha for a giant, peach-coloured anthill, almost double (or triple) the size of your average human being—if they don't notice the two tiny feet underneath, that is. Feet so close to the rest of her almost triangular body that she appears to be moving more lackadaisically than a snail. And if that passerby's eyes aren't sharp enough to make out that those two little flaps near the peak of the hill that blink every now and then are Ispha's eyes, they might overlook the fact that the gentle rise and fall of her body is just her respiring a little too emphatically, a little too sonorously. We'll discuss the workings of Ipsha's ears, nose, and mouth another time because they are all the same thing—an opening at the top of her anthill body, leading into her—a wormhole, as it was most often called.

Oh, and she has never had any hands, neither of her own nor of friendship extended to her by any other human being. People mostly forgot that she was a human being, too. Deformed, yes. Terribly deformed. And the size of a giantess. But still a human, if you looked closely. And I couldn't have, but now that I stood in front of her.

I learnt of Ipsha's forced isolation only after she began speaking to me. She was yet to tell me that, as a child, she used to wail relentlessly at the top of her voice, regardless of the hour of the day. People used that as a ready pretext to banish her from the kingdom and send her off to live in the Mahogany Jungle, where she still kept wailing. That was until her vocal cords gave out, and she lost her voice. The only sounds that accompanied her now were those of her melodious breathing and the occasional whisper, which is how she spoke to you if you were close enough to her, both body and soul.

That day, however, Ipsha did whisper to me. "Help her," she said, which I didn't know then was such a deviation from her usual stance.

But it was at those words that I first noticed the fallen fairy lying near Ipsha's feet. The fairy was about the size of my arm and was oddly blue, which I guessed was the natural hue of her feathers unless they changed colours and had turned this strange shade of blue because she was hurt. Her tightly pressed eyelids had long, green eyelashes, though. But the peculiar shade of blue also recurred on her skin, which was patterned with another lighter shade of itself. Those patterns in blue grabbed my attention, so it took me a few moments to notice that the fallen fairy was naked.

"Help her," Ipsha repeated, and I knew then why she had pulled me here with the melody of her breath. What I didn't know, however, was that it was no coincidence that she had chosen me to help the fallen fairy. No, such things are decided years in advance by forces so mindless that it would be pointless to term their workings as conspiracy, even if those chains of events could trigger an entire kingdom's downfall.

It was neither a conspiracy nor a coincidence that I met Ipsha on the day the first fairy rained from the skies, spelling doom for the kingdom of Bishadnagar.

ACT II

Then One Day, Your Love's at Stake

When I was a child, people used to call me the boy with an unhealthy curiosity about curiosities. Sometimes, they added the term 'orphaned' before 'boy', but that hardly changed who I was. I lived in a hut beside the jute fields, but unlike the other villagers, learning the art of crafting saleable items out of jute was the last thing I had on my mind. Instead, my tiny hut was a museum of sorts. Inside it, you'd find the golden tongue of a frog that, in its lifetime, had been cursed to woo ladies instead of flies. Or the eye of a tiger that reflected your deepest fear if you stood in front of it. Or the purple toenail of a firebird that had burnt its own fingers.

In those days, my two best friends were a sixty-year-old dwarf who used to tell the most amazing tall tales and a girl named Tanii who had eyes behind her head and emptiness in front of her face. Tanii was my age, or used to be, until she was burnt at the stake for being a witch, which is what she actually became after they burnt her. Then, she stopped ageing and began haunting our village and killing people with her childish pranks. So, I had to break off my friendship with her. But the old dwarf and I missed her for many years after.

When the old dwarf passed away, I no longer had anyone to take care of me or encourage my curiosity about curiosities. My knack for collecting such rare items without caring about worldly affairs became untenable. I wasn't an artisan like most of the other villagers, much less a gifted one like the old dwarf. So, I became a jute trader. I bought items from the village artisans and sold them off on other shores for a profit. It would be wrong to say that I didn't still keep an eye out for curiosities when I travelled to those distant shores, and indeed, my collection kept growing, as did the size of my house. Now, I had a dedicated room for my compilation of curiosities. But that dedicated room was in my house and not in my heart. Inside me was the same emptiness as had been on my former friend Tanii's face.

So, I cannot describe to you what emotions churned in my empty heart, that fated afternoon. My first glimpse of Ipsha was at once a reminder of all that I wasn't and a negation of all that I was. The fallen fairy set off a deep discontent for the second-hand fakeness of a room dedicated to curiosities in a house where a stranger lived—a stranger whose face I couldn't bear to look at in the mirror. In that labyrinthine Mahogany Jungle, the two ladies, together, created a realm that reminded me of who I used to be a long time ago before becoming a jute trader, before the old dwarf passed away, before I lost my childhood friend to a cruel fire.

I picked up the senseless fairy and asked Ipsha, "How do I help her?"

"Take her into the Night," Ipsha whispered. "Only darkness can heal her now."

"The Night?" I asked, confused. *Act quick when Night*, I remembered. Wouldn't the Mahogany Night forever trap the senseless fairy in its ever-growing viscosity?

"Yes, the Night." Ipsha's tone said she would have shrugged if she had shoulders. "Go now."

"But what if the Night gobbles her?"

Ipsha's sigh was a symphony. "I see; they've poisoned your mind, too. The Mahogany Night is nothing like they've told you. So trust me, and don't waste any more time."

I don't remember if I trusted Ipsha right then, but I know I wanted to. I let myself, fairy in arms, be pulled back into the Night. At the heart of its pitch-black viscosity, I put her down in its invisible waters, hoping that Ipsha was right after all and that the Mahogany Night would help her heal. But I had no way of knowing for sure since the nightly current took her away from me in no time. I had lost her to ambiguity. With nothing else to do, I resorted to my free strokes.

Back in the Mahogany Jungle, I asked Ipsha, "You think she'll be fine in there?" but Ipsha no longer spoke to me. She had no reason to.

We sat beside each other, breathing: hers a melody, mine incertitude.

On that fateful day, it took me a while to gather my thoughts and leave the Mahogany Jungle. I still had jute items to sell, and they were waiting for me on my boat. But that afternoon, Bishadnagar wasn't quite the busy hub it used to be. I was greeted by empty streets with the occasional fallen fairy strewn in the middle of the road or some corner of the pavement. These fairies looked no different from the one I had helped in the forest, except for the pattern that the two hues of blues made on their bodies, which was unique for each of them. No doubt those patterns did what our faces do: make them distinct and recognisable.

I found it strange that everyone in Bishadnagar had closed their doors to this spectacle instead of being curious about these dainty creatures. At that time, I didn't know about the standing order from the king regarding anomalies. I didn't know that the same principle of censorship extended to the present event of fairies raining from the skies, lying about in a near-death state on the streets. If the residents were allowed back on the streets, there'd soon be a rumour that those were the signs of impending doom, of imminent deaths looming over the kingdom. So, the residents had to stay inside, and the fallen fairies had to disappear, swept under the proverbial carpet.

And I didn't know on that fated day that the royal guards were supposed to take care of the fairy situation on the streets. But I remembered Ipsha's first words to me. *Help her.*

And I remembered Tanii before they had tied her to the stake. The two of us were sitting, hidden inside the jute fields, when she shared her fear. "I'm afraid of you growing up," she said.

I smiled. "Growing up is nothing to be frightened of."

"It *is*, for people like us." Tanii pointed at her blank face before turning away to stare at me. "Grownups like order in their world. They'd rather not be reminded of freaks of nature like us. When you grow up, you may start to see things like they do."

I put my hand on hers. "I'm not like them. I'll always be there for you."

Yet was I there for her when she truly needed me? Did I save her?

Now, I repeated what Ipsha had instructed me to do: I picked one fairy at a time and left them to the nightly current in the jungle. In each fallen fairy, I saw Tanii. I don't remember how many trips between Bishadnagar and the Mahogany Night I made that day, and I can't say if my efforts were successful in getting all fallen fairies to the healing of the Night. When I think of it now, I imagine the royal guards must have removed as many fairies as I had retrieved.

Have you ever felt you were carrying on doing something even though you were no longer sure what your end game was or why you still carried on doing that thing? That is precisely how I felt that day. The more fallen fairies I ferried into the Night, the deeper I sunk into my own uncertainty. Did I have any reason to trust Ipsha? I had just met her. By giving in to her designs, where was I allowing her to take me?

And more importantly, why did I think my journey with Ipsha had only begun?

Even though I stayed back in the Mahogany Jungle for the next few weeks (and I don't know why), Ipsha had stopped speaking to me altogether. We sat beside each other in silence. Or in Ipsha's melody, to be precise. When we spotted a falling fairy in the sky, we tried to locate the spot she landed in the jungle, and once found, I left her to the waters of the Mahogany Night. That was the only time I felt useful, even though I couldn't say how I was helping the fairies by that act.

At other times, when I was sitting beside Ipsha, I mostly felt small, which was less because Ipsha was a giantess and more because, by then, I had learnt to recognise the deep regret in the melody of her breath. Not the sort that comes from repenting a mistake, but one that springs from the terrible absence of something important in your life. I wanted to help her but didn't know anything about the origin of that regret, much less how to help set her free of it.

Because we weren't talking, whenever I was lost in thought, I stared into the Mahogany Night in the distance, waiting for the fairies to emerge from it again, flitting back into the light. Healed, like Ipsha had said they'd be. But they never emerged.

Then one day, Ipsha spoke to me. "Your waiting is pointless," she whispered. "They aren't coming out."

Her words were so sudden that it took me a few minutes to let that joy of being spoken to sink in. And then the import of her words dawned on me. "What do you mean they aren't coming out? You said the Mahogany Night would heal them."

"Why do you think they're healed only if they step out of the Night?"

There are times in life when you come across a question that you feel a deep urge to answer, yet no answer you come up with is flawless enough to utter aloud. Then, silence is the only recourse and wise counsel.

Ipsha whispered to me the story of a young boy who had fallen in love with the Mahogany Night, and when his mother strongly objected to that relationship, she said her son deserved a bride as fair as the day and stated in no unclear terms that she'd rather die than accept darkness as her daughter-in-law. The boy first protested, saying that the Mahogany Night, too, had once been human before she was chased into the jungle for her darkness, then he corrected his mother, saying he loved her for the woman she still was even in her formless existence, and lastly, he forever disappeared into the arms of the Night.

I instantly recognised that tale, for it was one of the most popular stories here in Bishadnagar, except that in the version the residents told, the Mahogany Night was an evil entity that had lured the son in. The name of that boy's mother was Haimanti, and that boy's disappearance had first cast Bishadnagar into the clasps of a relentless gloom and then set off the chain reactions that left the kingdom reeling under a patient shadow of immortality.

"The Mahogany Night is a woman?" I asked Ipsha.

She sighed. "She used to be, perhaps, a deformed one like me and, thus, banished from the kingdom. Then, the phantom loneliness of the jungle must have slowly changed her into this all-encompassing presence with no definite form."

"Wow! No one in Bishadnagar tells that version of the story."

"There's a second chapter to that story, too, that the residents of Bishadnagar won't tell you," Ipsha said, "because that one's about me."

After the Mahogany Night gave birth to Ipsha, the fairies gathered around her. Because the Night, with little volition left of her own, would make for a poor parent and Ipsha's father was yet invisible in the dark, they carried the newborn child on their wings and placed her inside her grandma's hut.

"Of course, I have no memories of that time, and my account of these events from my early infancy is based on how the fairies later recounted them to me. They say that my grandma was too mesmerized to speak for the first few seconds after she saw me. Then, when she came to her senses, she yelled, *what kind of monstrosity is that?* And she might have said a few untoward things afterwards, but the fairies say that most of her words were drowned out in the shrillness of my wailing. I had been wailing ever since I was born. Ceaselessly so. And I understand now why it was so. Because even on those very first days, I must've been in just as much pain."

"Why *are* you in pain?" I asked.

The melody in Ipsha's sigh was unmissable yet again. "Because everything's wrong about the geometry of my anatomy. These bones, they're all oddly twisted. Any tiny movement and the joints and tendons revolt against the exertion. Pain has been my only constant companion. Terrible and ceaseless pain that would even wake me if I ever turned sides in my sleep. Pain, as a reminder that my deformity is a curse indeed. Yes, you get used to that pain over the years. You learn to live with it. But pain is still pain. The punishment for being a monster."

"I don't think of you as a monster," I had to retort. "I think you're beautiful." I was telling her the truth, sharing my real feelings, as I had with Tanii many years ago, but I couldn't have chosen a worse time for that confession now.

"Please don't patronise me. There's nothing I hate more than that," Ipsha whispered, yet, for the first time, the scales of her melody felt imbalanced and inharmonious. "More importantly, why do you think a monster can't be beautiful? It has to be one or the other?"

Yes, so as I was saying—necessary questions with only flawed answers. Only this time, the interval between the instances of them was a little too close for comfort. But instead of resorting to silence, I followed it up with the stupidest response. "I didn't mean it that way."

"That's what the people of Bishadnagar told me too, and my grandma Haimanti as well, when they left me here in the Mahogany Jungle to fend for myself. But what they mean doesn't matter to me. I just want them to fulfil the only wish I ever made to them. I don't care for the rest."

"What is your wish?"

"You make it sound as if you're a genie." A calmness returned to Ipsha's melody. "Well, my only wish is to be set free of this suffering. I wish for them to help me attain death. How I've longed for that! I would've taken things into my own hands, you know. If I had hands. Still, I've tried to starve myself to death, but even the air of this jungle keeps me nourished. I've tried to drown myself, but Mother Night's waters only know to heal and not to choke.

"So I turned to the residents of Bishadnagar. I called them here and requested them to gift me freedom. *Please put an end to my pain,* I told them. But they only looked at me in shock, murmured among themselves, and shook their heads. You'd think they'd rather not have the monster keep on living in their jungle, but no, in Bishadnagar, death is a curse word. No fear is greater than that of death. So, they told me, 'You should never choose death over life, no matter the suffering.' What they meant was, 'You have no choice over the matter, and we'd rather keep it that way.'"

"No one should decide for you." Anger rose inside me. I was reminded of Tanii once again. She needn't have become a witch if others had listened to her pleading. Her desperate pleas for justice when they were dragging her to the stake to fulfil their own crooked ends. "You shouldn't have given up."

"I didn't. When the six children slashed their throats, I thought that was my chance. I put all the living children in the kingdom into a trance and called them to me, hoping that now that the residents had experienced death, they'd be afraid enough to get rid of the monster in the jungle once and for all, to make sure the rest of their children were safe. But they proved me wrong, yet again. They'd rather close their doors and wait for their streets to be cleared of any lingering evidence of death than accept that death as a part of their lives. Much less accept it as a gift, as in conditions such as mine. They'd keep clinging onto their hundred-year-old children rather than release them, release me. Those six kitchen knives made little difference."

"You don't need those other people any longer." By then, I was decided on that. I had to right the wrong. From Ipsha's past. From my own past. "You have *me* now."

When I said so, I was already aware that perhaps those were the exact words Ipsha wanted me to say, that maybe that was the sole reason she had been painstakingly sharing all those details from her past with me. But even if so, it mattered not. I didn't mind being used to fulfil her cause. Because now I knew the source of her regret and its solution, too.

"Tell me what I need to do," I said.

ACT III

Asking for a Hand

The ancient cartographers say that at that very moment when I agreed to help Ipsha, the wormhole that gave access to her true rapture awakened. The wormhole deepened into her being and began widening too. I have no way of ascertaining if this were the case. At that time, I didn't even know about the wormhole. Since Ipsha was so much taller than me, I couldn't have seen it or known of its existence.

Until she invited me in.

"I realised long ago that, no matter how severe, pain cannot kill me," Ipsha said. "This ill-formed body has gotten too used to it and won't accept it as an agent of change. I can only die of that which is the opposite of pain. Something akin to ecstasy."

"How do you attain that? Help me understand. I'll make it possible."

"You have to do two things for me. One of them might put your own life at risk. So, decide carefully."

Should I have been afraid of that warning? Instead, I shrugged, and not because I was brave. "This life I've been leading isn't worth much to me, anyway. I know that now. I've known that ever since I met you. Just tell me what that thing is."

"You have to lead me to pleasure. Put yourself inside me."

Yes, those words, whispered in straight notes, perplexed me. If Ipsha was indeed asking me what I thought she was, I didn't know how to carry that out. So far, I hadn't even wondered about that side to her, but now I found myself asking, if her body was indeed capable of attaining actual physical intimacy, wouldn't she have longed to be loved too? But I shook off that thought right after; I was being presumptuous again. Even if her body was incapable of physical intimacy, couldn't she have still craved love?

And how did I feel about her longing for love? Would she have asked for that from just about anyone who was willing to help her because she needed to be released from pain? Therefore, instead of wondering about the nitty-gritty of her proposition, I ended up asking her something else. "Why do you want *me* to do that?"

Ipsha stayed quiet for about half a minute. "I understand it's a very personal choice. Risky, too. Feel free to say no. And I'm sorry that I asked you for that. It wasn't easy for me either."

"Wasn't easy because you aren't attracted to me otherwise?" I asked.

"How do you keep asking the wrong questions?" The inharmony returned to Ipsha's breath. "Must be an inherent talent."

"I'm just trying to understand. You must agree that these are not the most usual circumstances, Ipsha." I realised that was the first time either of us had uttered that name. I had only heard it mouthed by the residents of Bishadnagar during my previous visits when they spoke about the monster in the Mahogany Jungle. I wondered who gave her such a beautiful name. "Who named you Ipsha?"

"My mother did. At least, that's what the fairies told me later. Because in her current state, Mother had no way of communicating with me, the fairies used to carry her messages to the little me. But then, since I was born to the Mahogany Night and in this deformed body, people somehow assumed I would be naturally immortal and didn't bother to bathe me in the waters of river Haimanti. So, I started growing in the phantom loneliness of the jungle, not knowing then that growth would be an endless process for me."

"So, you're saying that you still keep on growing up to this day?"

"Yes. You may call it a curse of *junglee* loneliness. I believe both my mother and I still keep growing. What happened in between this is that the fairies slowly stopped visiting me. I don't know why they did. Perhaps fairies aren't allowed to visit adults. But before they disappeared from my life, they told me the meaning of my name. *Ipsha means desire,* they said. Now, I often wonder why Mother named me that. Was it because I was a fruit of her own desire? But even then, isn't it strange that you'd like to name your child that, knowing well that she may never truly feel desired all her life by another human being?"

By then, I already knew that I desired Ipsha. I desired her more than anyone else alive. If I told her that, she'd only assume I was trying to be kind to her. "What is the second thing you'd want me to do?"

"The one I shared with you is my second wish. My first wish is that you hold my hand."

"What? How can I…? I don't understand."

"For many years now, I've wished to hold someone's hand and look into their eyes, to experience what desire feels like." Ipsha sighed, this one like a soft, billowy cloud. "I know I have no hands, but I can imagine I have one if you believe I do." She stopped for a few seconds, but I knew she wasn't done speaking. "Think of it this way. If I say I dream of holding a hand and only you can fulfil it, will you?"

How could I say no to that? I extended my right hand towards her, my palm open. "May I have the honour?"

"Okay," Ipsha whispered, readily.

I closed my palm around hers, her phantom fingers around mine, soft and warm. Then, I threw my head back to peer into her eyes.

We stayed that way for the next few minutes until she asked, "Will you come up to my nest?"

"Nest?"

"Well, people like to call it a crater, a tunnel, or a wormhole, even though there are no worms inside. I like to refer to it as a nest because it houses so many of my organs. It's simultaneously my mouth, my ear, my nose, and much more. In truth, however, it's just a hole above me. So, maybe a wormhole indeed. But it's also my… you know… my pleasure organ."

"Your…?" No wonder I fumbled with my words. "How do you know that?"

"Because whenever a bird or something perches on its tip, it makes me feel all kinds of funny inside. A warmth spreads all over my body. Takes my mind away from the pain."

Now, I had started to grasp what she expected of me. "Then, allow me to take that pain away from you," I said, as I readied myself to climb up her anthill body.

Sometimes, life is a straight line: the shortest distance between two points. At other times, it's a dot: a point often overlooked. Yet an entire universe may quite effortlessly fit in that dot. We have many different names for that dot: a breakeven, a turning point, an orgasm, a childbirth. A universe each.

Ipsha's ecstasy was one such dot: it defined her entire life, the universe inside notwithstanding.

The opening on top of her—the wormhole, or the nest, as she called it—was a song. It was composed to perfection and was meant to awaken your senses, to make them receptive to the oncoming experience, the rise and fall, the crux, the aftertaste.

The wormhole was wide enough for an entire person to step into. Peering inside, it was a deep orange glow reminiscent of an active volcano as the wormhole twisted itself deeper inside her being. Yet, when I dipped my hand inside and touched its glowing wall, it was lukewarm and soft.

When I dipped my hand, the rhythm of Ipsha's breath paced up momentarily. Then, she said, "I'm ready. Dive inside. Come to me." When Ipsha spoke, the orange glow inside changed patterns in sync with her voice—some parts burned brighter; others faded to lightness.

The allure of the wormhole became unbearable. I undressed as if readying myself for a swim, then deep-dived into her. Headfirst, I went. The orange ripples brushed past my skin as I swam deeper into her. I turned at a twist, and the light from the mahogany forest above me was gone. All that remained was the sparkle of various shades of orange.

The walls of the wormhole vibrated when Ipsha let out a soft moan. Never have I heard such a potent melody. And while I was drenched in its spell, that melody travelled outwards. It flew into the forest, took a dip in the dark waters of the Mahogany Night, awakened the fairies inside, and then journeyed towards the kingdom of Bishadnagar.

As I pushed deeper into Ipsha, the wormhole tightened around me. Tender was its touch, blossoming like a dance of sensations on my skin. And there was a soft suffocation about it that pulled me deeper. I let myself be carried forward.

Ipsha's moans repeated more frequently now, each a wave I could surf on. What I didn't know then was that each of those potent melodies rippled forth outside, not only making its way towards Bishadnagar but increasing the radius of the Mahogany Night as the fallen fairies, now awakened, pulled the dark curtains of the Night outwards, slowly extending the long-banished woman over the kingdom, returning her dark self to her home.

I didn't know any of this because, at that moment, I could think of nothing beyond Ipsha. I didn't even care that the suffocation was slowly taking my life. And even if I did, I equated it to Ipsha's own experience: ecstasy, as a whisper postponed. Deep inside her, the orange glow made me one with her. I knew she wanted to tell me something as simple as, *This, what I feel for you, is love*, something as simple as, *Take all of me away with you*, something as simple as, *Let me die in your arms*. Her ecstasy spoke to me on her behalf. What could be sweeter than death at the climax?

But Ipsha's death was climactic in more ways than one. When the potent melody of her moans penetrated the kingdom of Bishadnagar and poured into the houses where the families stayed, sensuality rolled over the skin of every family member inside like a continuous fabric of silk brushing past their bodies. The awakening was irrefutable, the arousal undeniable.

Then came the Mahogany Night that the fallen fairies had pulled into town. Meticulously and dexterously, the fairies wove the Night around the residents and cocooned all of them inside. And when the fairies flitted around each of them in the dark, that odd hue of blue on their bodies, which I later realised was a deep shade of inspiration, washed away the many coatings of gloom that had accumulated on their beings over the decades and centuries. The residents' hearts became overwhelmed with a sudden need to love, to touch, to explore each other. It was unlike anything they had allowed themselves to feel in all this time.

With the coatings of gloom gone, the floodgates had opened, and the ageing that lay in hiding in various bends and contours of their bodies for many years now came rushing forth. It began with a middle-aged woman named Haimanti. Ipsha's grandma aged faster than the speed of thought and crumbled on the floor as nothing more than a skeleton being hastily dressed in a terribly wrinkled skin. The process repeated itself all over the kingdom, for the parents and their hundred-year-old children alike, only varying in the wrinkle of skin on their corpses.

I wonder sometimes if their deaths had been at the height of ecstasy like Ipsha's and mine were to be. Were they pleased when death approached them? Did they resign from the insidious wear-and-tear of immortality with a smile?

The ancient cartographers state that at the centre of the stretch of scorched earth that once used to be the Mahogany Jungle, the place where a sinkhole now exists is where the kingdom of Bishadnagar used to stand. Archaeologists and geologists have backed this claim. But the ancient cartographers also state that the sinkhole that now attracts aeroplanes and meteors towards it, is what remains of Ipsha to this day, and the soft orange glow that it emits at night are the memories of an endless wormhole that once passed through "a giantess named Ipsha" and led to a nothingness that defined the universe. The archaeologists and geologists rubbish this claim. To this day, I don't know who to agree with. The truth is I don't know. Yes, my soul still glows orange in the sinkhole, but beyond that, I know nothing of what succeeded Ipsha's death or what became of her afterwards, or why I remain in the sinkhole to this day, all alone.

All I remember is Ipsha whispering my name and repeating it over and over again in her ecstasy. *Arko.* I remember that sensation of my name being uttered in her potent melody. I remember swimming deeper and deeper inside her, not looking back, just as I hadn't looked back that one time, many years ago, when they set the stake on fire where Tanii was. My childhood friend screamed my name, pleading for help. *Arko.* The radiance of a fire that burns forever. *Arko.* And I ran right into the fire to save her. The fire gnawed at my skin; it lent me a new look, a bit grotesque, but the old dwarf managed to pull me out in time. Saved my life, but not Tanii's, leaving me cursed to look back forever since that day, just like she used to.

No one was going to pull me out this time. Out of Ipsha. Out of this sorry life I had tried to cover with wealth. Breathless, I pushed forward into the orange melody, watching my burnt skin peel away, watching my breath peel away, and then my regrets, until Ipsha uttered my name one last time. *Arko.*

The last time Ipsha said my name, she screamed it at the Mahogany Jungle in a voice she had lost back in her childhood. That voice was fresh like the mahogany scent around us, deep like a woman who had turned into an endless night, innocent like the children who thought slashing their throats would solve anything, selfless like the old dwarf who had dedicated his life to taking care of me, and truthful like the promise Tanii and I had made to marry each other when we grew up—a promise that I would ask for her hand from her drunkard father one day. When Ipsha screamed my name, Bishadnagar dissolved into that final moan of her ecstasy, and I learnt to forgive myself.

READING LIST
Diane Lefer

Ladies, shall we resume on Zoom?

Being called a lady was reason enough to quit the book group though I could have pointed out there was a time in the South when "ladies" was a progressive political statement, back when white women were ladies and Black women weren't. But when it's 2020 in the suburbs and the only POC in our group is Amina who was a doctor in India but only her husband has a visa to work here so now she's a stay-at-home Mom, we have an agreement to keep anything even remotely political out of bounds.

I wanted to read *We Need to Talk About Kevin*, the novel about the mother of a disturbed boy who kills his classmates. I'd already read it but I wanted to talk about it because we really needed to talk about Taylor Burnham. The little freak. It was one thing when he was a little kid, the butt of everyone's jokes, Burp-him they called him. From the time he entered kindergarten, he only had to walk into the classroom or down the hall when all the boys would start burping, he'd cry, then everyone would laugh at him for crying and the teacher, in whichever grade, would humiliate him by telling him boys don't cry. After Sandy Hook, I began teaching my daughter: *Don't tease him. Always be nice to Taylor. If he brings a gun to school, he'll spare you.*

The book group started out as a Mother/Daughter group. I don't know about the other mothers, but I joined because Portia doesn't talk to me. When you talk about fictional characters rather than about yourself, it can reveal a lot and Portia, on the High Honor Roll every damn marking period, doesn't mind talking as long as it's on an intellectual plane. I've tried to warn her, intelligence won't get you very far in life. She does give me a lot to be proud of, as though that's enough.

I know it's hard for her, being a suburban high school's academic star. Taylor isn't the only outsider who was bullied. First they asked why her parents named her after a car. Then they started calling her Portia-Potty. I hoped the book group would help her meet other girls and make friends. She quit right away, rolling her eyes at any fiction labeled YA. Sometimes I think the normal kids are right: My daughter can be a pompous ass.

The other kids quit the group, too, as little interested in reading as their mothers. With them gone, we were free to bring out the wine and forget about YA. I felt kind of bad about the wine becoming central to our meetings—Amina doesn't drink—and even without YA, no one wanted to read anything adult or disturbing.

Like *The Perfect Nanny*, suggested by Jill. Katie read the first line. *The baby is dead.* "I don't think that's a healthy book for us." And yet she's the one who disagreed when Serena said motherhood was too damn hard: "You've got to watch them all the time."

"I don't," said Katie.

"And if they jump off the roof?"

"They'll never do it again."

And this is the coastal elite.

Serena vetoed *The Hidden Life of Trees* because she couldn't pronounce the author's name—Peter Wohlleben. "How are we supposed to discuss it if we can't say it?" Katie added her own veto. "It's science, isn't it? Science is divisive."

The problem of consensus, which our gender presumably values: It's easy to reach consensus on No. Harder to get to Yes.

We—at least I—assumed the virus would be contained in a month, maybe six weeks, but here we are, winter, hunkered down, trying to take heart that at some point it's bound to end. For us, at least, fighting Covid is a passive struggle: what we refrain from doing rather than what we do, though to maintain mental health we are advised to count our blessings, find the advantages in the day's challenges.

Such as:

I think it's great the schools have shut down. Portia was always nice to Taylor, just as I told her, and then they were teenagers and he started asking her out. And we all know that rejection by a girl is enough to set off a rampage. "He's texting me," she says. "Did you answer?" "What do you think?" she says. I don't know if that means yes or no. She flounces off. But as long as we stay at home, she's safe.

We're getting through this "together," but—another blessing—that doesn't mean (at least so far) with my sister.

It turns out I like—even prefer—Zoom. I can put up a background or a photo of myself instead of live feed. Then the ladies can't see when I roll my eyes.

When you're hermetically sealed, you can think your own thoughts and no one can read your mind. Which can be a trap: I did such a good job of hiding my feelings Tommy married me hoping I had none. Oh, but I did. What went on behind the shield? When I was Portia's age, it was mostly sexual fantasies, sometimes about my favorite actors and musicians, but mostly about Chaz after his brother's OD. Everyone whispered about it. No one talked about it. People avoided Chaz, too shameful and how do you talk about death when you're a kid? I wonder if I already sensed the OD's—though not fatal—in my sister's future. I wrote to Chaz—a snail mail letter, this before we'd ever heard of email and text. I wrote him how sad I was, that if he wanted to talk, if there was any comfort I could offer… Those days, it's not like you could carry your device with you, so that whole spring break, I sat by the front door and waited. Suspended animation. I stared into space, unable even to read the books that in those days were my best and closest friends. I waited for the mailman just in case my letter was answered and if it was, I had to grab it before anyone else—my mother, father, sister—could see.

I wonder what's going on inside Portia now—what secrets—when she presents that pleasant blank face to me. Fantasies, or memories? For all I know she could be sexting, but why would she? And with whom? If Portia is a social outcast—and I don't know for sure she is—it's because she doesn't follow the crowd. She doesn't do what the other girls do just because they do it. But the point is, I don't know. I'm not the kind of mother who pries. I allow her privacy, her secrets. I don't go snooping through her drawers or her phone or try to find if she's on Instagram or TikTok. If she doesn't have friends to share with, I can imagine she hopes to be popular with people who don't know her.

What I need is not the knowledge of what she has or hasn't done. I want her to offer it to me.

I actually imagined Portia and I would spend the lockdown getting to know each other. I imagined a lovely time of mother-daughter bonding. Yes, we do Zoom yoga together in the morning, sharing an activity rather than feelings which I've been brought up to believe is the way fathers bond with their sons.

I stay in, just sit around, but unlike that time during spring break, I've got nothing to wait for.

"I don't want you going out," I tell my daughter. Of course she rolls her eyes. "It's not safe." I know she's always got a mask with her. She's constantly washing her hands. "He could be out there. Taylor. Watching for you."

"You think I want to be like you?"

"That's not an answer."

She says, "You're not in a risk group. You stay inside doing I don't know what. You have the groceries delivered. You haven't even stuck your head out the door."

"It's cold outside."

"So put on a coat! Go for a walk. Or at least stand outside. Look at the snow on the branches. Watch the birds. See the sunset." A conversation, at last. She says, "What is the matter with you?"

The other mothers have problems with their teenagers too. Katie says, "When she was growing inside me, we were one person. It's hard to accept she's her own person now."

When I was pregnant, the cells that would end up developing into Portia were not me. They were an infinitely mysterious manifestation of Life itself. Mystery then was a bit of a turn-on instead of a slap in the face. Once Portia was born, even when she was sucking at my breast, I never felt *this baby loves me*, only that she was furiously blindly tenaciously inexorably relentlessly uncaringly attached.

Now, she doesn't need a mask or a Plexiglass shield to keep me from reading her face.

Just an example: She pulls down her sleeve so quickly it wouldn't be fair to say she does it furtively to hide the tattoo I've already seen.

"Is that temporary, or did you—?"

Kids these days get tattoos. She's really young but still, it's what kids do and it doesn't mean anything, but hiding it, that's another story. She walks away. It looked like a butterfly. If that was a real tattoo, when did she get out of the house to have it done, and how did she pay for it, and why? I look up temporary tattoos on the internet. She could have ordered a set online, applied the ink herself, a process taking about as long as it takes me to color my hair, something I no longer bother with during lockdown. I think the gray is reassuring to the clients I meet with over Zoom.

Why hide it? It's not like it's a gang tattoo, I imagine saying.

I want it removed. They can do it with a laser, can't they?

But why?

I thought I was being an ally, but Karla Cornejo Villavicencio is fucking tired of migrants being compared to fucking butterflies.

I hold my breath, hoping she's not going to use that ridiculously hip compliment and call the author a badass.

She's fucking brilliant, says Portia.

If we'd actually read *The Undocumented Americans* in our Mother/Daughter book group—which we could have done if Portia hadn't quit and we'd chosen it even though Serena couldn't pronounce Villavicencio and if Katie had been willing to read about day laborers, a subject she would have objected to— intended to make her feel bad when these days we all need cheering up—I don't even want to imagine how the discussion would have gone. I figure Amina would have felt canceled the way the author isn't concerned with the unfair treatment of educated professional immigrants like herself.

When I hold imaginary conversations, I'm happy to attribute admirable political sentiments to my daughter, and I allow her to say *fuck*. The book, if we could read it together, might give us an opening to talk about people dying, the cruelty, the incompetence, the threats to our democracy, and the lies, and more lies, and lies, and lies.

We agree about all that, she'll say. *There's nothing to talk about.*

As for this business of separating children from their parents, what if Portia thinks it's a good thing? In my imagination, she would never say so. We communicate with mutual respect and feeling just as I used to with junior high and later high school boys who didn't know I existed or, if they did, didn't care or whose apparent indifference was most likely a veneer over their distaste, while in my imaginary conversations, they saw and heard me with appreciation, and shared their own usually unexpressed feelings of passionate love for me. In real life, I loved them unconditionally no matter how unrequited that love. They remained indifferent if not hostile and unattainable, exactly like Portia, which has to mean that I love her.

While I'd hoped talking about books would reveal Portia to me, there were things about the other mothers I preferred not to know. If we read *We Need to Talk about Kevin*, and I brought up Taylor Burnham and my concern that he might have access to weapons, how would I react if one of the ladies doubled down on the Second Amendment? That would most likely be Katie, who pretty much outed herself when she objected to Zoom and wanted to continue meeting in person. What was she thinking? Masks are tyranny and Covid-19 is a hoax? That could have been the end of the group, but as though she understood she'd brought us to the breaking point, as quickly as she'd refused to Zoom, Katie changed course and said it would be fun.

Then she vetoed *Educated*. "Isn't that the one by the girl [woman? lady?] who overcomes a brutal background? No, I don't feel inspired by someone rising from adversity."

"Above her family," said Amina.

"It's only the adversity that makes it interesting and I don't want to read about that."

They don't even like books. When they *can't get into it* or insist *it's boring*, I try to convince them there's satisfaction to be had in seeing a thing through to the end.

Serena says, "We could do screenshare and watch a movie together and discuss it afterwards."

My ex-husband got annoyed when I wanted to talk about the film we'd just seen. *I go to the movies to escape. Where's the escape if I have to talk about it?*

We didn't talk either—Suzanne, my mother, and I—the afternoon Mom called us to sit with her in front of the TV to watch *Bad News Bears*. The movie was funny, yeah, the cute little boys swinging their bats and missing—the losers, then suddenly connecting and running the bases like mad, but what I mostly saw was my mother. She looked happy. I saw a joy I'd never seen in her before. Certainly she got no joy from her daughters. Would it be different with a son? The movie first came out the year of my birth. Did Mom watch it then hoping for a boy?

I fell for the little boys, too. They made me think of the new boy who'd just moved to our town and immediately started following Suzanne around and I thought of him and realized I wasn't jealous of my sister but of his mother. She knew him when he was a baby. She knew him when he was a little boy. It was awful to think even if he loved me I would never know all of him.

Mom wrapped one arm around me, one around Suzanne, and this was so out of the ordinary, we both stiffened.

Most of the time she was—I wouldn't say angry—but exasperated, annoyed. I was a kid. I used to drop things, spill things, break things, throw up at the kitchen table. My mother expected me to be dainty and clean. My father was patient, indulgent. I thought he loved me more than she did till I suspected from his daughter he expected very little. For a while that hurt till I realized when people have no expectations, you are free to be yourself. I decided what he gave me was a gift.

Still, they labeled us. They named my sister for Leonard Cohen's *Suzanne*. Dad would play guitar and Mom would sing. For me they did duets on *Mary Ann*. Not Harry Belafonte's *Mary Ann* but the Canadian folksong. I can remember my mother's long unwashed hair wrapping around Suzanne as she sang to her, Suzanne saying, *You smell funny*, Mom blinking rapidly, but saying nothing, you don't punish a child for speaking her truth. From then on, for how long I can't remember, we taunted our mother, *Mommy smells funny, Mommy smells funny*, though children are supposed to see you as akin to god, they aren't born to humiliate you.

When Portia was born, a little animal, all red and squalling life, was I already thinking by the time she's a teenager, she'll hate me?

She says that Burp calls his mother *Honey*. There's a lot I don't know about mothers and sons but we agree that's pretty weird.

This one looks interesting: *Sons and Other Flammable Objects*. But it's by Porochista Khakpour. Not gonna happen!

With so many contemporary topics off-limits and books rejected rather than read, what is there left to talk about?

"Can we talk about Taylor Burnham?"

The ladies respond with laughter, Serena with giggles, Amina's laugh more like a cackle.

"A face," says Jill, "only a mother could love."

But he's just a boy and they like to talk about men.

I talk about my ex-husband Tommy, and so Jill insists that means I'm not over him. Really, there's no one else to talk about. Aside from a few insignificant lapses in judgment, I've kept to myself since I learned nice guys do as much damage as bad boys.

Lionel Shriver, the author of the book I wanted us to read, has called today's feminist campaigns neurotic and pathologically petty, which infuriates me even though I probably agree and in spite of which I'm a feminist. I'll probably need to boycott her now and it occurs to me even though Serena could pronounce her name, she'd surely be confused as to Shriver's gender.

I told the group I'd experienced sexual harassment many times, and three times from women, which is why I sometimes think we're not in the era of #MeToo but of wide-eyed, blameless #WhoMe?

On my first job after I finally left Tommy I was delighted to work for a female boss. One afternoon she called me into her office. "This is a three-hole punch," she said. "Your choice which of your orifices I will insert it in." What could I do but decide she was joking? Then she showed up at my apartment one night. I was surprised but I told myself two women in the business world, sisterhood, mentorship. She lay down on the couch, spread her legs and said, "Lick me." She said, "You work for me. You do what I say." I told her quietly to get out. When she didn't, I hollered and Portia woke and wailed until my boss stood up and left.

I would have reported a male boss, at least I think so. But a woman? In solidarity, I didn't tell.

The ladies found this story so distasteful they didn't press me to tell about the other two incidents, which was lucky because while I'm sure I wasn't lying, I can only remember the once.

"There was something odd about his penis," Jill told us after she slept with a famous man. I won't name him because my intent is not to gossip. I bring this up because what were we to think? That she was bragging about her conquest? That she was sexually inexperienced and found a perfectly ordinary penis "odd?" Was she showing off or testing us, to see which of us would be first to ask questions for the prurient details? Most likely, she just wanted our attention.

What was odd about Tommy's penis was—though I didn't share this with the ladies—it didn't get hard. Now I suspect without good sex you can't make living with someone tolerable and so it got to where I couldn't stand being around Tommy or he with me and that's why it's so hard for a mother and daughter to live amicably together. Of course back then I assumed there was something wrong with me. At night, I disgusted him with my tears.

"Don't you want to be happy?" I asked him.

He said, "I'm not sure I would like it."

"Is there someone else?"

"Don't be ridiculous," he said.

"Then what is it? Why?"

"I've found I don't like you as much as I expected to."

It's years since Portia has said a word about her father. Either he mattered to her as little as she mattered to him, or she doesn't ask because they've been in secret communication all these years. He may find the relationship easier from a distance.

After we separated, he moved back to his parents' place. Portia must remember our drives up to see him but he was never there—though he'd always have left some expensive gift for her behind. His parents grew tired of "entertaining" us. The real reason the visits ended, I don't know if Portia remembers, it was the time she came home crying. "Does it hurt when they nail you to the Jesus cross?" I assured her no one was going to do that. "Nana says if I'm bad, the Devil will get me and not even God can save me."

"What a nightmare," Jill let me know. "Why on earth did you marry him?"

I'd been attracted to a man who seemed gentle. He wasn't like the charismatic bad boy I fell for in college when being in love was a matter of life and death. It wasn't that way at all with Tommy. I thought that meant the relationship was healthy.

Jill asked, "Why didn't you leave?"

"I did leave. I'm here, aren't I?"

Katie isn't here. She hasn't joined us for a couple weeks now. Smart move, I thought, till Amina says she must have taken a turn for the worse. We didn't know. Only Amina, a physician, was the confidante. Katie's cancer treatment put on hold because the hospitals are overwhelmed. "So if she dies," asks Jill, "will it be attributed to Covid?" Jill, inappropriate as ever, though I'm not much better. I'm taking precautions, I'm bored, I'm free and have to restrain myself from asking what's the big deal? Hundreds of thousands of people are always dying horrible deaths somewhere from something.

The CDC warns people not to spend the holidays with family and with any luck, that will keep Suzanne away. I don't understand why more people don't use the excuse. For Christmas, Portia's getting wool socks, rhinestone-studded face masks—she won't use disposables, the planet! the planet!—and subscriptions to all the streaming services she desires. She points out I get the benefit of those too, but after a long day of Zoom, my eyes are too tired to stare at a screen for fun. I think she finds me annoying and exasperating.

Then the faucet knob in the shower/tub breaks and Portia and I can't turn on the hot water. It should be a simple repair but the maintenance staff is maintaining isolation. We fill buckets from the sink and take sponge baths like hospital patients, which is what in this era we hope not to be.

I'm not complaining. Portia and I live in a "luxury" townhouse, purchased at bargain-basement price from the senior partner who even helped me get the mortgage. He'd invested in a few residences just before the crash in '08. I thought he was merely overextended. I later learned he was going through a divorce and began selling off assets at a loss just to cheat his soon-to-be ex-wife.

Honestly, this is why I have to stick up for men. All of my opportunities have come about through their weakness and perfidy. My townhouse. My very-well-compensated job as Trademark Assistant. The senior partner I work for used to be too drunk after lunch to function. Come afternoon, the clients soon learned they had to rely on me. Once we began working remotely, he stayed drunk all day so filings, trademark licensing (for legally licensed fakes), infringement litigation, it became my sole responsibility. Pleadings, briefs? I draft them. An associate reviews and checks my work and takes it to court. I made it clear to the partnership they could either hire an attorney to cover for my boss or they could double my pay. We negotiated a 40% raise, fine with me!

You would think after Tommy I would not want anything to do with another alcoholic. I'm not sure how it happens, but once you've coped with a drunk, it is, maybe, one of your transferable skills.

At first, alcohol just put Tommy to sleep. The day came when being drunk released all the pain and anger. At first, against bosses and politicians. At first I confided in my women friends. They warned me his rage would soon enough be turned against me. They warned me about escalation. They told me I'd end up beaten, maybe even dead.

They were wrong. It wasn't my life he threatened. If I left him, he said he'd pour himself a glass of whiskey and drive straight into a tree. I never thought he'd do it. It had to be a cry for help, and in those days I stayed because it was in my nature to be helpful.

There are so many reasons a person doesn't leave. Maybe I was too demoralized to imagine any other life or brought low by what some might call depression. Anyway, leave to go where? My parents were off teaching English in Saudi Arabia. Like my sister and unlike me, they were adventurous though even then it occurred to me they might've gone to the ends of the earth so my sister could no longer ask them for anything. I thought it's about time they cut her off but then I got scared. The way it works, I always thought they'd do anything for us. Even if I didn't feel loved, I always believed they would die for me if need be.

I imagine Portia feels her life is slipping away. She's at the age when everything feels important because you have no idea you'll grow up and discover that it wasn't. The pain still marks you. So my daughter must suffer, ruminating on all she's missing when all she's missing is the usual daily tedium, the boredom and frustration that can drive anyone to despair. She still goes out running though I wish she wouldn't.

"I saw him," she says.

"He was watching you. Is he stalking you?"

She says, "I kept running."

I'm the one who's running out of time for something good to happen. For years I chose safety, what some would call deprivation, but this isolation is no longer my choice. When the country opens up, I'm afraid I'll be reckless. I'm afraid of what I may do. I need to be touched—right now—and not even my daughter will hug me.

I find I don't like myself as much as I expected to.

I find myself wondering when Mom stopped singing and when Dad put aside his guitar.

I used to sing a duet with Portia—*If I needed you,* and she'd respond *If you needed me…* We sang it as a round. You can harmonize without even trying.

Her name, something to ponder and probe. At her age you try to figure out not only who you are but what your parents blessed or cursed you with. Suzanne, an enchantress. Mary Ann, a source of pain. In the song, the man who longs for her suffers more than the lobster in the pot. Why didn't anyone want me? If I were going to believe the song, someone was pining for me, if only I knew who, but what if it was someone creepy, better not to know, better not to be in the position of having to dodge him, reject him, deal with him.

And what did I bestow upon my daughter?

I wanted her to be a lawyer. She was going to be Portia or, if a son, Perry. I still believed then in the rule of law, that for every wrong there is a remedy. She was born. I named her Portia. Was I already thinking, Oh, child, be merciful.

She can look me straight in the eyes, still nothing gets through, nothing is revealed. I'm sad. She's sad. Easy prey for TV hucksters with the promise of life-changing results. I know a surefire way—just ask Burp—a bullet.

I'm not asking for it.

The first time I tried suicide, which was not the first time I thought of it, I was 9 years old. I found a bottle of iodine in the bathroom closet, a skull and crossbones on the label. Poison. So I spilled some on a KitKat bar which I ate in bed expecting I wouldn't wake up. Then there was the time I cut my finger and wrote in blood on my parents' mirror. If I really wanted to kill myself, there were more effective and permanent ways. I thought of suicide all the time, but what I did I suppose would be classified as a call for help. What did I need saving from?

I've never actually met Taylor Burnham, just seen what he looks like in class pictures, like a boy who's just wet his pants, holding himself stiff and at the same time squirmy with distress, trying to decide how to compose his face.

It occurs to me Tommy probably looked like that years before I knew him, when he was still his mother's little boy, fearing the clutches of the Devil.

Burp looks harmless.

"You told me to be nice to him," says Portia.

Well, yes, but at the same time, girls have to learn not to be nice. We can't be nice all the time. It's not safe to be nice.

I wouldn't compare it to The Talk Black parents have with their sons, of course not, no comparison, though…

She says, "I told him you don't allow me to date."

"I'd rather you didn't. You're just 15. But we can talk about it."

"Mo-om. It was just an excuse." Taylor Burnham gives us something to talk about. "He says he'll eliminate the threat to our happiness." She says, "He means you."

By the time I was Portia's age and classmates started to slit their wrists, when Suzanne flirted with self-destruction, I couldn't understand. I played it safe. I hadn't thought of killing myself for years. I was well past the days when I enjoyed thinking my parents would grieve if I died. Just hold on, I told myself. A few more years and you can get away. Finally, you'll start your life.

I think Portia is counting the days till she can leave me. I think she's counting on me to talk to the boy.

If he listens, I'll tell him to be patient. What feels so overwhelming now, it passes. You'll move away and no one will know what they called you, or what you called your mother, or how they laughed at you, and how they shunned you. But I won't lie. I won't promise that someone someday will love you.

A good book, I'll tell him, can be a friend. I won't tell him it can also be a fuse.

You think you're different, Taylor Burnham, but in the end you're like me, you're like everyone. You'll arrive where you're going, you'll hunker down, you'll wait for it all to be over.

THE MOTHER HIVE

Christina Hoag

Al told Lyra not to worry, she'd killed twenty-six people.

"I knew I liked you," Lyra said.

Al snuggled closer to her, sandwiching their upper arms. Lyra leaned in. Al did the same so their hoodied heads touched, formed a triangle with their joined shoulders. They sat like that for a while in the darkness, feeling the wind cyclone through the empty building and their bruised souls.

Then Al said, "You should get some sleep."

"What about you?"

"Don't need much. I'm a real light sleeper anyway."

Lyra wriggled her body downward so her head pillowed on her backpack. Her lower back still hurt where the asshole had kicked her. She'd curled herself around her bag, embryo tight, until Al came along and brained the guy with a cricket bat. Of all things. Then she took Lyra to the abandoned building. That was two days ago. She finally stopped peeing blood yesterday.

A loud clap echoed from somewhere in the building. Al stiffened. "I better check that." She grabbed the cricket bat, a souvenir from Afghanistan, and made to get up from their small camp on the floor.

Lyra clutched her sleeve, suddenly wary of being left alone. "It's just a loose board, or a door. We can check it in the morning."

"I better do a perimeter check. It would be just like them to come when the wind is wild. Good cover."

As her footsteps thudded into silence, Lyra banked Al's sleeping bag against her like a bulwark and jack-knifed her knees, staring at the door. The angry wind had lifted up a torrent of dust. She held back a sneeze, afraid to release it in case someone heard her. The urge passed, replaced by a seizure of panic. What if Al didn't come back? She got a grip on herself. *I'll be fine. I got myself out of rehab jail, didn't I? I got myself here, didn't I?*

Time passed with aching slowness. Then the low pitch of a long whistle shot through the darkness. Lyra relaxed. The silvery light of a cell phone bounced off the walls like an echo. She detected shuffling footsteps in between Al's stride. She straightened. There *was* someone.

Al entered. "This is Ruby. She was hiding in the alcove of the back door. I told her she'd be safe up here with us."

In the rinse of light from the phone, Lyra could see Ruby's mouth was a smeared mess of crimson lipstick. Blood trickled from a nostril, bright against her olive skin, and her cheek was puffed, but it was the lipstick that got her. There was something shipwrecked about a woman with lipstick all over her face.

"Sure," Lyra said.

Ruby sniffed. "Thanks."

Lyra unzipped her sleeping bag and spread it flat on the ground. Al shifted her duffle bag to the center like a pillow. Lyra did the same with her backpack. Then she lay down and patted the space next to her.

"You can sleep here, Ruby."

Ruby lay down with her head on the duffle. Lyra dug out a roll of toilet paper from her backpack as Al cloaked them with her sleeping bag. Lyra pulled off a stretch of squares and started cleaning the lipstick off Ruby's face. Tears spilled from Ruby's eyes.

"Keep crying," Lyra said. "It's helping to get the lipstick off."

•

Tess raised her face for a wash of early morning sunshine as she stood on the expanse of terrace. The sea stretched before her, sapphire blue, flat as paper. She felt an upswell of gratitude.

Lyra had finally agreed to go to rehab. Jake had finally agreed to shoulder half the cost. And she was finally getting her writing career back on track, sending out story pitches and queries after years of living in a tailspin driven by her daughter's addiction.

The chirp of her mobile phone interrupted her reverie. She padded into the kitchen, the sash of her dressing gown trailing on the floor in a cartoon cat tail, and grabbed the phone on the table. When she saw who was calling, her body tensed. This can't be good. Not this early in the morning.

"Ms. Henkel? It's Daisy from Refreshe Life."

"Yes." Tess braced herself. Once again on the edge of the precipice.

"I'm afraid Lyra left the campus during the night. She wasn't at breakfast. We checked her room and found her backpack and clothes gone."

The morning's ease vanished. "When I enrolled her, I specifically asked about locks." A chisel drilled into Tess's temple, tightening her voice.

"I'm sorry. Maybe this wasn't explained properly to you. According to fire code regulations, we can't lock clients in. We've already reported this to the police. We're confident they'll find her. She can't have gone far."

After exacting Daisy's promise of updates as soon as she received them, Tess hung up. It was useless to get angry at the place now. She'd save it for later when they'd likely refuse to refund any of her $30,000.

The money was the least of it. She'd tried everything with Lyra over the past four years. The gentle approach. The tough love approach. Outpatient rehab. Inpatient rehab. Therapists, psychiatrists, addiction counselors. Anti-depressants. The last time Lyra had disappeared, Tess was called in the middle of the night three weeks later from an emergency room. Lyra had been sexually assaulted as she lay nodded out on the street. It scared Tess enough to push Lyra to go to Refreshe Life, and scared Lyra enough to finally agree to go.

Tess thought it would be a relief to hand Lyra over to the rehab place, to replace the duty of caring with her own ambitions again. It was, at first. But after two weeks, with her inbox remaining stubbornly empty of replies to her queries, she felt a pang that built into a tsunami of sadness. She missed Lyra.

Now she was being summoned back to the frontlines. Should she call Jake? He was covering the war in Ukraine. Undoubtedly shacked up with a young nubile photographer or a starry-eyed NGO volunteer. Phoning him would only lead to more disappointment. More resentment. The tragedy of his own daughter was always too small for him.

She switched into hunt mode. It felt as comfortable as pulling on a pair of yoga pants. She sat at her laptop and researched the areas where drugs were sold in the city where she'd left Lyra, then booked a cheap motel on that side of town. She slid open the bottom drawer of her desk and took out the well-worn envelope containing photos of Lyra to show to people, then crossed to her closet and pulled out her roller bag. She paused for a moment as she recalled what her therapist said during their last session.

"Do you really miss Lyra or being needed to save her?" the woman said.

"I miss *her*, of course," Tess said, indignation—or was it a sense of falseness? —coloring her voice.

She canceled the following appointment and never went back.

Light slid through the cracks in the boarded-up windows. Al's spot was empty. As soon as Lyra registered that, she detected a familiar scent, one she hadn't smelled in years. She followed it up a staircase to a metal door propped open with a hunk of wood. She pushed it wide and stepped onto the roof. Al sat on a plastic milk crate, puffing on a cigar, staring over the industrial sprawl punctuated with bright green of tree canopies here and there.

Lyra sat next to her on the ground, crossing her legs and leaning her head against Al's muscular thigh.

"I love the smell of cigars," she said.

"You may be the only one in the world."

"My dad smokes them."

"I started in Afghanistan. There's a lot of hanging around in the Army. More wait than war. Smoking was something to do. Everybody smoked cigarettes, but I liked cigars better."

"The twenty-six were from the war?"

"Mostly."

Lyra closed her eyes. She felt safe with Al. Protected. Something she'd never felt growing up amid the plates and glasses flying across the kitchen, the walls reverberating with recrimination and resentment. Her only solution was escape, physical and mental.

"I had a vision last night," Lyra said.

"Like a dream?"

"Yeah, but more real."

"Okay."

"Let's make a home here, like with furniture and stuff. We could barricade the stairs so no one could come up."

"You don't know them. They always find a way."

The Army was after Al. She knew too much, she said, and "they" were worried she'd tell. "There's only one way to shut people up for good. That's why I have to keep moving," she'd told Lyra.

Lyra leaned on her vision. Pushed it within Al's reach. "We'd stay on the down low. Nobody would find us."

A breeze blew. Al held up her cigar so the gust caught the ash, blasting it into wafer-thin shrapnel that fluttered away, then disintegrated. "Yeah, I could dig somewhere to stay for a spell. I've been traveling a good while."

"Me too."

Another long pause. "All right." Al slapped her free palm on her thigh. "Let's do it. You and me."

"Me and you."

They went downstairs a few minutes later to suss out what needed to be done. They walked around the top floor of the four-story building, wending through the warren of small rooms. They entered a room where dust motes made a milky way out of a shaft of sunshine.

"Looks like it was offices," Lyra said. "They even left some furniture. We can use all that."

She gestured at the chairs, desks, filing cabinets. In the middle of the floor, surrounded by the moat of the hallway, was the island of the elevator, stairwell, kitchen, and communal bathrooms, the kind where you had to ask at reception for the key that was attached to some oversized trinket.

"Can't you just see it, Al? Bedroom, living room. Get some pictures for the walls. Make a garden. Our own cocoon." Excitement flushed through Lyra at the thought of building something that belonged just to her without her mother telling her what she should do, what was wrong with her, the mistakes she was making, how getting pregnant and marrying her piece-of-shit father had ruined her career.

"We could grow vegetables for food," Al said.

"And flowers," Lyra said. "We have to have beauty."

"You're the beauty," Al said.

Lyra flushed with warmth and cast her eyes downward. No one had ever said anything like that to her. Al gently pulled her chin up.

A voice bleated behind them. "Can I stay? I got nowhere to go."

They wheeled. Ruby stood on the threshold. They'd forgotten about her. In the daylight, Lyra saw she was just a kid, a teenager. Al and Lyra exchanged glances. Who were they to turn her away? They were all women looking to shed unwanted lives.

"Okay," Lyra said.

"We share everything," Al said.

Ruby nodded like a bobblehead doll. She pulled out a wad of folded-up bills from her bra and offered it to Al. "What I made last night before I ran."

"You gonna have people coming after you?" Al said as she took it.

Lyra looked at Ruby, who was twisting her mouth at the wall instead of answering Al.

"Truth," Al said.

Ruby nodded. "I was his top earner. But I got this." She reached into the other cup of her bra. She pulled out a thin metal object and flicked it open. A switchblade.

"You got anything else in that bra we should know about?" Al said.

They all laughed. Light with relief, hearty with hope.

As they walked on, Lyra felt a pang of guilt. She hadn't told Al that she would have people coming after her, although Al hadn't asked. Lyra knew that at this very minute, her mother would be scouring a map to find her. Lyra was twenty years old, and her mom just wouldn't let her live her own life. She couldn't stand up to her, couldn't say no. In high school, she took the classes and signed up for the clubs her mom told her to, enrolled in the college her mom told her to, went to the shrinks her mom told her to, then it all would become unbearable. She'd start doing drugs, and then she'd run away from a life she didn't own. Her mom would find her. The cycle would repeat.

"You need to toughen up," her father told his daughter as he cleaned his lenses and packed them for the next war zone.

"Can I come with you, Dad?" Lyra said, a plaintive note in her voice. "Please."

"It's not a place for kids, honey," he replied. "I'll take you somewhere when I get back."

He never took her anywhere when he returned. Instead, he used her request to go with him as a weapon against her mother, which would cause another fight with Lyra. No more. Now she had Al.

Tess checked into a low-slung motel with dirty curtains and a stained carpet on the other side of town from Refreshe Life. After changing into her search clothes—jeans and a sweatshirt, tattered and frayed but still essentially whole, much like the state of her maternal love, she set out in the rental car. On the flight, she'd studied her map, marked bridges and highway overpasses, riverbanks, soup kitchens, homeless shelters, parks. She knew that searching by night was her best chance of finding her. By day, drifters seemed to melt into the asphalt and concrete.

It was twilight when she reached the first park. Arms jughandled on her hips, eyes narrowed, she scoured the place for young people who looked like they were living rough. Sure enough, a guy sat in a lotus pose on the grass playing a set of Pan pipes, his dirty blond hair a bird's nest of nascent dreadlocks, a spotted dog sitting Sphinx-like next to him. She approached him with a photo of Lyra. Asked if he'd seen her. He asked if she had any cash. She peeled a dollar off the stash that she'd brought for that purpose, making sure he saw she had more. He took the buck and shook his head. "Sorry."

Asshole, Tess thought. At least she'd only wasted a dollar on him. For the next three hours, she went through the same routine at two other parks, a street corner, and a small encampment in some bushes. She returned to the motel under a gibbous moon, exhausted and famished. She'd rise early and check the soup kitchens and homeless shelters, then go to a copy shop and print some flyers. Pin them up around town. She flopped onto the bed and checked her email. Holy shit. She'd received a response from a national magazine to her pitch for a story on the effect of climate change on the global food supply. She clicked on it.

"Good timing. I just had a story fall through, so I need something ASAP for next month's edition. Let's set up a time soonest to talk," the editor wrote.

Tess felt a pinch of fear. She couldn't take the assignment. She had to find Lyra. Always Lyra. Like when she applied for the editor's position at her newspaper and didn't get it. Like when she'd put in to join the investigative team. The day after the managing editor told her that the open spot on the team had gone to someone else, Tess took leave for "family reasons" and then resigned six weeks later. When the investigative team won a big prize that year, Tess said saving her small family was worth more than any prize. Jake tossed back his head and laughed. "Come off it," he said. "They had to run three corrections on your last big piece. You were never going to get that assignment. Face the truth. You're over."

Tess decided not to answer the magazine editor. She was back in action, on a mission to save her daughter.

•

Over the next days, Al, Lyra, and Ruby cleaned the top floor. They pooled their cash and bought groceries and utensils, a propane camping stove and candles. Ruby turned out to be an adept shoplifter, tucking soap and shampoo under her voluminous sweatshirt and inside her sleeves. They moved furniture from the bottom floors into the stairwell to block off two landings and rearranged other furniture in their home. Lyra took over meal prep, heating cans of baked beans and chili. She delighted in the empty plates and smiles of appreciation.

After one shoplifting expedition, Ruby brought back a woman she'd spotted doing the same thing in a drugstore. Chantelle was fleeing a boyfriend who had given her a broken arm and a swelling belly. She'd been riding freight trains for seven months and was now living out of a decrepit van she'd stolen, staying mobile so the guy wouldn't find her. Ruby figured they could use the van and Chantelle could use a stable place to hide. She moved in.

Once they had wheels, they drove around wealthier neighborhoods and picked up stuff people were throwing out, plates and glasses, cushions and chairs, a chest of drawers, a plastic tub for laundry, mattresses, paintings, and vases. Al only wanted to go out at night to avoid being seen by her pursuers.

On the way home, with the van loaded to the gills, they sang along to the radio with the windows open. Their favorite song was "Killing Me Softly." Lyra noticed that Al didn't even mind that people stared at them at traffic lights. Maybe, she thought, Al was feeling the same as she did. Round and full. Or maybe the people that were after her didn't exist outside her mind.

With some scrap lumber they collected and tools and nails Ruby lifted, Al cobbled together garden boxes. Lyra used a large cooking spoon to shovel earth into plastic bags from a patch of woods next to the building and filled the boxes. Chantelle pocketed some packets of carrot, tomato, zucchini, and lettuce seeds from a nursery, while Lyra dug pansies and marigolds and sunflower plants out of gardens by night.

"If we attract bees, maybe we can have a hive and make honey. We could even make it to sell," Lyra said.

Al looked at her with a bemused smile. "Is there no end to your vision?"

"I never really had a vision before. Are they supposed to end?"

"Maybe not," Al said.

"Maybe they can go on forever," Lyra said.

"Yeah, I never thought of it like that," Al said.

"You know what our place is?" Lyra said. "It's the Mother Hive."

"The Mother Hive," Al repeated. "I like it." She brushed a shock of hair out of Lyra's eyes. Lyra realized she hadn't even thought about getting high since leaving rehab.

At a soup kitchen, a young woman with eyebrow piercings and chapped lips advised Tess to check the rail yard. A lot of young people hung out there, waiting to hop freight cars, she said.

"People still do that?" Tess said.

"You'd be surprised," the girl said. She looked in need of a hot bath and a meal that contained all food groups. Tess handed her some money, aware that it would more likely be snorted, smoked, or shot up than spent on food, but at least she could say she tried to help.

Tess didn't get far into the rail yard. A bull-necked security officer sped up in a golf cart and bumped to a stop. She was relieved. Thought the fact that he carried a gun in a hip holster meant he was there to help.

"Ma'am, you're trespassing. You have to leave."

She told him why she was there. He twisted his head and spat a gob of chewing tobacco on the ground. It sat there, glistening in the sun. Tess's stomach turned.

"If we catch her, she's allowed a phone call."

Outside the yard, Tess sank to the curb in the shaded lee of the fence as the old hailstorm of self-pity pelted her. What did she do wrong? Why was she such a bad mother? What had she done to deserve this? What happened to her happy little girl? Why hadn't she had a second child? Why had she ever married Jake? Why had her life turned to failure? The hot bristles of tears pricked her eyes and then spilled over.

"You're not a cop, I take it."

Tess's head jerked up. An older man with stringy hair stood in the doorway of a shabby RV parked at the curb.

"No."

"But you're looking for someone."

"My daughter."

He nodded like he expected the answer. "I seen you at the soup kitchen this morning. At the park too."

She hadn't seen him, but she was focused on young people. This guy obviously got around. Was observant. She walked over to him, pulling out the photo from her back pocket. It was now creased and covered with greasy fingerprints. As he studied the picture, she switched to breathing through her mouth. The man stunk, a rank mixture of stale urine and unwashed body odor. He handed it back with a shake of his head.

"If she's riding the rails, she could be anywhere in the country right now."

"So, I should go home. Is that what you're saying?"

He stroked his whiskered chin. "I know some of the young ones. We share food now and again as they pass through. I did hear some talk about one of the girls going to live in a squat on the east side. They call it 'The Hive.' Just for women."

"The east side, you said?"

He nodded. "There's a bunch of abandoned buildings by the river. Used to be a nice neighborhood before the developer went bankrupt. Used up all his money for bribes to the city council."

Tess fished out her phone from her purse to look at the map.

"Something else," the man said. "The girl who left, she drove an old white van."

Nights were when Al grew restless and worried about the Army finding her. "I'm going to have to leave. I don't want to, but they're getting close," she said as Lyra drew her into her arms. "I can feel them."

Then Lyra remembered reading about castle keeps.

"I know what we can do, Al," she said. "We can turn this into a keep like in medieval times. They'd have a tower, and when invaders were spotted, they called all the serfs in from the fields to take shelter. The only entrance to the tower was a door high up on the wall. They entered by a ladder and then pulled it up after the last person. The only windows were narrow slits to shoot arrows out of. They kept stocks of food and water there in case of a siege."

Al's face brightened. "You're so smart, Lyra. That's exactly what we'll do."

Lyra beamed.

Al bought two long rope ladders and hung them from windows at the front and back of the building. They only used the front ladder, designating the one at the rear as the secret escape route. Anyone watching would assume the front window was the only entrance. Al also devised a pulley with a basket to hoist goods.

"At least I learned some skills in the Army besides killing," she said.

The night after they set that up, the four women lay around a fire they made in a rusting tractor-trailer rim. Somehow, they naturally shifted their bodies to make a connected square, heads resting on legs at the angles. The flames coated them with a sheen of molten light. Lyra felt serene. Free of expectations. Of judgment. Free to be herself, whoever that was.

The next day, she started drawing on the walls with a piece of charred wood from the fire. Shapes and squiggles of nothing in particular. She let her hand roam wherever it wanted, propelled by some unknown force like a Ouija board. Suddenly, it pushed her arm to sweep the wall with large loops and lines as high and wide as she could stretch.

"I like it," Al said. "You didn't tell me you were an artist."

She stood back and looked with surprise at what she'd just done. "I didn't know it myself," she said.

Later that day, Al and Chantelle arrived with half-used cans of paint of all colors, even some crazy ones like neons, that they picked up free from a recycling site, as well as brushes of all sizes.

"Now you can really go for it," Al said.

Lyra smiled.

•

For forty minutes, Tess drove up and down the streets on the city's east side down by the river. Some of the graffitied brick buildings were still occupied. Some looked abandoned. It was late afternoon. The air baked with the daylong heat. Tess's shirt was soaked with sweat. She braked at a stop sign and reached for her water bottle. Almost empty. She slugged what was left.

At what point was she going to give up? Return to her life? But rescuing Lyra was her life, and as much as she complained about it, she had to admit it was exciting. Dramatic. Purposeful. She and other parents she met at support groups exchanged emotional stories of the ordeals surrounding their addict children. Every night on this trip, she'd been calling other mothers to both seek and offer consolation. Sharing her experience made her belong to a community. Without Lyra, what would she have?

As she lowered the water bottle, she saw it. A rusting, dented white van. Wasn't that what that man had told her? It was parked inside a fenced area of an old building down the street to the right. Her stomach lurched. She pressed the gas pedal hard and veered to the right without looking. An oncoming truck honked loudly, and she slammed the brake, her heart clutching. Wouldn't that be the irony to cap all ironies? Killed as she found her lost daughter.

She parked in front of the building and got out of the car. A new padlock gleamed on the gate. This must be the squat. She'd have to wait until someone came out. A copse of trees at the side afforded the only shade in sight, plus a good vantage point to view the building through the chain link fence. She crossed into the patch of trees. One of her feet fell sideways into a shallow hole in the ground, wrenching her ankle. There were several holes around the trees, as if someone had been digging there. An animal maybe. She limped to a leafy tree and sank against its slender trunk. Her ankle pulsed with pain. Garden beds sat on the asphalt outside the building. New ones, by the look of them, with plants growing. People were definitely living there.

Tess struggled to stay awake in the hazy heat. She let herself doze off. She awoke in the voile of dusk light and licked her dry lips. Something was moving beyond the fence. She focused. A figure wearing a wide-brimmed straw hat, frayed around the circumference, puttered around the garden beds, lugging a heavy watering can.

She recognized the wide hips. They were hers. The figure turned her back to Tess. The tail of a dark red plait hung like a bell rope down the plumb line of her spine. Jake's hair. Tess stood, limped to the fence, and hung her fingers in the wire diamonds. She opened her mouth to call out, but no sound emerged.

Lyra deposited the watering can by the garden beds, then disappeared around the corner of the building. Tess clung tighter to the fence, relaxing her hold when Lyra reappeared, arms full of coffee cans containing plants. She placed them by the watering can, then knelt by the boxes, picked up a large spoon from the box, and dug a hole. She took a plant from a can and deftly sowed it in the earth like she'd been doing that her whole life.

Lyra was gardening? Since when? What else didn't she know about her daughter? It struck her that for years now, she'd mourned the little girl she'd lost and the addict she'd turned into. She didn't know who her daughter really was underneath the false layer of drug-addicted personality. She didn't know her at all.

When Lyra finished watering the seedlings, she stood, removed her hat, and swiped her perspiring forehead with her forearm. Her face was puffier than Tess remembered. Tess wanted to call out to her again, but another person appeared. A woman, tall and wiry, cornrows that draped the nape of her neck ending in a row of small hooks. Lyra turned towards her and smiled. A radiant smile that Tess also didn't recall ever seeing. Who was this person who was her daughter? Lyra and the woman kissed. On the lips. Another surprise.

Another pair of women appeared. One had long dark hair. The other was wearing a hippie dress of Indian cotton, tiny braids with colorful beads in her hair, and bare feet. Pregnant. Jesus. They vined their arms around each other's waists, backs to Tess, forming a crescent around the garden.

She stumbled back into the shelter of the trees, wincing with the pain of her twisted foot, and fell on the support of a trunk. For once, she was at a loss for what to do. Should she make herself known to Lyra? Offer to help her, take her home, give her money? Threaten to report her to the cops or call the rehab place?

Paralyzed, she stared at her daughter through the trees. Lyra looked fine. Healthy, in fact. Tess felt a corkscrew twist within her. Lyra was happy without her, making a life without her. Maybe she should do nothing, let her live the life she's chosen.

She watched the quartet of women until they disappeared around the corner of the building. Then she heaved herself to her feet and walked out of the trees into the night, feeling the press of the heat. As she drove back to the motel, she felt the click of release, the unlatching of a seatbelt. She would reply to the editor.

EVERY NOOK AND CRANNY, CRACK AND CREVICE

Shelley Lavigne

Pushcart-nominated purveyor of moist literature **Shelley Lavigne** lives in Ontario, where they roam the neighborhood in search of haunted houses and cool bugs. Their short fiction—mostly queer horror—has been published or is forthcoming in *The Dread Machine*, *PULP Literature*, and other independent anthologies. They are the author of *Sick! Stories from the Goop Troop* and co-author of *The Flesh of the Sea*. You can find them online at shelleylavigne.com.

The elevator doors are the gated type. They rattle with charm rather than squalor as Emily and I ascend. When we stop on the fourth floor and pull them back open, they hardly protest, well-oiled.

The hallway is like the rest of the building: well-maintained art deco, cone-shaped brass sconces, peach wallpaper, red carpet. I turn left without needing directions. Lefty instinct or a pull towards the apartment?

"Thank you again for doing this," I say to Emily as we arrive at the door. She places the keys in my hand and motions for me to use them.

The lock is slick, sucking at the key. I struggle to extract it, Emily's gaze—like a supervisor looking over my shoulder as I punch in produce codes—making me fumble.

The door opens with a warm sigh. Picture frame moulding decorates the walls. Milk glass pendants dangle from plaster medallions.

I follow Emily inside.

I see hints of the high schooler with whom I'd bonded over unacknowledged queerness—two gangly, awkward ducks who refused to wear the school kilt—in small-town Northern Ontario. We lost touch when she went away for uni so when she showed up at the grocery store a couple years after graduation with an undercut and a girlfriend, I was shocked but not surprised.

"You should visit, Nico. It's better in Ottawa. More open. You'd like it," she whispered as I handed her the receipt.

I resented her for the implication: that my hometown was backwards, I was too queer to fit in. But her statement opened a door I could no longer close. Four years of savings and remedial classes later, I landed a scholarship for mature students at the faculty of architecture. When I'd reached out to Emily to tell her the good news, she'd offered this house-sitting gig.

"The apartment has issues, but it's free until September. It's easier to house hunt in town."

When Emily throws the curtains open, the large living room floods with city light—hazy, yellow. The furniture is mismatched, a futon, an antique settee, a square coffee table—abandoned remnants of previous tenants. To my right is a bitten-lip pink marble mantle. The fireplace is filled in with bricks.

It's nearly perfect, its issues cosmetic at best; baseboards and panelling are outlined in dust, a city-painted cloisonné; the floor varnish is worn away in places, wood the faded beige of old straw.

If the slight disrepair were Emily's "issues" I'd hate to hear what she thought of my house—the dishes on the counter, discarded sports equipment in the halls, the twins screaming at some videogame blasting in the living room.

"Thanks for letting me crash here."

"Us small-town lesbos need to help each other out."

I flinch. That term never felt comfortable to me and the casual branding makes my skin crawl. I don't want to bring attention to it, especially if that's the reason she's helping me. I'm not even sure what I would say. I don't yet have the words to explain my gender and I don't want to confuse or inconvenience folks if my thinking changes down the line.

Better to explore it on my own first.

Better to wait until I am not reliant on her for shelter.

"Right."

"Inheriting this condo was a curse. The fees and taxes are so high and tenants keep breaking their leases. I barely break even."

I cannot imagine why anyone would leave this place. It has charm.

I am charmed.

"The vibes here are off. I feel kinda bad luring you here and not telling you about it but Betty—my girlfriend—says she can come by and purify the place with sage if you have issues."

I feel none of these *vibes*. The apartment is old, sure, but that doesn't automatically fill it with spectres.

Unburdened, Emily speeds for the door, fumbling with the lock. She only looks back once she's over the threshold.

"Stagers will be here on Monday, showings start Tuesday. I'll be looking for a September first move in, just over a month away. There should be a bunch of apartments available, you'll find one easy-peasy."

"Thanks again," I say, pushing the door closed.

It slams shut.

The pendant light swings, making my shadow nod.

I should re-open the door, apologise to Emily, but her footsteps quickly recede. There's a rapid-fire triple beep as she summons the elevator.

Then silence.

No siblings, no clients or colleagues.

My brothers bet I'd last two days max on my own, driven insane by the lack of distraction from my "deep dark thoughts." I'd thought they might be right.

Until now.

I don't need to worry about passing—is my voice high, posture right, smile bright? I don't need to be *Girl Enough* for those around me—I can just be myself.

I could get used to living alone.

Especially in a place like this.

I should rest—or eat—but the dirt and dust keep me from closing my sandpaper-lidded eyes. Experience tells me I'll be too bothered by the mess to sleep.

As a kid, I'd checked out sun-bleached architecture books from the library. Every page was a window into a fantasy life; the quiet calm order of the picture-perfect homes, the way everything had a place. I held them inches from my nose, blocking out reality. This place is better.

In the entryway, I run a dampened cloth along the moulding. The unveiled whiteness is pure, radiant. Slowly, I peel back the city soot. After an hour, the mouldings gleam like new.

The kitchen tile is refreshingly cold underfoot when I finish. I bring my wrinkled, wet hands to my neck, letting the cool liquid trickle down my back. The golden hour light streams through the window like a blessing.

My stomach emits a gurgle that's echoed by the sink drain.

I scrounge the cupboards and dine on canned tuna and stale soda crackers.

I'll tackle groceries tomorrow, I promise myself, before slouching towards the bedroom to be reborn.

"Miss, do you need a bag for your groceries?"

My skin crawls, ill-fitting like a dollar-store Halloween mask.

It's just a stranger, not worth correcting.

I should be used to this by now.

It's just old-fashioned, drilled in by training, more polite.

"No, thank you."

Cleaning products dig red canyons in my knuckles. With no one telling me to stop picking at myself, I pull at hangnails and suck on bleeding fingers. A constellation of bruises form on my legs, almost as if they absorbed the blemishes and imperfections of the apartment.

I avoid the bathroom, daunted by the tiles and grout and nooks and crannies, putting it off until I've dusted and cleaned every other inch of this place. But on the third day, there's no more putting it off.

The yellowed grout bites at my knees. It's like kneeling on sandpaper. I soap and scrub and rinse and scrub until it turns light grey. The place looks fresher even with such a small change.

As I stand, I catch a glimpse of myself in the mirror.

Freeze.

The face looking back at me is not the one I've made peace with for 25 years.

My hair is nearly buzzed, the haircut I've never been brave enough to ask for. My jaw and cheekbones are sharper, dusted with hair and glitter. My nose fits my face, dignified, strong. It flares like a bull—and oh gosh—I have a nose ring. Red lipstick that's too feminine for me to wear in public accentuates the bow in my upper lip and pairs with my dusting of strawberry blonde facial hair.

I blink. The image shifts back to the face I'm used to.

I move around the bathroom, trying to find the reflection from before, trying to catch one more glimpse of the face I wish I had.

It never shows itself again.

The roommates-wanted ad says "Safe Space: women/AFAB only" and I want to peel off my own flesh. The rent is decent, the place looks nice, but is it worth hiding a part of myself they find repulsive? Would I be safe in a space that seeks to exclude folks like me?

I have over a month before I need to leave.

There's no rush.

A dream: I am in the apartment, transformed into the home I'd make if I was allowed to stay—dark walls, art, cozy antique furniture.

The door has scabbed over, and red inflamed skin around it feels warm to the touch, infected. I rub ointment onto it, big handfuls from a paint-can-sized tub.

The windows in the living room are big brown eyes. The curtains hold me in place, stroking my inner thigh as I lick the cornea and chocolate and whiskey coat my tongue.

I crouch in the hallway to flatten peeling wallpaper. The maroon wall underneath is liver-dark—similar to its colour in my dreams—and fuzzy like the skin of a peach. I stroke the crimson down but instead of a firm surface, my finger ruptures the soup-skin membrane.

The space beyond is flesh-warm, custard-thick.

Something like a tongue strokes my finger from the base to the tip. Lips suck on the end.

I've never been touched like this, too uncomfortable with my own flesh to let someone else get this close to me. It's a rush of *no, stop* paired with *flay me alive*.

Panic wins and I pull out my finger with a damp pop.

The digit tingles but is otherwise unharmed.

Lying flat on the floor, the hardwood digging painfully—pleasurably—into my hip bones, I smell chocolate and whiskey. The flap looks like an open mouth. I want to lick into the gap but instead, I sink my index and middle finger into the soft crimson. I press deeper, my fingers slipping past the knuckles.

The hole is fever-warm, hungry. Its peristaltic motion pulls in my wrist, my forearm. It massages the tension from my sore arms, a thank you for my hard work.

I close my hand, fisting it. Filling it.

The walls shudder, pulling me in with more force. I skid on the hardwood, sweaty palm squealing.

The sound snaps me out of it; I'm about to be sucked in. My nails gouge the floor, scrambling for purchase. My shoulder passes the threshold.

I brace my feet against the wall and push—

Pop.

I'm all there: five fingers, five nails, skin sunburn red. I scramble away.

In the living room, sunlight has been replaced by streetlamps. My arm grows cold and I feel the wall's temptation once more.

It was so warm. And nice, being held.

I give the wall a wide berth, afraid I'll be sucked in again, afraid I'll push myself into it. But perhaps most afraid that, like the mirror, it will be ordinary upon further inspection. Another hallucination fuelled by my unchecked desires.

In my dreams, strips of wallpaper reach out and wrap me in a cocoon. In its protective warmth, I liquify like a butterfly.

I wake up before I finish my transformation.

•

Two older men cross the street behind me.

"I fucking love summer."

"Yeah, all those pretty young things in shorts and dresses."

I feel their gaze like hands on my body—I wish my body made clear that to desire me is queer, that communicated to straight men I'm not *for* them.

They follow me for a block, two, before I arrive home.

The intercom buzzes.

"Hello?"

"It's the stagers."

"I'll let you up."

One is carrying a clipboard, the other two carry a hypermodern couch. Its bulbous protrusions should fit through the doorway, according to Clipboard's measurements, but it gets stuck in the jamb.

Emily arrives as they reinstall the door. Her eyes shine as she inspects the place.

"This place is sparkling! Don't take this badly but you'd make some power-dyke a good housewife."

Now isn't the time for this conversation.

"How about you go see some apartments while we work? You've done so much, it's our turn," Emily suggests.

"Can I keep the old furniture? I don't have anything for my new place."

"Yeah, put it in the storage unit downstairs." She extracts a key from her ring. "It's got a bunch of my aunt's shit, so I'm not sure how much will fit."

The "shit" are some boxes and wrapped frames but there's plenty of room for the futon, lamps, folding chairs and bedside table.

"Heading up?" a stager asks, holding the door. Even though I'd rather stay, I follow him back to the lobby where Emily is waiting. She points me in the direction of campus.

She doesn't ask for the storage key.

"Good luck!"

As I near the University, rental signs sprout on lawns like dandelions, promising a host of different living accommodations: studios, one or two bedrooms, rooms to let.

Call! Inquire! Tours today!

The only places I can afford are the rooms in joint housing. Shared kitchens and bathrooms. No privacy. Like living with family, but worse.

And I'd have to out myself and hope for the best from some complete strangers. Or continue in Cis Girl Mode for another four years.

I head back home—to the apartment, loitering a block away before Emily texts that the stagers are done.

Be careful with the furniture, you'll need to pay for damages.

The front door opens with a whine and I shudder at what the place has become. The too-modern furniture clashes with its old-school elegance. It looks like me in a dress. The new couch is sculptural, the dining table too chrome for the surroundings, the dresser bulbous as if conceived during an acid trip.

I tug the futon out of storage and into the sunroom. As I drift off, the walls squeeze in, swaddling me. Like a protective kind of smothering.

We have showings today from 11 to 2:30.
So soon?
Yeah! The new furniture really helped!
LOTS of marketplace nibbles!
How's your search going btw?
I have a couple leads.
SO relieved to hear that!

I wait out the tours in the storage locker. The limestone walls weep hard, slick slime and the bare bulb that dangles from the ceiling does little to lessen the cave-like atmosphere.

It's still better than going outside.

And I can satisfy my curiosity.

The boxes open with a coquettish gasp. Inside, I find tchotchkes, old art books, clothes that are masculine of center. I help myself to a couple jackets.

There are also a handful of pictures. One face recurs in many shots, brown curly-haired bob, thick-framed glasses. The scribbles on the back name her Alexandra Taft.

Emily's aunt was hot, butchy.

I move on to the paintings, all signed A. Taft. The interiors they depict give me a sense of déja vu. Light falling on stuffed bookcases in the sunroom, a meal laid out in a dark, candle-lit dining room, a hand gripping the clawfoot bathtub's rim.

The apartment as it looks in my dreams.

I've been dreaming of how it was before Emily made it a greige rental.

The last one is a portrait of the former owner of the apartment. While I recognise the curly brown hair, glasses, full lips and freckles from the pictures, the cheek and jawbone are more defined, dusted in a five o'clock shadow. There's even a triangle of an Adam's apple visible between the open collar of a button-down shirt.

Emily's relative—I fell into the same trap others do with me and I try not to lapse into self-loathing—had been queer too, maybe even trans.

"I wish I could have met you," I say.

There's someone waiting for the elevator when I step into the lobby.

"Are you Emily's little lady friend? The one taking care of her place?"

She's just old, she doesn't know any better. If I explained, it probably would just confuse her.

"Yeah."

"This is such a lovely building and community. I hope you enjoy your time here."

In my dreams, the scabbed-over door heals into a scar, the skin raised and pink. Oversensitive, the walls in the entrance shudder as I run my hands over the new flesh.

The intercom to my right morphs into full lips.

"I've been waiting for you."

Emily's text dings around dawn: *call when you're awake.* The afterglow of my dream is extinguished when I read the message.

I know her news before she shares it.

"I found some new renters: a pair of pharmacists who just moved to town. They loved the place. Said they could really see themselves living there."

I pinch myself, hoping I'm still dreaming.

It just adds to my pain.

"I appreciate you cleaning up. Obviously, the staging helped, made it feng shui, but you made it shine."

My complicity in my own destruction makes the sting worse.

"What if I rented it from you instead?" I ask before realising how desperate I sound.

"Sweetie, there's no way you can afford it." She hears the whimper I fail to contain, becomes apologetic. "I'm so thankful for what you did, so proud of you for moving out of Sturgeon Falls, and for going back to school as a mature student. That's so amazing. Truly! But I can't rent this place at a loss. I might as well live in it then, you know? We'll find you something else, I promise!"

She's silent, waiting for me to agree, thank her for her *generous* offer. I don't.

She never could handle silences. "You always knew this was temporary and–"

I hang up, dissolving into tears. I count my days left. Thirty-three. That isn't enough.

There will never be enough.

This is my safe space. I still had so much to learn about myself, so much left to do to make this place really shine.

"You don't have to leave."

A crackling voice shakes me from my stupor. The intercom, like in my dreams.

I crawl to the entryway, desperate, palming my way up the wall. I press myself to the perforated surface, their sigh is warm against my cheek.

"But Emily won't let me stay. What can I do?"

"Come to me, baby."

From anyone else, that endearment would have made my skin crawl. But this place has seen the true me—it's shown me a face I've always wanted—and in that nickname I feel seen, because I do want to be taken care of.

By them.

A crash draws me to the living room. The bricks in the fireplace fall, revealing a dark tunnel inside the pink stone mantle. A re-birth.

An unbirth.

The darkness within has the same gravitational pull that drew me to this place. It's my fate, the force that has guided me my whole life; the obsession with architecture, the desire to find a place where I can be myself, the desire to be of use. The discomfort in my own flesh.

I duck under the mantle. Pigeon bones crunch underfoot.

In them, I scry my fate: I, too, will come to my end here.

Panic grips me as I back out, an explosion of light as I hit my head.

"It's not the end. Climb, Nico."

The voice comes from above. From the impossibly-bright-for-dawn light ahead.

Because it isn't daylight, it's something else. Someplace else.

My fingers find purchase on old brick, the light from above highlighting ledges to grip. As I move up the walls, they tighten around me, holding me.

"Don't let me fall."

"Never."

I stretch as I pull myself up, lengthening in the narrow space. My bones protest, growing pains shooting through my body like current in a wire. Sweat stings my eyes, watered down by tears. My muscles strain to function under such torsion, shaking, pleading with me to go back before I no longer can—what's a broken bone compared to this extranormal transformation?

My body fights me just as it always has, beholden to the rules and norms of the world that never did suit me.

Mind over matter, I continue forward.

My skin catches on the stone walls that press around me, a final grasp to hold me back. I pull up. My shoulders tear, flesh ripping off of me in ribbons. I hear the distant slop of my epidermis hitting the ground. Now unwrapped, I can see my muscles quiver, pulse, stretch as I grasp the rock, climbing ever further. My blood slicks the walls, lubricating my passage, easing my journey.

The pain becomes pleasure as I shed what held me back, as I'm stripped to my undiluted core. There are no gender markers left, there's barely anything that marks me as human.

The walls contract in waves, pushing me towards the light.

My fingers tingle, losing their grip. But I don't fall. The walls hold me too tightly for that. Nor do I need to pull myself forward. They'll do the work for me.

The light ahead explodes into a thousand stars.

THOSE THIN PLACES

Jon Lasser

Jon Lasser is an author of contemporary and speculative fiction. His stories have been published or are forthcoming in *Lightspeed*, *Fourteen Hills*, *Analog*, *Spartan*, *Interzone*, *Ampersand Review*, and elsewhere. Jon is a graduate of the Clarion West Writers Workshop. You can connect with him through his website, twoideas.org, or in the Fediverse @disappearingjon@wandering.shop.

Julia specialized in spirit macrophotography, the souls of departed mice or voles fleeing this world upon the backs of starlings and whatnot. The secret was going to the thin places, for example some Queens graveyards, where the dead pressed their faces up against the membrane between worlds and could sometimes be seen, could sometimes cross over as though via osmosis.

In certain other places, the opposite effect emerged: places where the living haunted the dead. Julia imagined hyper-saturated gatecrashers spoiling the stillness of the grey beyond. The spirits, she gathered, were not fans. Once upon a time, the thrum of the island's crowds seeped into the realm of spirits, scattering the shades. Now a wave of empty luxury towers loomed like cenotaphs in the Manhattan skyline.

She'd come here, one of those Billionaire's Row spires, to take photographs. Part of the never-ending stream of lawsuits that the leaky, creaky, faceless wall of glass had sired. Strange noises from the elevator shafts. Viscous fluids dripping where no pipes were documented in the engineering drawings. The run-of-the-mill problems endemic to these ultra-tall towers. Her contact whispered of a thin place in the middle of the city, but they needed photographs to prove their case.

Julia once believed she would never sell out her art. Never be reduced to taking snapshots for an insurance job. But she was sick of frozen French Bread pizzas and wine filched from art shows so vacant she worried ghosts might crash. Sick of her roommates' baleful looks when rent was overdue, the empty feeling inside her chest that expanded like a bubble, suffocating her when she realized she was being left behind.

The apartment was larger than her third-floor Brooklyn walk-up, larger than her childhood home in Cherry Creek. Larger than she could take in at a single glance, with floor-to-ceiling views that gave her the spins until she curled up in the center of the enormous living room and held tightly to the dazzling carpet, on which that nearly-new chemical smell still lingered. The floor thrummed softly as though alive. The vista hollowed her out as though she was one of those dying voles, perhaps in the same way that money had hollowed out this neighborhood. She caught her breath and stood.

Where to start? Julia was used to the way thin places stretched near the edges, in darker corners, but everything here was light and open. "Airy." "Modern." There was no place for the dead—and yet, off the record, they were here. That was how empty the building was, how empty this part of the city had become.

There was nothing in this apartment for the living or the dead to long for, nothing but the idea of money. Whoever owned it wasn't hungry for anything; they lacked the gut tug of true appetite. She felt certain they'd never lived here, never even set foot in it. This wasn't a home, only part of a portfolio—one cog in a money-laundering machine that extracted ill-gotten gains from Russia or China or some other benighted authoritarian regime and, through the alchemy of capital, transmuted that blood money into thousands of these desolate abodes.

People like this had ruined her city, these absentee billionaires, who had thinned out this neighborhood so much that the osmotic pressure had, after centuries, reversed. Here she was, taking their money to photograph the dead they had inadvertently engineered into appearing, photographs they would distill into money as they had this entire neighborhood.

Surely this dismaying environment could not attract the spirits—but its emptiness offered them the opportunity to cross over. Julia stared at her feet and shuffled toward the window to pull the curtains shut, take the edge off the acrophobia, and blot out that low-hanging sun besides. They had no cord or rod. No visible means of closure. One of the switches on the wall behind the wet bar? She trundled over to examine the panel.

The rich have too many light switches. If she lived in this place—she could scarcely imagine—she would have labeled the twelve in this bank. Lights flickered throughout the apartment as though Julia haunted it until she tried the last switch on the right. A quiet whir as the draperies were set in motion.

When the last curtain pulled itself closed, she breathed easier. The thrum of altitude still tickled her feet and would not go away. It's only the wind, she told herself, playing this empty tower like a flute.

Julia darted off through one of the doors into the back half of the unit. A bedroom, the bed alone larger than all the space she could call her own put together. The curtains here were closed.

She willed herself to peek out the window, to master the dizzy vacuousness the height provoked within her. She peered out from a gnomon whose shadow stretched across Park Avenue, marking time. She reeled back, dropping the curtain, and fell upon the bed.

Julia closed her eyes and reached out with her other senses in search of the thinnest nearby place. The air tasted antiseptic, as though some luckless maid came each week to dust and mop the empty unit. Back in the living room, she ran her fingers over the marble bartop but felt nothing beneath the cold, smooth stone. The distant roar of a jet engine. No, closer. The clock in the entryway, a two-and-a-half foot wide sunflower, ticked quietly. (Her friend Alan would know what it was; he knew all about clocks and watches, but he wasn't here.) The mosquito-like buzzing of a florescent light, an overtone carried atop the sixty-cycle hum infesting the modern world. Not the sort of light one would find in a place like this.

They were hiding. Was the presence of a single person enough to push back their incursion? Perhaps that was why she'd been tapped for this gig: The others, who did not believe, could not locate the spirits when they receded.

Where did the humming center? Another room, closer to the geometric center of the unit. Merely the elevator bank? No—the kitchen, which in so many houses would be the center, a-thrum with life, but which here was empty as the rest—emptier perhaps for that expectation of fullness.

The buzzing sound hovered closer. There was the induction range, the double electric wall ovens—but where was the refrigerator? A palisade of integrated cabinets slid aside, revealing the bare-shelved pantry, containing the now-suddenly-unfashionable stainless-steel refrigerator and freezer. Julia stepped in.

Yes. Camera in one hand, she opened the refrigerator's French doors with the other.

The completely vacant refrigerator—not even a ketchup bottle—boiled with spirits of all kinds. Spheres of fire; spheres of frozen mist; men without eyes, blood spattered artfully across their torsos; lizard skulls whose jaws silently jabbered; and one black-haired white-faced maiden whose hair pooled above as though she was beneath water. Julia snapped picture after picture of their sad and thirsty faces, which peered at her from the crisper drawers and egg tray.

A hand, spectral as the aurora borealis, reached out.

Julia jerked the camera away as though the ghost meant to steal it. Then, more slowly, she took the offered hand.

She'd seen the hands of thousands of the dead. Stranger's hands, friendly hands, cold-hearted hands, grasping toward the cemetery gates or clawing through newly lain dirt. This hand had belonged to a baker, a cobbler, perhaps a butcher. Strong hands, adept with a cleaver. Hands that had cured meat. Trimmed the steaks. Stuffed the sausages to feed the neighborhood. Here he was, trapped on the other side of an empty refrigerator.

She still held his hand. Was it a comfort to the dead to hold them, or did that excess of life burn like lye? It was a comfort to her to touch the past city, the one that had preceded these hollow monoliths. A hand that had seen work, likely also poverty worse than what had hounded her, poverty he had overcome to thrive.

It wasn't something she'd thought about, and afterward, Julia would never tell anyone why she'd done it, why she'd risked death or worse. Why she'd grasped for a line from a city defined by capital flows to something more atavistic. Why she was afraid of the emptiness inside herself. "If I'd seen someone hanging off a cliff by their fingernails, I'd've pulled them up," she'd say, but that wasn't it at all.

The ghost tumbled through, taking on corporeal form where he sloughed off the caul-between-worlds. Yes, a butcher once, from a time when that job could feed a family. A beard that could have been the twenty-tens but also a hundred years earlier down on the Lower East Side. What was he doing uptown? He didn't belong here any more than Julia.

"Hello?" she asked. "Can you hear me?" And, when he didn't answer, "Do you speak English?" For all his seeming solidity, the revenant did not reply.

She snapped a string of photos. This—this was her paycheck. The city's finest banks would roll out the red carpet for her after these photographs. She would become part of the city's movement on the back of this spirit.

He wandered out of the pantry, through the kitchen, back into the living room. Before he took a seat at the bar, he adjusted his dungarees, straightened his denim work shirt, and flipped the switch to open the curtains. Even this ancient remnant had more facility with the controls than Julia.

It was funny: She'd seen so many spirits on the other side of the caul, taken the pictures of animals whose souls fled to join them—but she'd never seen a shade that had so fully crossed back into this world. It was different, new. So many questions she wanted to ask. Who he was. Why he had reached out—was it merely impulse, or a choice freely made? Where he had come from. But the curtains were open now, and Julia found herself on the plush carpet, the room around her spinning.

"What do you want?" she croaked, hands shielding her eyes from the bright, hands-wide-open world.

This time, he heard her. His empty eyes fixed on her. He stood, lumbering forward.

For maybe the first time in Julia's career as a paranormal photographer, dread gripped her. A cold hand tugged on her gut. Sweat beaded on her forehead, droplets emerging like that arm from the refrigerator.

The dead were innumerable and unconcerned with the living. Whatever Julia wanted—a paycheck, artistic validation, a bowl of soup—was irrelevant to them, as immaterial as they to her when they remained on the other side of the barrier that was not entirely a barrier. The dead had their own plans, ones Julia perhaps could not understand. She crawled toward the sofa and pulled herself onto it.

She felt barely dizzy at all when she kept her eyes closed. His emptiness dazzled her. Whatever he had once been, the blank space inside had become a mirror reflecting Julia's emptiness back at herself—two mirrors, infinitely reproducing nothing.

"Come here." She patted the overstuffed leather next to her. "Tell me what's on your mind." But the spirit trudged forward toward the entryway clock, where he disappeared.

Julia slid off the sofa and crawled behind the bar. She pulled herself up and pressed the switch, drawing the curtains shut.

She pulled up her shots on the camera. There he was, outlined more starkly than in person, almost like Kirlian photography. The clients would be satisfied. She would be paid. She'd warn them about the refrigerator.

Despite that twist in her gut, the spirit had been docile. He hadn't harmed her, unless you counted opening the curtains on that vertiginous landscape. He would find his own way home.

But what would the insurance company do if they found out? Could they trace him back to her?

She pulled out her phone and rang Alan.

"Shit," Alan answered. He preferred to text. "Is everything okay, Julia? Are you in danger?" Alan worried about danger a lot for someone who spent his days taking "spiritual photographs" of inanimate objects. Julia wondered how he earned a living. He had a rich boyfriend and had once mumbled something about a family trust. Whatever it was, he was always charming and just a little too concerned about safety.

"No. Maybe. I don't think so. I made a mistake. I—I took an insurance job. That new tower on Billionaire's Row. They said it was haunted. I pulled a ghost through from the other side. He's—he's around here somewhere."

"Is he angry?"

"He scared me, but I don't think so. Do you think they could prove I brought him through? Could they sue me?"

"They can sue anyone. Even if you win, they'll ruin you." He sounded so certain. "You should send him back to be sure." She wasn't sure he was right, but Alan knew how wealthy people behaved. To her, they were as alien as the spirits. Even him, who she adored.

"I don't know how."

"You think I do?" Alan sounded more amused than angry. She could almost see the twinkle in his eye as he dropped his voice a register. "Is he cute? Should I bring bell, book, and candle? Or handcuffs and a bottle of chardonnay?"

"I'm not sure he's your type." That was a lie. Alan definitely had a taste for rough trade.

"Anything else? I haven't eaten lunch. I'm right by Szechuan Kingdom."

"Oh God. I could have a bite. The eggplant in garlic sauce?" It wasn't as good as it used to be, back when the Kingdom nearly lived up to its name with branches all over Midtown and the Upper West Side, but she'd been going there as long as she'd lived in the city, and it was something to hold onto when things got bad or weird, and this was definitely one of those.

"I'll pick it up and catch a cab. Should be to you in thirty minutes or less." He blew a kiss. "Hold down the fort a little bit longer and call if you run out of ammo." Alan hung up.

Julia sat on the floor behind the bar, not quite daring to get back onto the couch. It would feel easier with someone here. Not because it was, but because it was harder to admit she had a problem than to pretend everything was okay, that these vertiginous views didn't feel like she was already falling through the floor-to-ceiling windows.

Alan was as good as his word, arriving twenty-eight minutes later with a small duffel under one arm and, in the opposite hand, a paper bag leaking steam out the top and hot grease out the bottom. He stepped into the living room, dripping Chinese food all over a carpet that 'must have cost more than Julia's annual rent.

"Jesus, Alan!" Julia stood, tottering, and willed herself to not look out the windows. "You're fucking up that—"

Alan marched over to the bar, put the bag on the marble, and shot her a crinkled grin. "Tell 'em the ghost did it. Ectoplasm. The insurance will cover it." Even though the insurers didn't believe in ghosts, Alan wasn't worried he'd be blamed. He worried for her about the ghost, which wasn't her fault, and not at all about the grease, which was his. Guys like him skated across the surface of life while the gears beneath crushed all the Julias. She laughed, but her hand on the bartop searched for something to grip.

"You got eggrolls." A hint of awe crept into her voice. They didn't have anything like New York eggrolls in Denver, where she'd grown up. Crispy, flaky, with bubbling skin, shrimp and carrot and cabbage enough to keep your hands warm on a winter day as you nibbled while walking down the street. (In Denver, their skins were thinner, smoother, and the rolls thinner too—more like what New Yorkers called a spring roll.) All these years living in the city and she still wasn't over them.

Alan handed her a wax paper bag. She bit in, squirting hot grease all over her chin.

"You have any clean napkins in that bag, or are they all at the bottom soaking up the oil?"

Alan handed her a napkin, and didn't say another thing until she was done with the eggroll. Then he only said, "Eggplant?" before handing her the carton and a pair of chopsticks.

Julia put down the empty carton and wiped her face with another napkin. She would have killed for a cup of tea, even a Diet Pepsi. Alan would've brought either one if she'd thought to ask.

"Aren't you going to eat anything?"

"I did on the way over. Uber driver's going to hate me." He laughed as though that wasn't possible. Julia half-believed nobody could. "So where's the ghost?"

"He came in through the thin place in the fridge but disappeared in the entryway by the clock."

"Did you know that was a genuine vintage Nelson sunflower clock? Not the Vitra reproduction, the original? Someone put a quartz movement in, the heathens, but you can tell. The patina." Alan delivered the line with a sort of hushed reverence Julia saved for New York eggrolls. She'd known he liked clocks and watches, always wearing fancy ones he endlessly explained, but she hadn't guessed he had feelings for them.

"I had no idea." She wasn't sure exactly what he was saying, but to him, this was pivotal, a telling detail about the people who did not live here. Something he might have learned about from his family. He'd led Julia to believe they were wealthy but cold, not only because he was gay. He hadn't outrun them completely, not any more than Julia had outrun her own childhood.

"You pulled him through? You're lucky he didn't pull you through." Alan shook his head again.

"I took pictures." She handed him her camera. "He hasn't tried to hurt me. He's probably harmless."

"You think everything about the past is harmless," Alan snarled. What had she done to upset him?

"Fair enough. But they've ruined this city."

"Who? Ghosts?"

"Not the ghost I let through, the ghosts who own this apartment. Who treat it like an investment rather than a home. They probably have half a dozen, a dozen units like this in different cities, making them all the same wherever they are. Turning Manhattan into Dubai-on-the-Hudson or some shit."

Alan stared out the window and didn't say anything for a minute. He pointed somewhere Julia couldn't see. "See that building?"

She'd have to get up from the bar to look.

"Uh—could you help me? I get… vertigo… near the windows."

"Oh, Darling!" He was soft with her again. She preferred him that way, the gentle man who would help her to the window, not the one who was angry because they didn't see the city the same way.

The building he pointed at had a tall spire—well, it had been tall before these mega-towers—whose roof appeared to be the same blue-green as the Statue of

Liberty, beautifully patinated copper. Gold ornamented the windows, or perhaps that was simply sunlight reflected off masonry. Numerous roof decks were laid out with tables, chairs, and potted plants.

"That's what should stand here. Not this."

"That's the Crown Building, Darling. It dates back to 1921. Probably the same era as your ghost, maybe a few years later, but same ballpark. In 1981, Ferdinand Marcos bought it. That putz Spitzer bought it from him."

"Eliot Spitzer? That putz?"

"His dad. Eliot inherited it, eventually. And a few years back, a Russian billionaire bought it. That's a long list of people you don't want to piss off. All rooted in the old New York you've romanticized. The players are different now, but the game's the same. Forget those ghosts; this ghost is no joking matter—"

"You're right. I know you're right." She wasn't sure, but gentle Alan was better than angry Alan, so she played along.

"—Not anymore. You've let something loose in the world. It's powerful, its motivations may be unfathomable, its hungers bottomless. And without a doubt, it's angry." His face was red, like he'd been yelling, even though he hadn't raised his voice. His fingers trembled.

"Angry? It—he hasn't done anything at all. Just kind of wandered around. Like a dad looking for snacks." Whatever Alan believed, he was projecting. He hadn't seen him.

"You don't want to get sued, do you?" He dropped his voice to a whisper, hissing. "They'll ruin you." He went to the duffel bag. "We have to perform an exorcism."

The bell was smaller than Julia imagined. Tarnished silver, not brass.

"It's the only thing I kept after the fire," Alan said. Julia didn't know and didn't ask him to explain; she'd already fixed her gaze on the Bible he removed from the duffel.

It was old. At first, she wondered if it was handwritten, illuminated by monks centuries before Europeans invaded this country. (Surely, in those ancient days, the dead must have pressed through the thin places more often.) But no, it was printed on a press—still, perhaps older than Plymouth Rock. The leather shone with oil; it had been well taken care of.

The candle could've been from a child's birthday cake: pink, with sparkles. Julia barked a laugh but shut it when Alan glared.

"All right." Alan pulled a lighter from his pocket. "My Patek—" He indicated the lighter, then melted the bottom of the candle and stuck it to the bar.

Julia sucked in a breath. The carpet, now the bar—she'd be lucky if she came out ahead on this job.

He lit the candle's business end. "Are you ready?"

"For what?"

"Watch." Alan pulled a rosary from his jeans pocket.

"Are you even Catholic?" But Alan—she loved him. Everybody loved him. Surely he knew what he was doing?

"Lord, have mercy," he intoned. "Jesus, have mercy. Lord, have mercy." He dropped his eyes and mumbled under his breath while Julia watched, eyes on a Bible worth more than she'd earn in a lifetime and a candle she could buy at the dollar store.

The bell rang. Alan wasn't holding it, wasn't anywhere near it. Julia screamed.

A noise came from the pantry, rattling and shaking. She heard it but didn't feel it through her feet the way she would have in her own building.

"What did I tell you?" Alan grimaced smugly. "It's angry."

"It wasn't angry before. You made it angry." She was on to that trick, the way at twelve she realized her mother had always been angry at her and it wasn't anything she had done, only that she existed.

"I didn't do anything," he whined.

Julia's heart sank. They would believe Alan. He was charming and rich. Whatever happened, he would get away scot-free and she'd be on the hook. He'd fucked it up; she'd be left holding the bag.

Alan took Julia's arm and silently walked her away from the window. She didn't want to, but he was in charge now. He pointed toward the kitchen. They walked hand in hand until she slid open the hidden pantry door.

The spirit lunged for her, spectral meat cleaver in hand.

She dove through its legs, beneath the ghostly blade, pulling Alan with her. Could it hurt them? Better not to know. Something cracked as they hit the floor, but Julia felt no pain. The ghost slid through walls and into the kitchen.

"Are you all right?" Julia brushed imaginary dirt off Alan's pants. It was easier than apologizing for what wasn't her fault than being made responsible for it. He held out a hand, and she pulled them up. "That was—"

"That was crazy, Julia. We should leave."

"You said—"

"I was wrong. It's too dangerous."

"But I have to fix it. I fucked this up—" She shook her head and fought back tears. If she left, the insurance—and the building and the tenants and everyone else in the city—would sue her. She'd never work again.

Banging came from the kitchen. Alan sighed, and she knew she'd won for now.

By the time they were out of the pantry, the glossy black induction cooktop was spidered with cracks. Lumps of colored plastic—Julia couldn't remember what they had been—melted on top of a tilted cookie sheet and oozed into the cracks.

The ghost surveyed the damage he had caused, a wicked grin shimmering across its still-not-quite-there face. Julia snapped more photos.

"Let's go," Alan whispered. "You have the pictures."

"I need the money." Julia was no longer sure whether this was true or sufficient. "The ghost is ruining everything!" Of that, she was certain. Easier to blame the dead than the rich charmer next to her. She buried her hands in her face and sobbed.

"The ghost is how the money ruins everything." He was repeating her own words, her own ideas back to her, but she nodded like an idiot. "This thin place, it's where people aren't because money is. Billionaires hollowed out this city, right? And it's the need for money that drove you here. Money's haunting you. You thought the ghost was from a time before capitalism turned vicious and destroyed the city. But it was always like this. Maybe worse. The Triangle Shirtwaist Fire. The whole damned gilded age. The Boston Molasses Flood."

"Wrong city."

"What's driving the city, what's driving you—it's money. The city's a sort of clock, and money's the mainspring."

"What winds it?"

"Desire." Alan searched with his eyes for something. He didn't find it; he turned back toward Julia. "This room is terrible. I can see why the ghost wants to destroy it. If you're going to break down, let's at least do it on the couch?"

He led her to the sofa. Julia sat and began sobbing.

"The damage. They're going to take everything I own."

Alan patted her on the back. "That's not true, Julia. There's insurance. The owners of this unit lead a charmed life." It took one to know one, didn't it?

"These aren't nice people, Alan. You said so. They're—"

The ghost tromped into the room, leaving ectoplasmic footprints on the carpet. Julia wondered, almost as though she was another person, whether ghost stains were easier or harder to get out than Chinese food.

When the ghost reached out, she had expected that in her most secret heart: He would brush her skin, they would connect across more than a century. Neither of them would ever be the same. It would be a passionate, if incorporeal, connection.

The ghost stole her camera, lifted it off her like a pickpocket.

"Shit!" Julia shrieked. "Give it back, you motherfucker!"

The ghost shrieked back.

Alan doubled over, howling with laughter. Tears streamed down his face. She glared at him, but he did not stop.

In a feat of supernatural prestidigitation, the ghost disappeared the camera. Julia moaned.

"Shit," Alan said. "I'm sorry. I shouldn't be—" He broke up laughing again. Rage rose in Julia: He'd fucked everything up and would hang her out to dry, by accident or inattention if not on purpose. Things just happened that way.

And the ghost—

The ghost pulled plumbing out through the walls.

No, that wasn't copper pipe. (Did buildings like this use copper, or had they switched to that plastic stuff?) It was golden and lumpy, as though it had extruded a precious metal model of her camera. The expensive electronics, the matte-black metal casing and high-end German lenses—now gold, literal gold.

The curtains turned to gold and fell with a thud. The spirit tore apart the wall, chunks of plasterboard and pipes and wires. The building groaned. He would bring the whole tower down—for gold, same as the people who'd raised it, bought and furnished units. Alan stood and grabbed her hand.

"We've gotta go." He pulled her toward the entryway.

Julia ran beside Alan, hand in hand, her tunnel vision so acute her acrophobia vanished.

The elevator wasn't there. More precisely, the outside door had been transmuted into a melted golden heap resembling a sleeping cow. Julia plopped onto the carpet and closed her eyes. This time, she would not panic. She would assume control of the chaos—somehow.

"Come on!" Alan shouted, tugging her toward a door with an exit sign: the staircase. Perhaps they could make it before the spirit turned the stairs into gold. Buried them in precious metal.

"Let me go." Calm grew in her.

"We have to get safe." By which he meant down, and out the front door.

"I'm not safe downstairs, Alan. I'm not safe anywhere. You should go." His family's money would cushion his fall. Julia had no cushion. If she lived, she was ruined.

"I can't leave you here." He tugged harder, but she thought heavy thoughts and would not rise.

"You can. You have people, Alan—your family."

"You're my family." She saw his face quiver as though he, too, was barely holding it together and he might break down in tears at any moment. "Come with me."

"I'm right behind you," Julia lied. Alan's eyes shifted oddly; he understood she was giving him a way out, plausible emotional deniability. The rich get richer, the poor get left holding the bag. He nodded curtly, sprinted for the stairwell, was gone.

The thin place was still inside the refrigerator. It quivered as Julia pushed her arms through. On the other side, where she couldn't see, she grasped some sort of handle.

Before she pulled herself through, she took a deep breath and wondered: Would it be better on the other side, haunting the dead?

YONDER, TWIXT THE VINES

Bert S.G.

I remember Candy, all shivers and smoke, her toes touching grass off the side of the hammock. We'd stretch out together on them long summer nights, swaying in the breeze all slow-like, sharing each other's air under the shadow of nodding pines. And she'd press that cigarette to her lips and inhale and blow, then reach over with one willowy arm and press it to mine, and the whole world would shrink down, smaller and smaller, till it was just me and her alone, hearts beating and burning together, watching that nicotine cloud swirl and dance and dissolve.

"See, Junie," she one time said, "this town got a way. Like to remind you without reminding you. How they keep folks in line." Candy knowed this well enough, I suppose. Her daddy run off with the meter man while she was still in diapers, and though she was too young to remember, she wore the weight of it every step of every day. Even after her mama was married up again, even after Candy growed into a young woman, that weight was still there, getting heavier with each raised eyebrow and folded pair of arms. That judgement-weight, that weight of letting-you-know.

Bert S.G.

I remember Candy, how old her eyes looked in that young face, like she was put together from two different people. We figured out early there weren't no escape from this place, so we escaped into each other instead. For a time, that was good enough.

Course, that was before the vines got her. That was before the vines got us all.

Most times when we ditch, maybe once a week or so, Trashcan takes us down to Lover's Lanes, the old bowling alley, so we can hang around the arcade and smoke and drink whatever beers he lifted from the bait shop. PeePee's sister works the shoe counter and she don't care much what we do so long as nothing gets broke and no one calls the cops. She's on the pollen real hard most days, you can tell by the way her lips turn green in the corners, no matter how much she tries to paint over it. I pretend it don't bother me, but in truth it makes me sad to think about. She used to be so beautiful, so alive.

Anyways, today takes a different turn. Our whole school is packed in the gym for some presentation about water safety, which is a real laugh when you figure all the docks and banks and beaches been vined up for years now. And sure enough, here comes Half-Face Jimmy, microphone in hand, teachers applauding his bravery and strength of character like we don't know he's just another pedo who lives at the roadside gator zoo. Jimmy survived a close encounter with a boat motor and now he wants to warn us all about the dangers of choppy water. Figure someone could chime in about the dangers of huffing gold spray paint before a fishing trip, but it ain't like he could go back in time and pass that advice on to himself, retroactive-like. And besides, who am I to judge? Lord knows I've got indiscretions of my own.

So it's me and PeePee and Lindy sitting together, hearing all about this deadly river that we'll never get back to, when up pops Trashcan's head from under the bleachers, right between my shoes. Let's go, his lips say, and that's all the motivation we need to scoop up our bags and hustle for the nearest exit. Jimmy's speaker-voice squeaks at our backs as we trickle through the door. No one tries to stop us from leaving.

Now Trashcan, he's good people, even if he ain't from around here. Story goes he got his name after dropping a trash can off an overpass, and that trash can just happened to be full of pig guts, and those pig guts just happened to hit a cop car. I don't know if all that's exactly true or not, but either way his folks sent him to live with his uncle here in town, and then his uncle died, and after that he just kind of kind of stuck around, staying in that old house alone, no school, no work, no one to tell him what's what or make him be a certain way. Most everyone I know steps around him like a dead cat in the road, but he ain't never showed me nothing but kindness.

Soon as we get in the van, Lindy and PeePee go for the pollen. PeePee's real name is Petey, but when he was young he had this stutter, so everyone called him "Pee-Pee-Petey," and it just evolved from there. He and Lindy declared their love all the way back in third grade, about the same time me and Candy first met, and they've stuck by each other's side ever since. Surely you seen them types, the ones who grow old together and hate each other for it, after decades pass and romantic notions turn to bitter obligations. Petey and Lindy, they was born into that life. And now, here they are, nodding off together, eyes glazing over, lips all greenie grey. It twists my guts to see them like this, so I turn away and watch out the window as the buildings pass by. Sometimes the whole world smells like dead plants and burnt up oil.

Trashcan peeps them in his rearview and hangs a left at the abandoned donut shop. He says, "Reckon that stuff's gonna kill y'all someday."

"Gonna kill you too," PeePee moans. "Gonna kill all us. In the air, don'tcha figure? All us hooked now, one way or nother."

I know he's right but I don't want to say it. Most days the air is so dark with dust that the street lights never go out. And the trees keep pushing in, closer and closer, clasped by some endless shadow that gets heavier by the day. Folks pretend not to notice but everyone knows the truth. It's them vines, thick as ever, squeezing our lives away, suffocating our dreams.

Downtown rolls away like a strip of old pictures: Church, diner, pool hall, church, movie theater, VFW, Masons, church, city hall. Figure most everything looks like it did fifty years ago except places are a lot more empty now. Even the old fountain is dry, the centerpiece of our community, now a bowl filled with beer caps and sandwich wrappers and bird shit. Trashcan circles it twice before tossing an empty bottle onto the pile. Then he hangs a left instead of his usual right, taking us onto a winding road out of town.

"We going up to the factory?" I ask, already knowing the answer, already feeling the dread tighten up my throat. The old shacks outside get smaller and smaller, eventually disappearing into the walls of devouring green. I remember mama taking me down this road to see my daddy at work, back when these shacks were homes full of families and light. But that was another life, another time, so long ago I can't even see it now. It's been a graveyard for so long I can't know it as nothing else.

Lindy says, "I don't wanna go to the factory, it's sad and there ain't no games."

"Hush now." Trashcan lights himself a cigarette by striking a match with one hand. "We going down to see Miss Candy. Long past time we paid our respects."

It started as a cosmetics factory, largest of its kind, fixing up all manner of cutting-edge lotions and lipsticks and ointments. They claimed their product was of the all-natural variety, concocted strictly from vegetable matter, so it figures they'd locate themselves down in the swamp, where there's an endless supply of sumac and death caps and wild boar shit to conjure from.

Course, honesty was never the cornerstone of industry. One day there was an accident, and a fire, and then the truth come spilling out like so many chemicals into the water. The company cleared out, lots of folks was out of work, and it seemed like the whole town ended up in court. There was a settlement of sorts, not that we noticed none. Money like that's got a funny way of falling in the wrong pockets.

Soon after, the vines started coming up, and ain't nothing been the same way since.

"Hear tell it weren't no chemical spill," Trashcan says as he leads us down the steps. The metal rail sweats beneath my fingers and the old plate windows give everything a green, ghostly glow. "That vine was always here, old as the swamp, old as the land. They started feeding it, like, and the whole thing got out of hand."

We descend behind the hot beam of his flashlight, one rusty stair at a time. There's no vines in our path but we can smell it, we can feel it climbing those unseen walls, glistening like black blisters, blossoming. The click and screech of mud critters follows us the whole way down.

Lindy says, "Why would they do something like that? I don't believe it one bit."

"Same reason y'all keep putting that shit in your face." The flashlight wobbles as Trashcan gets to the bottom step. His army surplus boots crunch on wet rocks and broken bits of glass. "Same reason Candy come down here and get herself et up. That pollen, PeePee. That good-good."

I come down right behind him and let my eyes adjust. A row of rusting locker doors surrounds the old break area, and past that is the employee entrance to the main room. I think about my daddy, how he'd walk through here every day, punch his card in the clock, maybe talk football and sneak a drink before heading to the floor. Used to be this was far as we'd come; we'd share some beers or smoke some weed at one of them broken tables, watch our friends waste their brains on pollen, then split before the cops showed up to enforce curfew. But we ain't been down here in months, not since Candy went missing, and now Trashcan's got other ideas in mind. He pauses with his palm on the door handle and flips the flashlight beam under his chin, horror movie style, and says, "They put that shit in everything. Get the customer hooked, like. Brush they teeth with it, wipe they ass with it. Reckon that's always money in the bank."

He takes us through the door and then it really hits me, that vine-smell, like an old pumpkin you stepped in or a bag of rotten broccoli at the back of the fridge. There's a chitter and flutter of many wings and the whole room fills up with sound. We stop and we listen till it all rattles away and Trashcan leads us on, deeper into the factory.

The main room is vast, like midnight on the river, it seems to expand over us forever. We walk a narrow platform above it all, far enough from the walls so we won't get grabbed. Rusted-out machines stretch from floor to ceiling and everything is vine, pure vine, it snakes around and layers over itself and knots the whole world together, sagging in big loops from the rafters and noosing up the giant contraptions down below.

This is where your daddy died, my brain tells me. This is where Candy died, too. And all the blood rushes to my face and my throat, hammering out a rhythm in my ears, like a roar, the music of my old friends SHAME and REGRET, noises filling me so full and heavy that it makes my knees buckle low. I'm like to tip right over, follow Candy down into the muck and the mire, until a reassuring hand steadies me from behind.

I feel their eyes on me, concerned and curious, and I wonder, do they know about me and Candy? Does everyone know? About each whisper and promise? About how my heart broke and bled when I heard the news? My secrets have always been my own, but who knows how other folks talk. Have I been walking around exposed this whole time?

Trashcan says, "You okay, Junie?" He waits for me to find my legs, then sweeps the light down to the far corner of the platform, where it connects to the opposite wall and turns the other way. "Jacket was hanging over there, like," he says. "They reckon it got snagged on the rail when the vine pulled her in. Guess she was in here clipping flowers, getting pollen to sell, same as always. Let her guard down."

"Possible she throwed herself down there on purpose," PeePee says, his shadow heaving with sigh.

"Now, why you say something like that?" Lindy hollers. Her bracelets shimmy and clank as she slaps his arm, his shoulder, his back. "Putting them evil thoughts out there. Ain't right to speak that way about your friends."

"Just saying what I heard is all."

Trashcan tells them to hush up and be respectful, so we sit there all quiet for a spell, breathing that poison dust, thinking them poison thoughts. A light rush of air waves through, rustling the leaves, drawing us closer together. There's a kind of voice to the vines, a slight humming or buzzing, like TV static in another room, it sometimes rides in on the wind, rising and falling, passing through the back of your mind, and right now that simmering breeze whispers against my neck, and I think about her kisses, her kisses and her smile, I think about our last night together, how our fingers clung beneath them ragged motel sheets, her same fingers now turning to dust in the carnivorous jungle below. And I weep and I wonder about the sadness of it all, knowing that there's no end to it, no forgetting, just waking up to darkness every day and looking for some kind of beauty in the sorrow, looking hard through the scraps of this life and not finding nothing at all.

On weekends I work the closing shifts at Fast Taco, pushing powdered beans and liquid cheese onto pervy truckers who I swear just come in to stare at me in my uniform. The highway runs past us before disappearing into the trees, and across that is the old Pump-n-Run station, oldest operating business in town, still hanging on after all these years. Most nights I run over there and grab some lotto tickets to scratch while Turtle Tim pushes the mop around. This has been my life for two evenings a week, every week for the past year: truckers watching my tits, scratchers coming up bust, and Turtle Tim carrying on about his stupid band. Saying how famous they gonna be, how they gonna blow off this town and never come back.

Most everyone I know has talked about leaving one time or another. I once fancied notions of being a famous poet, of packing my notebooks of writings and running away to see the world. But no one ever stays gone too long, and you can only watch so many failed escape attempts before you start to wonder if it even matters. I truly believe PeePee when he says we all got that pollen in us. How else can you explain it? Obviously something in the air keeps us from drifting away.

At first the vine stayed near the swamp and no one paid it no mind. Sometimes a dog would go missing or one of the town drunks would wander off for keeps. But things like that happen regular enough, so it was easy to ignore. Then it started turning up in houses, those little shacks around the edge of town, creeping into basements and backyards, choking out gardens and pastures and trees. Never quite advanced into the town proper, but after it took some livestock and a couple little kids, folks got scared enough to do something about it. They organized a group of men to go down to the factory, down to the center of it all, and try to burn it out. Some of them fellas used to work down there and knew the situation pretty well. The first day, they made a lot of progress, came back into town swapping stories and high fives. The next day, they all disappeared. My daddy was one of those men.

After that, the whole town got busy forgetting. And if not forgetting outright, then just pretending things weren't so bad. Like if you don't talk about something it don't even really exist. And if it does exist, maybe it's your own fault for finding out. Like catching the clap or getting in a car crash. You careful enough, it won't never happen, and if it does, maybe you done something to deserve it.

So every now and then, someone you know gets took, like they don't come home one day and you know they never will. And folks will put on their sad voice and touch your shoulder and say it was part of God's plan and all that. And they want you to know it's best to move on and keep them alive in your heart, and there's no reason to think this will happen again, but then their eyes get dark, same color dark as that shadow behind the trees, the ones keep closing in on us. That fear-color, the color of the vine.

Mama's not on the pollen but I guess she might as well be. That bottle got on top of her pretty hard after my daddy passed. She had a good couple of years, least that's how I remember things, but that hole inside her finally got too big to struggle against, and eventually every last piece of her fell inside. Didn't help folks said she brought these miseries on herself, shacking up with a drunk, having a baby out of wedlock, inviting the Devil into her home. Course, they'd never say it out loud, but between every bless-your-heart and God-love-you was a knowing glance or righteous sigh. Like Candy said before, folks here got a way of reminding you without really reminding you.

So mama found the bottle, and then she found The Lord. But not the same way as most churchgoing types. No, my mama's Jesus comes to her in the late night hours, in the privacy of her bedroom, and everyone on our block can hear her hollering about it, crying and praying and carrying on. Don't know that she's ever looked at a Bible, much less cracked one open, but she sure seems to know all the scary parts, the good stuff, all them bits about hellfire and blood rain and damnation. Sometimes she gets to talking to my daddy, like his angel come to visit and give her his blessings. Other times, she don't say words at all, just barks out weird noises, doing this whole chanting bit, till she finally runs out of air and pants like a dog into her pillow and passes out.

Tonight I'm lucky because the whole house is quiet when I come home. The TV is glowing in the front room but the volume is turned all the way down. There's a man in tights demonstrating some kind of new exercise machine and his moves bump in time with my mama's snoring overhead. I go upstairs and peek in her room, tuck a blanket round her shoulders and turn her on her side in case her supper comes up in her sleep. That's assuming she even ate something today. Most times, if I ain't home to remind her, she forgets to do nothing but drink.

There's a party at Lindy's and if I dally enough, I might get there in time to miss Turtle Tim's stupid band. I swipe a pack of smokes from my mama's purse and inhale three of them on the way, one right after another. I start my journey feeling agreeable enough, but as I get closer to her house, as the thwomping of drums and mumble of voices grows louder in my ears, the trueness of it all overtakes me, about how there's an empty spot waiting, a spot that will follow me all over that house, a spot that Candy used to fill. Without even knowing it, I slow down till I'm just standing in the road.

It could be minutes or hours when Trashcan finds me, lost in my thoughts, cigarette hanging from my lips. His old van chokes up along besides and he hangs one elbow out the window. "Best get to that party, young missy!"

I say, "Uh-huh," and he can pretty much tell my heart ain't in it. He pops open the passenger door and slaps the seat for me to come inside.

"Ain't missing nothing," he says. "Just PeePee and Lindy going at it. Let's go someplace peaceable and get drunk."

•

We drive back out to the factory, of course, and he parks in the old employee lot. From here, the building is a ghost of a shape. We can barely see it against the trees rising from the swamp behind it. Bits of moonlight hit the broken windows and reflect back to us like stars.

At first, I'm afraid he'll try to kiss me, and I'm even more afraid that I'll let him. But he don't even make a move, just slides back in his seat and cracks open a beer and stares out through the windshield, all contented-like. We sit like that for a spell, sipping off our cans and listening to the owls and frogs and crickets shout nonsense at each other.

Finally, he goes, "I know you loved her, Junie. It's okay to say so."

I look down at the can in my lap, at my thumbs against the metal, and I can see how gross my nails are, all chewed off and packed with crust. "Does everyone know?" I ask, and he shakes his head.

"Them kids couldn't pour piss from a boot with a hole in the toe. Reckon they don't know nothing about anything."

I try to laugh but then it all comes up, everything, all that pressure held by the weight of our secret, it explodes from the center of me, spilling out heavy from my eyes and nose and mouth. That fist I been clenching inside for all them years finally lets go, and it feels like breathing for the first time, and so I'm laughing through my tears, I'm so relieved to let it go, but I'm also sorrowful because I been holding on to it for so long I don't know how to go on without it.

Trashcan lets me empty out, then he passes me a stack of gas station napkins from on top the dashboard. When I'm done cleaning my face up, he says, "When I close my eyes and think bout her, know what I see?"

I ain't quite ready to speak yet, so I just let him go on without an answer.

He says, "I see that time when she busted Effie Birdbrain in the nose for stealing your bike, you remember that?"

"Course I do." The thought of it makes me smile all over again: Effie, holding her face with both hands, wailing and spurting, whole front of her cheerleader dress turning red with blood. "She throwed it in the pond behind the old Sack-n-Save. Used to follow Candy around and call her Homo-Baby all the time. Finally got fed up with her meanness and let her have it."

"Never knowed someone asked so hard for an answer they didn't want." Trashcan takes another swallow and his throat goes click. "Okay, your turn now."

"Well..." I throw my head back and sniff and let my thoughts wander. "Was this time, we was both 12 maybe, her mama and stepdaddy was off again, casinos or something, and I come over and she said, Let's go out to the barn, cause she got something to show me, right?" I can still see her, swaying through the yard, through the tall grass, hair trailing long and gold, disappearing into in the barn, waving for me to follow. "We climb to the loft and there's this little picnic blanket rolled out, and in the middle's a half-bottle of wine and a little plate with two cupcakes and a cigarette on it. This was right after my daddy passed and she knowed I was feeling low, real low. And I probably cried then like I cried just now, cause wouldn't you know that no one showed me a lick of kindness about it, not a single person, not even Lindy or PeePee. Candy was the first and only."

Trashcan nods and listens, eyes shining in the dark.

"So me and Candy, we ate them cupcakes and passed that cigarette back and forth, then we drank that wine, and it tasted so good, it felt so good. I wanted that day to go on forever. I wish it was still going on now."

Two more beers appear from the army bag in Trashcan's lap. He pulls the tab on one and holds it in front of my face. I trade him for my empty can and take a deep, bitter gulp.

"I got scared when it was time to climb down cause I thought I might fall off. All that wine and nicotine made my head all wobbly, see, I hadn't never drank or smoked none before then. So Candy, she got on the ladder first, then had me come down so I was kind of between them like, and then she sort of just guided me down with her hands over mine. She said, If you fall, Junie, we both fall. But neither of us did."

Something screeches out in the dark, and then a wind picks up, twirling bits of litter across the asphalt around us. And with the wind comes that hum, that static sound, faint but distinct, rattling around like a pebble behind my thoughts. Trashcan raises his eyebrows at me and I know he hears it too.

Bert S.G.

"Vines is talking again," he says.

"Yeah. Hardly never stops no more."

After that we go back to just sitting, not talking, lost in the whispers, letting the night fold us into its arms. My thoughts stay with Candy, then drift to my daddy, and I think about all them other people that was lost, all them other empty spots around town. Further back even, following those roots through the centuries, before folks like us come along to poison the land. How many souls been swallowed since then? Are their spirits still moving through the vines somehow? Are their voices still calling for us, too?

Next morning I wake up resolved to feel better about things. But it don't last for long.

Mama has breakfast going when I come downstairs, a big pile of toast and scrambled eggs, but she ain't touching it none. She's already parked out in the living room, feet up on the coffee table, watching her stories, half into an asspocket of gin. I push some food around my plate for a bit and have a little coffee, but then it's already time for work, I got a double shift today and it's a long walk down to the highway. So I go out to give her a kiss goodbye and that's when I see it, the face on the TV news, the man in the tie telling us that the vine is spreading, they seen it come up in other towns and cities outside our own. Mama reaches over to grab my arm and her fingertips feel like fire, her madness burning right through my skin.

The whole day moves slower than ever. I can't focus on nothing but my breathing, on the front door, on the trucks groaning down the highway beyond. I count change wrong on four separate orders, so they pull me off register and make me hand out bags at the drive-thru, and I want to scream at every customer who pulls up, let everything come out till my vocal chords are a shredded mess and blood sprays all over their lips and eyes. Don't you know? I'd shriek. Where you going now? There's nothing left out there. There's nothing left. But instead I just fill their pops, give them extra hot sauce, and send them on their way.

A bit after night shift rolls around, our manager comes down to say Turtle Tim won't be coming in to work no more. When someone asks why, he just

130

drops his head all shifty-eyed and retreats back to his office. All them boys in the kitchen start telling stories, saying Turtle Tim took some kind of shortcut home from the party last night, saying he weren't born with the brains God gave a rock. And at first I kind of frown and nod and pretend to go along with it, but when it hits me that I'll never again hear about his stupid band I lock myself in the bathroom and I cry and I cry and I cry.

After work I walk down to Lover's Lanes and see Trashcan sitting alone at the bar. He's got a paper cup in front of him that he fills with whiskey from a flask. I ask him about PeePee and Lindy and he rolls his eyes, shakes his head.

"They over in the arcade," he says. "Been on that pollen all day. Great for conversation. Real engaging, like."

He pushes a basket of pretzels at me but I don't want none, I ain't got the stomach for it. The music in here sounds like someone farting in a cave.

"Hear the news?" Trashcan asks, munching.

"About Turtle Tim?"

"What? Naw. Bout this place." He sneaks another shot into his cup. "They closing it down next week. Closing it for keeps."

I always knowed this day was coming but somehow it don't feel real, that they would take this last thing away from us, that this whole town is finally sucked dry. I want to cuss and scream about it, but all I can do is look down at my feet, at my shoes digging into that ugly carpet for probably the last time ever. "Where we gonna go now?"

"I dunno. Maybe time we moved on. Get away, like."

"But don't you know? Ain't you heard?" My voice rises up, barely able to squeak from my narrowing throat. "Them vines is everywhere now, it's growed up in other towns all over."

"So what, Junie? Gonna get us all one way or nother anyhow. Don't you wanna see what else is out there fore it does?"

Maybe he's right and maybe he ain't. I got no answers neither way. All I can do is push away from him, make as much space between my body and his words as possible. I catch a fast peek in the arcade on my way out the door and see the whole room is empty except for PeePee and Lindy, drooping by the ski ball machine, lips all mossy, goo leaking down their chins. The walls flash and ring with color, blasting rainbow lights against their faces, and a scrolling sign on the wall above PeePee says YOUR CHANCE TO WIN! YOUR CHANCE TO WIN!

I spill out onto the sidewalk, dust blowing in my nose and hair, surrounded by boarded-up storefronts and not much else, watching the light above the intersection blink yellow over and over again. I know I should go home and check on my mama, but I can't, I just can't, my feet won't move that direction at all. And I can hear Trashcan hollering after me but my feet won't move in that direction neither. There's a compass needle in my guts that keeps spinning, keeps spinning and spinning, and all I can do is stand here and squeeze my fists and bite down on my jaw to keep my pieces from flying apart.

Then the wind lifts up, and that buzzing sound fills me, and suddenly I know which way to go.

The old door opens with a yelp and I'm back in the factory, back in the main room, smelling that vegetable smell, wondering at the bigness of it all. When I was little, real little, my mama and my daddy took me out of town to see the state capitol. When they got me inside, under that dome, I looked straight up into it, and it felt like the whole world flipped around. Being in this room alone gives me that same feeling, that feeling of being shrunk down, of having no meaning. I take a few steps along the platform and let the whole thing stretch out overhead.

The vines are really buzzing now, singing even. My skin prickles up at the sound.

"Candy?" I whisper, and my words whisper back: Candy? "Is that you?" Is that you?

Leaves rustle up and down the walls and machines, making the sound of a giant, crashing wave.

"Candy?" Candy? "Is that you?" Is that you?

Another long wave. That singing gets louder and louder. In my heart, in my head. A warmth kindles in my chest and starts to spread. I keep going forward. Shadows of vines bob against them old windows, calling me deeper, encouraging me, agreeing.

My body moves on its own now. My feet move and my hands grab that rail and I can't do nothing to stop them. And I start thinking maybe my mama ain't so crazy after all, and maybe I was right before to think there was spirits in these vines. Maybe they been talking to us all along and we just don't know it yet.

A ladder hooks off the platform to my left. It's too dark to see over the side but I know it goes all the way down to the floor. Down to the center of it all. Down to the heart of the vine.

I step down into it. I start to climb.

The song is blasting my ears now, the hum of a thousand voices, hundreds of thousands, and my hands find the rungs, one below the other, I'm pulling my way down. Leaves brush against my skin like fingers, and the touch of them sends me back, back to that night in the barn, all them years ago, Candy's body pressed up right against me, her hands over mine, rung by rung, her voice in my ear, like the voices in my ear now, whispering, singing, soothing. Breath against my hair, my face, the feel of her, the smell. And as I climb, deeper into that bottomless dark, I know she is here with me, that fire in my chest burns hotter and hotter, a heat like I ain't never felt, and that heat is my love, that heat is our love, and I know by her voice, I know by her singing, I know I know I know that she is burning with me too.

EL RATÓN

Bucket Siler

Bucket Siler holds an MFA from Rainier Writing Workshop and has been a Vermont Studio Center Fellow and recipient of the Fulcrum Fund Award. Her writing has appeared in *Storm Cellar*, *The Offing*, *Atticus Review*, *Bracken*, *The Smart Set*, and others. She lives in Santa Fe, New Mexico, where she organizes Santa Fe Zine Fest. Find her online at bucketsiler.com.

Daniel didn't want to leave Colorado, but only Denver wasn't blackened toast and after twenty years of breathing crisp mountain air and living ten miles from his nearest neighbor, he had no desire to return to the city. Michigan was out, too—he didn't have enough cash saved to go north—and he couldn't tolerate the evacuation camps. Screaming kids, uneatable food bricks, sleeping like sardines on a hard gymnasium floor, and—worst of all—a total lack of privacy. A man needed a proper residence, one with four walls and a door. And there was only one place left, god help him, where he could afford it.

The half-acre he bought in central New Mexico wasn't glamorous. A square of desert, a stucco box, and a field of waist-high tumbleweeds. No porch, no fence, no trees, no electricity, no plumbing, no personality. Afternoons could hit a hundred degrees as early as March, water delivery didn't come cheap, and the air was so dry his lips cracked and bled onto his pillow at night. But even a one-room shack in the scorched desert was an upgrade from living out of his truck. Plus, there were no fires to worry about, and no smoke. That far south, there was nothing left to burn.

When he arrived, it took him less than ten minutes to unload the boxes from his truck and then he got straight to work fixing up the house. Over the next few weeks, he built a bed frame and a kitchen counter, re-painted the nicotine-stained walls, patched the cracks in the stucco, set up an outdoor cistern with a pump that connected to a dry sink inside, and mopped an extra layer of tar onto the roof. Once the house was in livable condition, he set his sights on the property. He wanted the place to feel like home and it would never come close without at least a gesture of landscaping.

The only nursery in the state was a three-hour drive away. He browsed the maples and ash trees first, dreaming of a re-creation of his backyard in Colorado, but they were priced dear, and besides, the woman who owned the nursery practically insisted he buy an elm. She'd just had a new shipment yesterday, she said, taking him by the elbow and steering him toward the back corner of the lot. Siberian, she said, her eyes twinkling. Fresh off the truck from Socorro. She claimed the variety would grow three feet a year with water, a foot without, and was basically impossible to kill. Just be careful, she warned, not to plant too close to a municipal water or sewer line (there were none within a hundred miles of his house, anyway), and watch out for rodents.

That last bit of advice threw Daniel for a loop. His Spanish was only so-so, worse when he was distracted, and now he was busy fumbling with his bungee cords, trying to figure out how to secure the tree into the back of his truck. He eventually gathered that mice or rats might be attracted to the wet soil as the tree was getting established, and he said as much to the woman, but she wouldn't let it go.

"Sí, sí," he kept saying, hoping to appease her. "Sí, entiendo. Los ratónes son muy peligroso," until finally she seemed satisfied and let him drive away.

On the way home, he kept looking into his rearview mirror, watching the sapling's wire-thin branches quiver in the dusty wind. He imagined the tree growing thirty feet tall with a wide, leafy canopy. Maybe he'd build a fence, too, and a bench where he could rest in the shade and have a smoke on hot days. Maybe one day, he thought hopefully, this hot, barren place would actually feel like home.

•

Daniel had scoffed when the woman suggested he rent a backhoe—it was only a tree he was planting, after all, not a coffin—but once he started digging he regretted not taking her advice. The soil, if you could call it that, was unbelievably dry and hard, more like pottery than dirt. Swapping his shovel for a pickaxe sped the process up slightly, but after half an hour the hole still only measured eight inches deep, and the scorching afternoon sun had left him heat dizzy and shower-wet with sweat.

It wasn't like he'd never lived with hot, dry weather. In the summers, Colorado regularly hit ninety-five degrees with humidity so low his bedsheets sparked. But New Mexico was something else—an ungodly, almost supernatural combination of heat and aridity that made him feel like he was living inside a fiery oven: parched mouth, flaky skin, heat exhaustion, headaches. Even the H_2OMax (a cheap electrolyte powder they passed out like candy at the evac camps, cherry-flavored and gag-worthy but usually effective) didn't help his dehydration. Since arriving three weeks ago, he'd chugged bottle after bottle of the stuff, only to piss the same measly dark yellow puddle they warned about in all the heat illness brochures.

Flattening himself against the stucco on the east side of the house, Daniel rested for a minute in the thin shade, emptying a twenty-four-ounce bottle of water, followed by another half bottle of H_2OMax, before getting back to work. At the ten-inch mark, the soil changed color, bone white instead of sandy brown, and so hard it chipped off like pencil shavings no matter how fiercely he swung the axe. A minute or an hour later (he was losing sense of time), he heard a small voice and sluggishly raised his head. It was one of the neighbor's boys, a skinny thing about ten years old with knobby, scabbed knees and a hand-me-down black t-shirt three sizes too big.

"What did you say?" Daniel slurred.

"You have to fill it with water," the kid repeated. "That's what my cousin does."

"I thought of that, but… uh…"

"It doesn't get any softer," the kid said. "Under the clay it's calcite. You've got to dampen it. Careful, though," he said with a knowing smirk.

Daniel wiped the sweat from his eyes, trying to focus on the kid's mischievous smile. "Careful? Why?"

The kid laughed. But after taking in Daniel's blank stare, his smile dropped. "You really don't know?"

"¡Mijo!" Across the street, a woman wearing a blue apron was waving her arms overhead like she was trying to flag down a passing car. "¡Mijo!" she shouted again, more urgently this time. "¡A comer!"

"¡Ya voy!" The kid glanced back at Daniel apologetically, then took off running, a cloud of dust billowing around his sneakers.

Daniel gave it another twenty minutes with the pickaxe before calling it quits. The kid was right. It was useless without dampening the soil first. He put the cistern hose inside the hole and watched the water pool, catching wavy glints of light, until it spilled over the edges. Full absorption would take at least a few hours, if not a day. For now, there was nothing else to do but wait.

The real problem was what to do with the tree. It wouldn't fit inside his house (too tall), and he didn't have a way to lock it up without risking damage to the fragile branches. In Colorado, he wouldn't have hesitated to leave it outside overnight. But he'd heard too many crazy stories about desperate southwesterners—armed men stealing pallets of bottled water from government warehouses, emergency water relief vehicles driven off the road and hijacked at gunpoint, guard dogs found hanging from fence posts by their necks. Not to mention your run-of-the-mill muggings and robberies.

But after pacing his yard for several minutes trying to come up with another solution, he realized he didn't have much choice. He settled on leaving the tree under his bedroom window, figuring he'd wake up if anyone tried anything and scare them off with his shotgun. Then he went inside to make dinner.

His house was hot as a kiln and, even after a fresh coat of paint, still perfused with the smells of the chain-smoking previous resident. After opening all the windows so that a slightly less hot breeze could flow through, he commenced his nightly ritual: fired up his stove, cooked a single serving of chili in a dented pressure cooker, played a round of solitaire, and flopped into bed.

He wasn't intending to sleep. He just wanted to listen to the wind knocking the elm tree's spindly branches against the window and imagine he was back in the mountains. But after spending all afternoon digging, two minutes of a supine position pitched him head-first into a dark tunnel of sleep—the cool, damp earth against his cheek, an overpowering smell of water, footsteps pounding overhead, and a distant, muffled voice echoing through the darkness,

"Mister! Hey mister! ¡No entres en la casa del ratón!"

In the morning, he'd forgotten all about the dream; he rolled out of bed, made a cup of instant coffee, pulled on his pants, and ambled out to the shed. But once he stepped inside, he started to feel funny, as if a shadow were following him, nipping at his ankles like a little black dog. He stared at the pickaxe dangling from its hook. Don't, said the shadow, and he turned, squinting into the bright doorway where the sun was already blasting the day to cinders. Then, forgetting what he'd been looking for, he grabbed the axe and walked out the door.

As soon as the tree came into view, he knew something was wrong. He hadn't heard anything in the night, but some creature—not human—had disturbed the pot, and half the soil was missing. The root ball, threaded and tangled like brown yarn, sat dry and exposed in the pot, and a long mound of dirt, two feet wide and almost a foot tall, snaked along the edge of the house. Daniel followed it into the front yard where a miniature mountain range of upturned earth zigzagged between a dozen gigantic holes—entrances, he could only assume, to a maze of underground tunnels.

He thought: rabbits.

The little black dog circled his ankles, trying to block his path; Daniel kicked him aside. Then he stormed into the house and grabbed the keys to his truck.

In Colorado, the road to Daniel's cabin was lined with lush evergreens and towering aspens, and through the trees he could see the white peaks of a surging, snow-fed river. It had a name, that river, something beautiful and melodic, but he couldn't remember it anymore.

The tree, he felt confident, would survive. He'd buy another bag of soil and get it into the ground tonight. Those bastard rabbits, however, were as good as dead. So was the hardware store employee if he didn't look up from his book and acknowledge Daniel's presence at the counter soon.

"Did you hear what I said?" Daniel shouted.

The man slid a bookmark into his paperback and undoubled his chin. Dead eyes and stoic silence—the official greeting of the state of New Mexico.

"I heard you," he said tonelessly. "Just not in the mood for jokes."

"Jokes? Who's joking? Damned rabbits turned my yard into an excavation site. I don't think that's funny—do you?"

The man raised an impatient eyebrow. "It wasn't rabbits. But I think you know that."

"Know what?"

He looked at Daniel like he was stupid. "Only El Ratón could dig that many holes overnight. And you know as well as I do there's nothing in this store that can kill him. So go play your prank on someone else."

"El Rat… Oh, no. You've got to be kidding me."

Daniel's strange conversation with the nursery owner made perfect sense now. Ratón, she'd said. Cuidado. Peligroso. In Daniel's half-distracted state, he'd assumed she meant rodents in general. Mice and rats in the lowercase plural— los ratónes. El Ratón was something else entirely, a freakishly large, mythological creature who'd single-handedly caused the Great Drought by burrowing under the earth and drinking groundwater until the aquifers ran dry. In Colorado, they had Inferno, a fire-breathing coyote who'd ignited most of their forest fires, but no sane person ever mentioned him without a heavy tone of sarcasm. El Ratón, meanwhile, was still blamed for everything from cracked earth to dry wells and lost dogs (in his desperation to quench his insatiable thirst, he sometimes resorted to eating animals, sucking blood, digging up fresh corpses, etc.).

The man found his page and put his nose back into his book. "I don't kid. You have yourself a good day, now. Bye-bye."

Daniel took a few deep breaths, calming himself. To be fair, the rabbits had been a guess. He had no idea what had actually destroyed his yard, and a rat couldn't be ruled out. Who knew—maybe New Mexico really was home to some rare, oversized species of Rodentia. In either case, the solution was the same: capture and kill, and this was the only hardware store for a hundred miles. He craned his neck, trying to see down the aisles.

"You carry dog food, by any chance?" he asked.

"Aisle four," the man said tightly.

Daniel yanked a green plastic shopping cart from a long chain by the door and forcefully steered it (one wheel was broken) up and down every aisle, loading up with everything he could find for rodent control: repellent, poison, traps, netting, gauge wire, dog food (for bait), a small water trough (also bait). The man followed him around the store, his finger tucked into his book.

"I've got to hand it to you," he said, "you don't give up easy. You've got, uh, what's it called—that acting thing. Commitment. I like that."

But as Daniel kept shopping, the man seemed to realize he wasn't joking—Daniel was actually intent on killing this thing—and his flippant comments became grim warnings.

"El Ratón weighs two hundred pounds," he said, glowering at Daniel from the end of an aisle. "His skin's two inches thick and tough as leather. My buddy once shot a bullet straight into his haunch, and he just—"

"Traps?"

"Aisle six," he said, following Daniel around the corner. "His teeth are like railroad spikes. He can outrun a horse. You have no idea what you're getting yourself into."

Using his cart as a shield, Daniel pushed the man's stout body out of the way so he could look at a live animal trap. The door trigger was quick and snappy, but it was too small for anything bigger than a mouse. "You got any crates? Like for a dog?"

By the time Daniel steered his overflowing cart to the cash register, the man had given up trying to talk sense into him. "You don't get it, do you?" he said, shaking his head in defeat. "You just don't get it."

"You're right," Daniel admitted cheerfully, shoving a wad of cash into the man's trembling fist. "I don't get it."

The drive home felt especially long. In his haste to get to the hardware store, Daniel had forgotten his hat and sunglasses, and now the morning sun (it was still only nine o'clock) blared through his windshield and straight into his eyes. The day didn't start or end gradually in New Mexico, he'd discovered. No muted yellow, soft light, shade-dappled mornings; no orangey, long-shadowed evenings. If the sun was anywhere between the two horizons, you were getting a full-blast assault, white-hot and blinding, no shade, nowhere to hide.

He licked his lips. His mouth was cotton-parched, and he'd forgotten to bring a fresh bottle of water—he only had the gallon of old gas station water he kept in his truck for emergencies. He reached behind the seat and flicked off the blue plastic lid with his thumb. After boiling in his truck all morning, the water was so hot it could brew coffee, but he slugged it down anyway, wincing as it scalded his throat.

He wondered if he'd ever adapt to living here—or, it struck him sadly, anywhere, since nowhere, in recent years, had been spared a dramatic change. Colorado was barely recognizable: blackened skeletons for mountains, a trickle of salty water through the gorge, washed-out trails and roads. He looked across the expanse of desert, bald chamisa and dead cholla cactus husks dotting either side of a bumpy highway in desperate need of repaving. What had New Mexico looked like twenty years ago? he wondered. Fifty? He imagined pine trees dusted with snow, cottonwoods clustered along the Rio Grande, summer thundershowers, swollen prickly pear fruits, piñon cones bursting with fresh nuts.

In the heat of his truck, his thoughts turned calm and liquid—ribbon of black asphalt running like a stream under his tires, horizon bending into a sleepy frown. It was the kind of dreamy mental space into which might pop, suddenly, your kindergarten teacher's first name, or the street number of your college girlfriend's house.

As he cranked the wheel, turning onto his dirt road, it struck him out of nowhere, like a spritz of cold water to his face.

No entres en la casa del ratón. That was what the voice from his dream had said. It meant, Don't go into the rat's house.

But dreams were dreams. If you put too much stock into that parade of nonsense that marched across your dark eyelids every night, you'd never get anything done.

Gleefully, he stirred a scoop of poison into a big bowl of dog food. After he killed the rat, he'd fill up the holes in his yard and rake the dirt until it was flat and smooth. Then he'd plant the elm tree right in the center, securely tied to a wooden stake, and spread a layer of mulch to keep the soil moist. In a few years, there should be enough shade underneath for a small bench. He could even build a birdbath—wouldn't that be something? Sitting at his kitchen table every morning, watching grackles splashing in the water outside his window?

He set the bowl of dog food near the entrance to one of the tunnels with a sly grin. So far, the only animals he'd seen in New Mexico were an abundance of red ants and—once—an emaciated coyote scrounging through a pile of roadside trash. But trees had a way of attracting life you might not otherwise have realized existed—squirrels, bees, finches, butterflies, hummingbirds, magpies, grackles— oh, grackles!—with their iridescent black feathers and spooky pinhole eyes. They used to descend on the grass outside his cabin in Colorado, staring around like they owned the place. Crazy, adorable weirdos. He cocked his ear to the wind. If he listened closely, he could already hear them cackling.

In the morning, there was no sign of the dog food, the cereal bowl, or the rat's corpse—just three new tunnels and a fresh pile of feces. Either the rat had a stomach of iron, or some poor dog had taken the bait and gone off to die in the arroyo. In any case, his first plan hadn't worked. No matter. He was not to be deterred. Using his supplies from the hardware store and a few odds and ends he found in the shed, he spent the day rigging up a wire cage big enough to trap a raccoon. By the time he finished up, the sky was streaked orange and pink, a rainbow twilight so dim he didn't notice the man lingering behind his truck, watching him. As he slathered a stale tortilla with peanut butter and positioned it at the back of the cage, he saw a shadow move in his peripheral vision and nearly jumped out of his skin.

"Jesus Christ!" he yelped, clutching his chest. "Where did you come from?"

"I'm Hector's cousin," the man said, as if that explained everything. He was lean and sinewy, with a wiry black goatee that was long enough to tie into a knot.

It took Daniel a second to make the connection—Hector, he finally realized, must've been the kid he'd talked to yesterday. "Hector's cousin, huh?" he said finally. "You know, oddly enough, this whole thing started when I followed your advice."

"My advice? I don't think so. I never would've advised this." He pointed his scraggly chin at Daniel's cage. "Not in a million years."

"I meant filling the hole with water. I was trying to plant a tree. That's how all of this started."

The man laughed. "Oh, no. This started *way* before that."

Daniel expected him to follow this statement up with something, but the man just stared at him with two inky, unblinking eyes.

"Can I… help you?" Daniel asked irritably. "Because I'm kind of in the middle of something."

The man clucked his tongue reproachfully. "Oh, man. He's got you right where he wants you. Pretty soon you'll be the one drinking gray water and sucking the blood from dead dogs."

"Alright," Daniel said, turning back toward the house. "I can see where this is going."

"El Ratón gets into your head!" the man shouted, wiggling his fingers by his temples. "Makes you think you're doing what you want, when in reality, you're doing what he wants. You're never going to win his game!"

Daniel stopped short, whipping his head around. "I just want to plant my tree!" he cried. His voice was surprisingly high and helpless sounding, with a little crack at the end. When the man saw his face, he frowned pitifully.

"Oh, now, there," he said, and his voice was so kind Daniel thought he might cry. "There's no harm planting a tree. It probably won't survive, mind you. But there's no harm."

The edge of a cinder block hit the back of Daniel's calves and he submitted to sitting. The man sat, too, gingerly patting Daniel's knee. "This place used to be filled with trees—beautiful trees—did you know that?" he said. "Piñons. Cottonwoods. Huge ponderosas. Red willows along the river bank." Despite himself, Daniel smiled. "But, that's all in the past," he added.

Something about how he said the past made Daniel feel like a brick had walloped him in the stomach. He wanted to tell the man everything—how homesick he felt for his old house by the creek, the grove of aspens where he used to walk in winter, the river where he fished for trout. But his throat had tightened and all he could manage to say was, "It's so hot here."

"Don't I know it."

"And dry."

"Drier than ever," the man agreed.

"And I'm always thirsty. No matter how much water I drink."

The man paused. "Is that so?"

"That's normal, isn't it?" Daniel asked, looking to the man for approval. Something about him made Daniel feel like a little kid.

"Depends on how you look at it," the man said.

"How do you look at it?"

"Listen," the man said, standing. "Just leave El Ratón alone and you'll be fine."

Sound advice. But Daniel just couldn't take it. He tensed up, clenching his jaw. "I can't. I have to… I need to take control of this… this situation."

The man grabbed Daniel's shoulder firmly and gave it a little shake. "He's playing you, can't you see that? You're falling right into his trap. Look at yourself—you're a mess. When was the last time you had a bath? Or a decent night's sleep? Or changed your shirt, for god's sake?"

"What does that have anything to do with anything?"

The man let go of Daniel's shoulder, shaking his head sadly. "You know what?" he said. "I feel sorry for you northerners, I really do. You think everything's about you. Your house is gone. You're hot. You can't get what you want when you want it. Well, guess what? We're all hot. Lots of people's houses are gone. None of us are getting what we want. But you can't just come down here and drink the world—"

"Drink the world? What the hell are you talking about?"

The man studied Daniel carefully, as if gauging what kind of reality dose he could handle. Finally, he said, "I didn't want to bring this up. But El Ratón was a northerner, back when he was still a man—New York, I think. Moved down after the flood and bought a place near Taos. Beautiful house, right along the creek. But New Mexico wasn't good enough for him. He was always complaining—our healthcare system wasn't advanced enough, our people weren't punctual enough, the swamp cooler didn't get cold enough, the air was too dry, his head hurt, he couldn't get a good night's sleep.

"After a while, his grievances overwhelmed him, and nothing at all could satisfy him, not even the things he used to love. Food didn't fill his hungry stomach; water wouldn't quench his thirst." He paused, giving Daniel a meaningful look. "They say he drank the creek first. Then the Taos reservoir, the Rio Grande. He ate the leaves on the trees, the wildflowers, the piñon sap. Burrowed under the earth and sucked the aquifers dry..."

But Daniel had stopped listening. What in the hell was wrong with these people? Couldn't they see what was right in front of them? He tugged at his shirt collar. He felt hot, like his skin couldn't breathe. Finally, he burst out,

"Goddamn it, you people will believe anything, won't you?"

The man raised an eyebrow. "You people, eh?"

"It was climate change, you idiot."

"Come again?"

"Climate change. That's what caused the Great Drought. It wasn't a shapeshifting migrant rat who dried up the southwest, just like it wasn't a fire-breathing coyote who burned the Rockies, or an ancient wind spirit that tore up the plains states. Are you listening to me? There is no El Ratón. We did this to ourselves."

The man gave Daniel a familiar look—the same one he'd gotten from the kid and the hardware store employee. A combination of smugness and pity, like Daniel was a stupid, petulant child. He wanted to smack it right off his face, but his rage was so intense it had frozen him to the spot.

"Just be careful," the man said, turning to leave. "He's fooled smarter men than you."

Daniel waited in the darkness for what felt like hours. Cloudless night with prickly stars and a white half-moon cutting a swath of light across his face. If nothing else, his conversation with Hector's cousin had convinced him that El Ratón was real. His origin story was obviously fiction, but too many people's eyes had gone wide at the mention of his name for there not to be a teensy bit of truth to the claims. Daniel's guess: an unusually large rat, or more likely a cadre of them, New York City style, had somehow flourished in the state's post-drought decay. What do you expect when you stop maintaining a public sewer system or collecting the trash, or properly disposing of dead animals? It was a once-in-a-century evolutionary opportunity, and rodents, as usual, had been the first to take advantage.

In that case, the trap he had built should be just about right—he was thinking eight, maybe ten pounds at most, about the size of an average house cat. A rat that big wasn't impossible, but it would certainly cause alarm, even hysteria, in the right people. As he sat outside his front door, struggling to stay awake, he watched the cage's wires catch silvery glints of moonlight and listened to the words from his dream looping through his head like a song: No entres en la casa del ratón, no entres en la casa del ratón, no entres en la casa del ratón until, eyes drooping, his chin fell south and he dozed off.

When he woke up—minutes later? hours?—he had a wet, slimy spot on his shirt. He wiped his chin and a smear of blood came off on his fingers—his lip, painful to the touch, had cracked open while he was sleeping. He rolled his leathery tongue around inside his mouth. It tasted like battery acid. Water. He needed water.

He staggered into the house and sucked down a twenty-ounce bottle, but drinking only seemed to make him thirstier, like he was pouring sand, not water, down his throat. Refilling his bottle, he guzzled another, then another, but his tongue was still scaly, throat shriveled, nostrils dry as dirt. What the hell was going on? He rummaged through the cupboard for the H$_2$OMax. He could've sworn he had an extra container in here somewhere…

Just then, he heard something outside and froze, listening at the kitchen window. Four nimble paws rustled in the weeds, followed by the sound of glugging water—his cistern! He grabbed a flashlight and ran outside.

At his first glimpse of El Ratón, Daniel stopped in his tracks. He was at least sixty pounds, roughly the size of a pudgy black lab—enough to give any man pause before approaching. Beyond his sheer size, though, he was more pitiful than frightening: ancient and sick-looking, he had a mangled, ropey tail, shredded ears, and numerous bald spots on his fur. Between gulps of water, he breathed through his nostrils with a wet rasp, like a dying old man.

Daniel stifled a laugh. This was the diabolical mastermind everyone had warned him about? The vicious creature who dug up fresh graves and sucked the blood from unsuspecting stray cats? There was only one word for this old, chubby rodent, and it was pathetic. Daniel almost felt sorry for him.

Still, he thought, readjusting his sweaty grip on the flashlight, that didn't mean he should let him off the hook. He was still a noxious pest that needed to be dealt with. But how? A shotgun would be ideal, but there was no time to get it or anything else—he might run off again. Trying to catch him with bare hands was off the table, too—for all Daniel knew, he could have rabies, or worse.

That left clobbering him on the head with his flashlight. It was one of those old-fashioned ones, a magnum something-or-other that weighed about three pounds. Daniel knew it could do serious damage—he'd once used it, in a pinch, to hammer a tent stake into hard ground; another time, he'd dropped it on his toe and it swelled up like an eggplant. If he was firm, and quick, he should be able to bash El Ratón unconscious with one or two blows.

He tried to creep forward stealthily, but soon as he moved, El Ratón bolted, scurrying around to hide in the narrow space between the cistern and the side of the house. The good news: he was stuck, as long as Daniel blocked his exit. Trapping him with a wide stance, he shined his flashlight into the rat's withered, trembling face. Suddenly, he understood why everyone believed he used to be human. El Ratón's eyes were soulful, self-aware, and… well… sad. He looked like a beleaguered old man trapped inside a hideous rat costume. Daniel shuddered and, steeling himself, raised his flashlight overhead as El Ratón's massive body quivered with fear at his ankles.

But it was a weird, narrow gap he was aiming through, with El Ratón tucked between the plastic tank and the side of the house and a mess of plumbing pipes blocking a clean shot, and even after a series of boisterous thwacks in the rat's direction, he hadn't made contact. He tried swinging up and under, but only succeeded in bloodying his knuckles against the stucco, and El Ratón was getting more difficult to aim at by the second. In the strobing white light, he threshed around in a panic, his weight flopping into Daniel's legs, claws catching on the loose threads of his jeans.

Finally, Daniel managed to strike the rat once, hard, in his torso. But his hide was so thick it was like hitting a horse with a pillow. Exhausted, Daniel paused for a breath and, seeing his opportunity, El Ratón bolted, running out through the gap between Daniel's legs and disappearing into a tunnel in the yard.

In retrospect, this would've been a perfect time to call it quits. Instead, in a split decision he would later regret, Daniel chased after him. At the entrance to the tunnel, he dove to the ground, tucked his elbows, and squeezed inside. He fit—barely. With no room to bend his knees or lift his head, he progressed only a few inches at a time, wriggling through the darkness like a man-sized worm.

He felt oddly proud of himself—those two weeks he spent in army training camp before he quit years back had really paid off. Tomorrow, he'd probably need half a bottle of Taos Lightning to wash out the dirt and tiny, sharp rocks embedded in his bloody forearms, but at the moment he felt invincible. El Ratón might fancy himself a unique phenomenon, Daniel thought viciously, but soon he'd meet the same fate of meddling rodents everywhere.

A few minutes later, though, a torrent of dirt and dust released from the tunnel walls by Daniel's squirming body began to make breathing difficult, and in the darkness, he fought against a rising panic. If an open space like a den or cave didn't appear soon, it'd be impossible to get back out. The tunnel was so narrow he couldn't turn his head side-to-side, let alone make a U-turn, and there was no way he could crawl backward out of this subterranean finger trap against gravity. Yes, gravity. Ever since he'd put his head into the hole, he could feel the blood draining out of his feet and into his ears, like he was falling toward the very center of the earth...

Breathe, Daniel. Just breathe. Inside his waistband, where he'd tucked it for safekeeping, he could feel his flashlight digging into his stomach. He focused on its blunt pressure, the heat of the metal against his skin. He might be trapped, he reminded himself, but he wasn't dead yet.

Finally, forcing himself forward, his spine snaked around a tight curve, down a steep incline, and then suddenly his head popped into a pocket of cold air. He gasped with relief. If he couldn't find El Ratón, he could at least turn himself around and get back home, which, he realized soberly, was probably the wisest choice at this point. He wriggled his shoulders free and hoisted himself into the open chamber. Then, after tumbling head-first five or six feet, he landed on a hard, earthen floor.

Compared to the surface, the air inside El Ratón's cave was damp-feeling and, Daniel thought with a twang of homesickness, pleasantly chilly, like a cool autumn evening on the Colorado riverside. Even so, it wasn't somewhere he wanted to linger. He fumbled with his flashlight. A faint smell was wafting up from the depths of the cave—whatever El Ratón had stashed away in his lair was giving off an oddly delicious aroma, like slightly turned peaches. Daniel imagined a pitcher of cool, fruity water gliding down his ravenously dry throat and found himself drooling.

Finally, his thumb found the on-switch, and the cave illuminated. But when Daniel saw the source of the smell, he nearly vomited. The underground chamber was filled with piles of rancid trash, spoiled produce, and the rotting corpses of smaller animals—mouse, gopher, squirrel, and something that looked like a Chihuahua with its head ripped off...

So the stories were true. He knew he shouldn't worry—El Ratón was too old and weak to pose a real threat to anything much bigger than a skunk… but still, a voice inside his head was screaming run away. This whole situation was just too weird; he'd figure out how to deal with his yard later, from the safety of his house, with the doors shut tight and all the rodent-sized gaps securely stuffed with towels and old t-shirts.

He panned his light across the cave's ceiling, looking for the tunnel he'd entered through. At least ten different holes darkened the earthen wall and they all looked the same. Pick one, he told himself urgently. Just pick one and go. The hole closest to where he'd fallen was probably the safest bet; however, he realized with a wave of regret it was at least a foot above his head.

Ten minutes later, he'd managed to stack up ten or twelve inches of nasty, half-eaten foodstuffs under the entrance hole, and was yanking on the tail of what looked like a cat's corpse when he heard the distinct sound of El Ratón's massive body shuffling along one of the tunnels.

He quickly abandoned his trash mountain and scurried into the shadows. At this point, he didn't care about getting revenge on El Ratón—he just wanted out of there, fast. He watched as the rat waddled over to the trash pile and began gnashing on a wet carton of milk. If he snuck up from behind, he should be able to catch him by surprise and buy himself enough time to escape. Daniel quietly crawled around the pile, to the edge of the shadows. He was getting close to striking range—the wet, rotting smell of garbage right under his nostrils; the sound of El Ratón licking an empty can of tomato sauce echoing in his ears— when he felt something juicy go squish under his knee.

He paused, looking down. Inside a puddle of rancid liquid, a slightly rotten orange, glistening with juice, lay smashed on the ground. His stomach churned with a strange mix of revulsion and desire. The liquid looked like a tropical lagoon, but the orange—half-eaten and speckled with white mold—was absolutely irresistible. He couldn't, though—could he?

The fruit was halfway to Daniel's mouth when he felt a searing jolt of pain in his leg. He whipped his head around; El Ratón was inches from his nose, his yellow fangs bared, hissing. His red, inflamed gums emitted a terrible odor, like rotting flesh. By this point, Daniel was so terrified he'd abandoned all heroic pretenses; he shamelessly cowered and cried out, "Please don't hurt me!"

As if he'd spoken the magic words, El Ratón closed his ghastly mouth, spun on his little pink feet, and scuttled off. At the entrance to a dark tunnel, he stopped, turned back, and smiled at Daniel with a row of squarish, distinctly human-like teeth. Then he disappeared.

Later, Daniel would be absolutely certain about what he saw. But at the time, he thought he must have been hallucinating. Once he was sure El Ratón was gone, he banged his flashlight on the ground until it submitted to one last dim flicker, then rolled up his torn pant leg for a closer look at his wound.

He'd been bitten before—as a kid, a pet guinea pig had nearly severed his index finger; another time, a stray dog sent him to the emergency room for stitches. So he knew what to expect: a thin laceration, a little exposed subcutaneous tissue, but no bruising yet. When he got back to the house, he'd need a good saline rinse and a strong adhesive to close the wound; in a few weeks, assuming the bite didn't get infected, it'd be like nothing happened.

How wrong he was. Although only five inches wide, the wound on his calf was bone-deep and copiously oozing a goopy, black fluid that definitely wasn't blood. He tore off his shirt and wrapped it tightly around his leg. The gushing was worsening by the second, and now, with the shock wearing off, so was the pain. He watched in horror as the remaining healthy skin surrounding the bite charred black and peeled away, revealing fat, then muscle, then bloody bone. He squealed. At this rate, even if he could manage to get to the hospital (it was three hours away on a dark, bumpy highway), he'd need his leg amputated for sure. He made one last feeble attempt to stand up, then slumped, moaning in agony, to the ground. The pain was worst in his leg, but every part of his body hurt, including his internal organs, which felt like they'd been vice-clamped and twisted up like a wet towel. Writhing on the cave's dirt floor, he thought:

They were right. He won.

Then his eyes fluttered and rolled back inside his head, and he passed out.

•

Darkness, and the bitter taste of dirt inside his mouth. He tried to push himself off the ground, but his balance was wonky, like his arms were too weak to hold up his body, and he face-planted in the dirt.

Wasn't this usually the part of the story, he thought murkily, when the hero woke up in a white hospital bed, surrounded by friends and family? Instead, the air smelled of rotting fruit and corpses, his flashlight's batteries were long dead (although, strangely enough, he seemed to have excellent night vision), and his leg...

He reached down for his pant leg, hoping to gently tug his wounded limb closer to his face, but there was nothing inside. His right leg seemed to have shrunken, leaving his jeans behind like an empty sack. Rolling away from his deflated clothes, he tugged on his hip until he saw skin and felt a bit of relief. Besides its unusual size and shape, his leg looked fairly healthy—a little shriveled and hairy, and his toenails could use a clipping, but...

A hollow fear settled into the pit of his stomach. Raising his tiny pink hands to his face, he pawed frantically at his features—his nose was elongated and cold at the tip; bristly whiskers protruded from his cheeks; his teeth felt like jagged tusks. He craned his head toward his posterior. A stringy tail had sprouted from... he shuddered to think where exactly. No wonder El Ratón had been gloating on his way out of the cave. His bite must have infected Daniel somehow, and...

Water, a voice inside him screamed. Water water water water water—

A tremendous thirst, worse than any he had known, consumed him. His throat wasn't dry; it was desiccated. Like it was made of dust from which the last molecule of moisture had been squeezed. The dryness traveled through his esophagus, into his stomach—right down to his soul. If he didn't drink something soon, he was sure he'd die. He lifted his snout to the cave's dirt ceiling and sniffed. Somewhere above ground, a plastic tank filled with water was sitting unattended. The cistern.

Rolling onto his stomach, he balanced four shrimpy limbs under his paunchy mid-section, then scurried up the cave wall and back through the tunnel. His thirst was so intense, so compelling, that he was a little surprised at how fast he was able to run; compared to last time, the journey was lightning, and soon he popped out into a labyrinth of dirt mounds and tumbleweeds. Passing a metal cage glowing faintly in the moonlight (the stale tortilla inside didn't tempt him), he darted along the side of the house until he reached the water tank.

The taste was like rain falling in the desert; for one precious second, Daniel's thirst felt truly satiated and, cradled belly-up under the spigot, he let out a contented sigh. If only he could suckle from the cistern's brass teat forever, he thought, he'd never want for anything again.

But his satisfaction turned out to be madly fleeting—next second, he felt even thirstier than before, like the water itself had somehow dehydrated him. It went on like this—drinking, getting thirstier, drinking more, until his belly got so full it threatened to burst. But even then, sloshing around on the ground like a water balloon with his stumpy pink legs in the air, he kept drinking. If it were up to him, he thought deviously, he'd never stop. He'd drink the whole damn world.

Later, as the moon set over the dirt mounds in the yard and the sky turned gray with the dawn, Daniel—gorged, but still thirsty—waddled away from the empty cistern in search of another source of water.

He didn't notice the man who, hours earlier, had emerged, naked, from a hole on the opposite end of the yard. After getting clumsily to his feet, the man had ambled past the elm tree and the bag of garden soil and the shiny wire cage and walked right into Daniel's house, yawning and stretching his arms overhead, as if he'd just woken from a long and bewildering nap.

BODY WORLDS

Tom Johnstone

Tom Johnstone is an author of horror fiction and a critic of genre literature. He blogs at tomjohnstone.wordpress.com and you can also follow him @tjohnstone.bsky.social.

Now, here she stands, statue-still, staring at the flayed figures fixed in grotesque, sardonic poses. He stalks around them, examining each tableau from every possible angle, his corpse-grey eyes drinking everything in, a tall black-clad bee hovering, sucking visual nectar. Not just looking—hearing too, apparently. He nods occasionally, as if in acknowledgement of words inaudible to her. If only he listened to her as attentively as he does to this unseen conversationalist.

Sometimes, he terrifies her.

She feels almost as paralysed as the figures are. Humiliated too, as they would be if they could feel anything. They can't of course, any more than furniture does. To think they were once people—not statues or other commemorative representations of the dead, but actual, literal people.

Here in this starkly lit, black-walled exhibition hall in Bruges, it seems like years since they arrived in Ghent, centuries since they visited Naples.

Ghent was a ghost town. Bruges was busier but also quainter, stiflingly so. All the mediaeval former guild houses and grain stores and breweries, now bars and restaurants, tourist traps with 'trap' gables crenellating the roof façades, what

Robert in his usual sardonic way called "Shrek Town", with the castle looming over everything, were in the centre of Ghent, on the banks of the River Lis. Catherine noticed the streets of Ghent were wide and clean, which made the faint whiff of sewage all the more disconcerting. The mostly electric cars and gleaming white trams sailed past with uncanny quietness.

It made a stark contrast with the noisy, narrow, bustling streets of the previous stop on their "European marriage-mending tour", as Robert called it—Naples, where scooters loaded with artichokes and asparagus and aubergines barreled down back alleys, forcing you to press your back against the cool, ancient stonework to avoid both the heat and injury. Still, she reflected, at least there you could hear the vehicles' approach. Here, in more environmentally conscious Belgium, the cars were lethal farts, silent but deadly, even if their emissions were arguably less flatulent.

Maybe it had been the Mediterranean heat that had made their time in Naples so fraught with emotional hazard. It had been there that Catherine felt the burning desire to ask him if he'd ever been on holiday with Maisa, Robert's 'affair partner' in their couples counsellor's non-judgemental therapeutic parlance (or 'that home-wrecking bitch' in Catherine's). With a downcast look, Robert admitted to a night in a hotel, muttering "Hardly a holiday really". when he sensed her pain. It was as if, a couple of months after the confession that had prompted this continental mercy dash to save their relationship, he felt as if she should be over it, and that this new revelation wasn't a big deal. He didn't have the sense to understand he'd hurled another grenade into the partly repaired structure of their life together with this. It might not seem much to him, but it had shattered the picture of brief encounters and stolen embraces in secluded places, or a cramped car seat, to which she'd clung like driftwood for the last two months.

After the mention of an overnight hotel stay, implying them sleeping together, waking together, she found herself drowning again. Instead of a lifebelt, he'd then thrown a depth charge into the churning ocean within Catherine, admitting a subsequent sexual encounter with Maisa after he'd sworn blind it was over.

Then she'd wandered the Neapolitan streets desolately, stomach churning as if she were a passenger in a boat on choppy waters, the way she had when he'd first confessed to the affair, clutching trees and walls for dear life, Robert following, looking on in childish confusion, hanging his head, offering apology after empty, inept apology, interspersed with sighs of irritation that she was still upset.

She remembered how sometimes, over the past two years that he had been cheating on her, he used to fidget with his wedding ring, turning it around on his finger, pulling it over the knuckle towards the tip of his finger, then pushing it back, as if toying with the idea of removing it altogether. Now she knew why: a red flag if ever there was one. In a sudden fury at his refusal or inability to comfort her, she tore hers from her finger, grasping it on her fist as if she might hurl it into the gutter. She had no intention of doing this of course, but he didn't know that.

"Catherine!" he gasped.

If she wasn't so devastated, she might have laughed at his pompous outrage.

Eventually, the storm of her anguish had subsided, and there she was—washed up in the Bay of Naples, by a castle on the shore, numbly watching the waves slop against the barricade of giant boulders that was all there was of a beach. Finally, she slipped the ring back on and let him lead her back through the streets, her head and heart pounding, in search of somewhere to hide from the glare of the sun and the stare of strangers.

"I suppose you want to go in there," she said, catching him looking at the sign pointing down a side street to the Neapolitan Museum of Torture.

"No, not if you—"

"Why not?" she said, with a shrug of indifference. After all, how could it make her feel worse?

But it did.

A spiked chair greeted them in the vestibule. An iron female giant opened spiked doors to swallow them in her transfixing maw. An exquisite line drawing of the Pear of Anguish decorated one of the walls.

"Reminds me of the thing I had for my cervical smear," Catherine said with a shudder.

"There's actually no evidence it was ever even used for torture," said Robert, reading the lurid multilingual commentary, then walking on with a dismissive shrug.

Crude wax dummies lolled in contorted attitudes of agony, in barrels, on wheels, hanging from gibbets, stretched on racks.

"Bet you'd like to use that on me," she said of the Scold's Bridle that confronted them when they turned a corner.

"Don't be ridiculous," Robert said, looking up at the helmet-shaped frame cast in rusty black iron, with its spiked tongue trap and ass's ears. "What the hell d'you mean?"

"I think you've just proved my point," she said with a bitter smile.

"I still don't know what you mean."

"You just want to shut me up. You think I should have moved on by now. You're angry I haven't."

"Well, come to think of it, why can't you? It's been two months!"

"You've been lying to me for two years. I'm still in shock, Rob."

He looked around, as if embarrassed that other visitors to the museum might overhear their row, but the place was deserted, their only audience a waxen woman, adulterous according to the plaque, sitting astride a triangular wooden structure the writing identified as the Spanish Horse, hands tethered behind her, ankles weighed down with papier mâché slabs, her eyes glassy, her mouth a grimace, as the sharpened apex slowly split her apart, dark painted blood oozing down between her legs.

"I wish you hadn't done it, Rob," she said in a small, sad voice, not for the first time and probably not for the last. She wondered if he really wished he hadn't, as he had claimed when he begged her to stay with him.

Previously he'd responded to this lamentation by muttering something about how you couldn't put the toothpaste back in the tube or the genie in the bottle, but genies granted wishes, didn't they? This time he just threw up his hands, apparently impatient at her continued pain at his infidelity, irritated at the plaintive reproach in her words and voice. She felt broken on the wheel of his scorn, choking on her own prickly pear of anguish. Yet she followed him into the next compartment of this nightmarish place, where a wax witch gazed blankly at the painted flames licking at her hempen skirts. Catherine remembered Robert saying he'd been like a man possessed when he'd cheated on her, and that such a claim in times long past could have led to a charge of witchcraft for *her*—the means for Catherine to avenge herself on her rival. It was a delicious yet nauseating thought. It struck her that so many of the devices on display here were punishments for women who talked or fucked out of turn; either that or their inventors had given them a female name—the Scavenger's Daughter squeezing men until the pips squeaked and their ears bled in her steel triangle, the Iron Virgin devouring them in her spiked womb. God! It was grim in here—the air felt warm and stifling, with a faint smell of her own sweat and something else, an obscure musk she couldn't quite place.

Why had he brought her in here?

No, she wouldn't just follow him further into another circle of hell. Let him follow her. Without a word, she turned. He didn't seem to notice, engrossed in the contemplation of a man suspended from the ceiling by arms tethered behind his back, or perhaps the woodcut reproduced nearby of two men using a giant saw to… She looked away in disgust.

In a heartbeat, she was out of there.

It felt good to be outside. It was possible to avoid the relentless glare of the sun by standing close to the tall, old buildings towering around the museum's entrance. In any case, it was clouding over now, the sky darkening with storm clouds. She wondered how long it would take for Robert to notice her absence. Minutes passed. He probably hadn't even registered that she'd gone.

A flash of long, black hair drew her eyes to the bustling main street at the end of the narrow quiet one where the museum stood.

She hadn't seen the face, but she headed off in pursuit of the woman as if pulled by invisible strings. She'd seen pictures of her on Facebook, enough to recognize her and fear the shock of accidentally meeting her in the street in their hometown, either alone or with Robert, or worse, catching them in some tryst somewhere. She ignored the sensible inner voice telling her how crazy it was to think she had followed them here to Naples.

But maybe it wasn't so incredible. Robert had managed to pull the wool over her eyes for two years, and she'd been unable to believe it when she'd first confronted him about a Google search on his phone for Arabic endearments. The rational voice also told her lots of Italian women could pass for Egyptian from behind. Yet here she was, wandering the winding streets of an unfamiliar city, following a stranger who happened to bear a passing resemblance to Maisa.

The very thought of the name pained her.

The rain came on suddenly, the large drops spattering the parched pavements, petrichor tickling Catherine's nostrils. The woman walked fast, probably in a hurry to get to her destination before she got soaked, or perhaps she sensed she was the object of a pursuit. But she never looked behind her to check if she was being followed. Either way, Catherine struggled to keep up as her quarry turned first down one narrow street, then another, thinking she'd lost the trail in the crowded areas, then finding her again in more deserted ones. It helped that people seemed to keep their distance from the woman, and that she herself gravitated towards the quieter alleys, taking what appeared a rather complicated path to her destination. Catherine began to have misgivings about this enterprise: The woman's route took her further and further away from the museum. Robert was surely wondering where she was by now. But a brief check of her phone displayed no messages or missed calls. If the worst came to the worst, Google Maps could guide her back to him.

She knew how unlikely it was that this woman was her. Yet the more she followed the stranger, the more convinced Catherine became that she was. Her clothes, elegant and tight-fitting, black skirt slit up the back, above equally black calf-length boots, pale-brown flesh visible in the space between, mutton dressed as lamb, she thought sourly, combined with bangles at the wrists and jangles of earrings that swung when she turned corners. Her walk, confident and sensual, suggested to Catherine someone brazen enough to plunder another woman's husband. Her very name meant 'proud, swinging gait' in Arabic—Catherine had googled it! Maybe it wasn't so far-fetched to believe she would come out here to taunt Catherine with her presence, flaunt herself before her rival. Catherine quickened her pace as the woman turned another corner, desperate to see her face to face. She knew what Maisa looked like from Robert's Facebook friends list, where Catherine had found her self-regarding, self-satisfied profile picture, dark-brown eyes gazing out at Catherine, mocking and provocative. She longed to grab her by the shoulder, spin her around, spit vitriol in her face.

Catherine had already confronted her on Robert's phone. Maisa had picked up unsuspectingly, thinking it was him. In front of him, staring into his eyes to see his reaction, Catherine had demanded to know when they'd last fucked. He sat shame-faced as a schoolboy summoned to the headmaster's office, fidgeting with that damn ring as if he were wishing upon it, wishing the ordeal could be over. Maisa protested that she couldn't remember, "It must have been an unmemorable experience then," Catherine had said, then hung up, her eyes still glaring at his downcast face.

At last, the woman paused outside an apartment block, fumbling in a black leather handbag for her keys, making her bangles jingle, her long black mane veiling the side of her face.

"Hey," Catherine called. "Maisa!" she all but spat.

"Prego?" the woman replied, turning towards her pursuer.

And Catherine saw the reason she'd been in such a hurry to get home and had tried to avoid crowds, who for their part seemed to shun her—the face a pitiful, distorted mass of scar tissue, where the flesh had melted and reformed.

"Scusa," said Catherine, summoning up what Italian she could remember, trying to hide her horror, and hurried back the way she came, thinking to retrace her steps.

It was then that she realized she didn't know where the hell she was.

By the time they reached Ghent, things had calmed down.

Maybe it was that Catherine was chastened by her ill-considered stalking episode in Naples. Maybe it was that Robert had been kind and patient when she rang him distraught, wet, bedraggled, in floods of tears, lost and too upset to be able to use Google Maps.

"Don't worry, darling," he'd said. "Stay where you are and I'll find you," and he'd calmly tracked her down through the winding streets of Naples, holding her close when he found her, as if he really did love her, as if he wasn't the man who'd robbed her of two years of her life and made everything they'd done together in that time seem a mocking lie.

It was as if the storm had lifted, as suddenly as it had descended, the mountainous volcanic landscape around Naples giving way to the flatlands of the Low Countries.

But in Ghent, their problems were far from over.

The hotel they'd hastily booked turned out to be one star, and the one remaining room they'd secured proved tiny and cramped, with just a sink. There was a shared bathroom along the hall. The room itself barely had space for anything other than the two single beds, so the only thing to do seemed to be to make the best of it as far as she was concerned. She set herself to pushing them together. They could make love like they used to as students, visiting each other's rooms in their halls of residence, spending days in bed.

But as she began kissing him passionately, she felt his lips stiffen, his eyes staring at the ceiling, glistening with unshed tears.

"What is it, Robert?" she asked gently.

He glanced down at his penis, which she saw was still a flaccid, wrinkled mushroom. His breath came out in gasping shudders, under the circumstances a parody of arousal.

"I can't feel anything," he whispered.

She managed to set aside her own pain enough to be kind, hiding her disappointment at his failure to achieve something of which he had no doubt been perfectly capable with Maisa, leaving him all used up, with nothing left for Catherine.

"It's okay," she said. "It's not all about that, you know. Here… Let me help."

Playfully smiling, she stroked his lolling member, which showed some tentative signs of life, but he still looked miserable, jerking away from her slightly. She sighed, trying not to let resentment take hold, determined to keep working at repairing their shattered relationship. It was a storm-damaged house, where some rooms were safe to enter, but if you walked through the wrong door, the floor gave way, plunging you into an abyss of pain and bitterness and recrimination.

She told herself not to take it personally. He was just getting old, that's all.

"Never mind about that then," she said, trying not to feel humiliated but hearing her voice growing tight and irritable. "Let's just have a cuddle, eh?"

He nodded and rolled next to her, burying his head in her shoulder. She felt like she should say, "There there," but sod it, she wasn't his fucking mother and didn't want to be, even if he'd betrayed her with someone old enough to be. Maybe that was it. She felt the warm rush of blood surge within her lower belly, the cramping pangs telling her she was about to come on. Was he disgusted by the rusty stench of her blood? Did he long for his coy menopausal mistress, who could never contaminate him with menses? She tried to ignore these humiliating thoughts, stroked his back, using her nails, something she knew he'd liked in the past, but it didn't seem to be turning him on, and God, she was wet, and needed a fuck. How stupid of him, to fuck up this crucial part of their life together, for the sake of a fling with someone he insisted he didn't even love.

"Robert," she said softly, "it's not all about your cock, you know. We can just… touch each other. That can be nice too."

He flinched away from her, and she saw his eyes were wet with unshed tears.

"But you don't understand," he sobbed. "I can't feel anything—anything at all."

"De rekening, alstublieft," said Robert to the young woman serving them, over the eviscerated remains of the two lamb chops on their respective plates.

Funny that the Dutch word for 'bill' sounded so grim and forbidding, Catherine thought, as if it were more than just a payment—a reckoning. It seemed as if everything they did now, every activity, every transaction, was highly charged. He returned Catherine's gaze defensively—she had been watching him, checking if any intimate looks or flirtatious banter had passed between him and the waitress. Listening wouldn't have been enough, as only he knew any Dutch, but she detected no tell-tale glint in his eye when he made eye contact with the young waitress. And it wasn't as if his recent infidelity had been with someone younger—on the contrary, which might or might not be a small mercy, depending upon which way she looked at it.

As they waited for the bill, both of them stared out of the window at the striking and disturbing image advertising the Body Worlds exhibition in Bruges, showing a sexless figure, flying on wings the colour of raw salmon, pectorals unfurled like flags, staring at them with lidless eyes from a hoarding on a tram stop shelter.

"Looks up your street," she said. "Want to go?"

"Are you saying I'm morbid?" he said, with a faint, wry smile that acknowledged that such a charge wasn't entirely unwarranted. "But why not? Plenty of chocolate there, so something for both of us, eh?"

She laughed. He had a point. She was on her period after all.

The ghastly figure seemed to beckon them to Bruges, a skinless angel with a mirthless sinewy grin.

"Plastination," Robert explained. "Corpses preserved and manipulated, put into strange poses. I heard something about it on Radio 4. There was a bit of a controversy about the exhibition coming to Britain, I remember. They didn't allow it in the end. So, this would be a chance to see something we couldn't see at home."

"I suppose so," she said. "Why not?"

It certainly was, she thought. They agreed to go the following day. Today was set aside for a riverboat tour of medieval Ghent. Their guide was a middle-aged woman in an orange cloche coat and hat. When she turned from the wheel to address them, her wide eyes stared at her passengers through round glasses, addressing them in French, English and Flemish. Robert whispered to Catherine that she looked like a seafaring Miss Marple, which made her smile. A castle loomed above them, grey and forbidding. 'Miss Marple' announced that the medieval punishment administered within its walls for counterfeiting money was boiling in oil, her voice echoing across the water, bouncing off the ancient stone walls.

"Bit harsh," Robert says.

Catherine smiled faintly, nodded, but inside she was thinking, He doesn't get it, does he? He still thinks lying's okay. What would it take for him to understand—to feel how she felt when she found out? Boiling in oil?

She wondered what it would take for him to feel anything at all. She thought of the plastinated angel, stripped of its skin, cerulean-blue eyes fixing their unblinking gaze into the distance as though experiencing a higher state of consciousness.

Later, they returned to the hotel and requested an upgrade to a larger, more comfortable room with an ensuite bathroom. The beds were still separate, single ones. She considered pushing them together so they could try making love again, but the thought of it was too humiliating. Instead, she tried to sleep. Robert insisted on reading, even though she'd extinguished the bedside lamp on her side. She peered at his face, still attractive despite the signs of age, tension adding to the wrinkles around his eyes. Seeing them begin to flicker closed, the book falling from his limp hands, she climbed out of bed and went over to his bedside, switching off his light.

At last, she was able to sleep, but it wasn't a restful one.

She woke up to go to the toilet, but from the ensuite bathroom, she thought she could hear bubbling chuckles from the bedroom. She convinced herself it must be a freak of the water pipes.

But when she went back into the bedroom, she heard sighs and rustles that abruptly stopped. There were two bodies lumping the twisted sheets in Robert's bed, two faces staring back at her, a pair of grey eyes and a pair of brown ones: His eyes, blinking with injured innocence, held the same guilty schoolboy look he'd presented to her when she first discovered his betrayal two months before; the face next to his was a melting, shifting parody of glee under a wave of black hair.

Waking up from the dream, she lay there, holding her breath as she listened out for Robert's voice, to hear if he mumbled her name between snores.

Now, after a tense breakfast in the hotel and a silent train journey, here they are in Bruges. They're in a Chocolatier, one of the many lining the streets. She stares at the serried ranks of cuboid delicacies lining the counter. Robert stands behind her. She turns to him.

"Which one do you think I should get, Rob?"

"I don't know—whichever one you want," he says, putting his phone away.

It isn't a hurried gesture like it used to be, but the way his grey eyes widen with alarmed secrecy is too familiar from before. She decides to let it pass. Probably just force of habit. But he couldn't be, could he? He wouldn't, would he? Surely, he couldn't still be in contact with her...

The corners of his lips widen into a grin, his eyes still fearful, but there's real tenderness there, too.

"Look at you," he says, a soft tremor in his voice. "You're like a kid in a sweetshop."

"I am in a sweetshop," she points out. A very expensive one, she decides not to add. He's paying after all.

"Come on, hurry up and choose," he says.

"Alright, alright. I know you can't wait to see all the flayed corpses."

Funny how the mood's lightened, despite his obvious disinterest in the chocolate side of the outing and impatience to climb onto his own grisly hobby horse. She believes they are in tune with each other, that they can make a go of things, in spite of his betrayal. He settles "de rekening" and they leave the shop arm in arm. They walk along the busy street, dodging a horse and cart taking tourists around the sights of Bruges.

"What d'you reckon?" he asks. "Fancy a ride?"

"No thanks," she says, laughing at the grim face of the man driving the horse and cart.

She feels giddy and light-hearted, but there is an undercurrent of unease in her. She dismisses it from her mind, munching a chocolate, the sugar keeping her buoyant. She knows it's not all going to be plain sailing and there will be choppy waters ahead, but at least they are afloat, on their way to see the formaldehyde freakshow called Body Worlds.

Like Saint Peter at the pearly gates, the skinless angel on the poster beckons them into the square where the exhibition is housed. Two monks, sculpted in gun-metal grey with green streaks, stand mournfully embracing. Robert draws her away from the figures, anxious to get into the exhibition. He seems almost to bound towards the doors, chattering happily about Gunther von Hagens' methods for preserving the dead. It's the most excited she's seen him all day—indeed for days.

"What's the hurry?" she wonders, but he doesn't answer, guiding her inside briskly. It doesn't matter. She likes him taking control. He's been passive for too long, with the affair the exception that proved the rule. But even that, he pursued with his characteristic reserve, exploiting the fact his default setting was withdrawal to deceive her with studied neutrality rather than outright falsehoods, lying by omission, the ultimate in passive aggression. It's good to see him animated and engaged. Nevertheless, she is somewhat unnerved by his eagerness to enter this mausoleum of unholy relics.

She thinks of a line she remembers from some old poem—I run to death, and death meets me as fast, or something.

A man in a Fedora rictus grins at them from a display.

"Gunther von Hagens," Robert explains. He looks almost reverently at the picture. "'Born in 1945 in German-annexed Poland, he grew up in East Germany. Hospitalised as a child because of injuries exacerbated by his haemophilia, he developed an interest in medical science, particularly anatomy. In 1979, he applied for a patent for his ground-breaking method for preserving dead bodies, plastination…'"

"I can read, you know," says Catherine, glancing around her as if embarrassed, but it isn't as if people are queuing up to get into the exhibition. Apart from the box office staff, there's no one else about. Hardly surprising given the ticket price. It costs an arm and a leg to get into Body Worlds.

Robert's still chattering away happily, reading out the blurb.

"'There are four stages in the process: fixation, dehydration, forced impregnation and hardening.' Basically," he continues, paraphrasing, "They preserve the bodies, suck out all the liquids—"

"Hang on," she interrupts. "Forced impregnation?'"

"In a vacuum—well, a partial one. They bathe the body in a liquid polymer while boiling off acetone. That leaves a vacuum in the cells, sucking in the plastic. You end up with a corpse that never rots, one that you can touch."

"Right," she says.

"What?" he asks, detecting an edge to her voice.

"Nothing. Sounds great. Let's do it."

He shrugs and walks up to the counter, leaving her standing behind him while he speaks in Flemish to the woman selling tickets. Catherine watches in a state of defeated inertia as he glances back at her, saying something that makes the ticket seller laugh, no doubt joking about his neurotic wife's squeamish reluctance. He returns with two tickets, a fait accompli.

If only people spoke French in this part of Belgium, she thinks. When they originally decided to visit the country, the French-speaking part was their intended destination, but the Airbnb in Brussels fell through and he booked a hotel in Ghent instead. She's beginning to feel as if he engineered that deliberately to put her at a disadvantage because he speaks some Dutch, unlike Catherine.

Don't be foolish, she tells herself. Everyone speaks English here anyway. It's only pride that's making her refrain from communicating in her own language. She finds it humiliating, especially after all the pointed remarks, full of mock concern, from Belgian EU border officials about Britain's exit from the bloc. At the time, she shot back a rejoinder about how she hadn't voted to leave. But paradoxically, this bloody-minded refusal to speak English has left her devoid of the power of speech, leaving all the communication to Robert, who now stands flapping the tickets at her.

"Come on," he says. "What are you waiting for?" he demands. "What's the matter? I've bought the tickets now. Don't embarrass me!" He lowers his voice to a hissing whisper as though remonstrating with a child who's refusing to separate at the school gate. "Come on… People have preserved bodies for centuries—and put them on display. And all the donors consented to this."

"You said… 'touch them'."

"Yes, but that doesn't mean we have to! Come on, Catherine, I've bought the tickets now and it's closing soon. It's no different from looking at Egyptian mummies at the British Museum."

"Of course not," she says, forcing a smile and taking the proffered ticket, trying to put out of her mind that Maisa is Egyptian.

The cadavers may never rot, but there's something very off about the poses.

Since they have been in here, Catherine has seen a male corpse wearing nothing but a firefighter's helmet as if he were a flayed stripper-gram, carrying a female corpse, a goalkeeper with a head splintered and splayed out to show the stress of participating in sports, an artist with no eyelids painting with an easel at a canvas. Another display shows the entire white stringy web of a human nervous system pinned against a black background. Now, she and Robert stand contemplating a body sliced into cylindrical sections, not unlike the lamb chops they ate yesterday.

Mummified pharaohs were at least allowed some dignity in death, she remembers. The exhumation and display of their preserved bodies was the result of colonial plunder, not something they consented to or, indeed, expected.

Seeing her look of horror, Robert again mumbles something about the subjects having consented, but he too looks unnerved, as if this is more than even his ghoulishness can stomach.

"So you keep saying," she says, wondering if Von Hagens offered generous financial inducements to donors facing hardship. "But did they bargain for this?"

He doesn't answer. Just says, "Come on," but maybe he, too, just wants to get through this as quickly as possible by now. "It's closing soon," he reminds her.

It doesn't help that the informational displays emphasise everything that can go wrong with the human body. There is a video on one wall showing the correct and incorrect ways to sit at a desk in front of a computer screen. Many signs and displays warn of diabetes and other dire consequences of indolence and indulgence, extolling the virtues of exercise next to dissected organs, photos of lungs both before and after a lifetime of smoking, and arteries jammed by cholesterol. Yet the goalkeeper's split open skull, dark-pink muscles fanned out, and blue-irised eye shooting out on a thread of optic nerve illustrates a sign warning of the strain sport puts on the body and mind. The exhibition seems to Catherine to present human life as a dangerous battle, a struggle for survival, where a living body's very existence is under constant threat of being snuffed out at any moment. While she has no doubt that there is truth in this, she doesn't necessarily want her nose rubbed in it to this extent.

"I'm feeling a bit judged here," she says to Robert.

He smiles. "You mean, after all the Belgian chocolate and beer and waffles? I know what you mean. Maybe we should get out of here…"

She looks at him hopefully. Seems he's had enough too.

"Yes," she agrees, "I mean, it's very educational and everything, but I think I know enough about how close I am to death now!"

"It's just…" He looks away awkwardly.

"What?"

"Well, on the blurb outside, it said you can see the figures playing sport, painting pictures, making love…"

"And?"

"We haven't seen the ones making love yet."

"Oh."

"Well, we can't leave without seeing that, right?"

"Right."

"Well, can we?"

"No, I suppose not. I mean… You've got to get your money's worth, eh?"

He chooses not to hear the edge of sarcasm in her voice.

So they continue along a darkened corridor, which Catherine is relieved to see leads to a door outside, allowing her to breathe in some fresh air before ascending a staircase up to the next bit of the exhibition, offering an overhead view of the grounds, reminding her there is a world outside Body Worlds.

Through the next door is a corridor with small rooms to the side. One offers you the chance to exercise before a video image of a skinless corpse that is supposed to imitate your motions, but in fact, it performs a jerky parody of them, limbs going into impossible spasms like one of those little puppets Catherine remembers from her childhood with a button at the bottom of the wooden base that makes them bend and jump, bend and jump. Another of the rooms contains a glass case full of tiny fetuses at every stage of development in the womb, from conception to birth. Catherine thinks of sideshow babies with two heads in jars and wonders if the fetuses, too, are real. And if their parents signed consent forms for their display.

There are other rooms in this corridor. Robert hurries past them. There are no copulating corpses in there, and he's anxious to continue his prurient quest, but the door out of this corridor does at least lead them back outside momentarily, taking the edge off Catherine's increasing queasiness.

"Rob," she calls after his back as he strides impatiently along the next dark corridor smelling of formaldehyde.

He turns, his grey eyes glaring back at her with irritation.

"What?"

"I'm starting to feel really nauseous."

He sighs.

Maybe she should just go along with him, uncomplaining. Maisa probably indulged him more, was more submissive and compliant. If Catherine makes too much of a fuss, he might use the invisible scold's bridle of his infidelity on her. If she's not careful, her tongue might trigger his preferred torture device, the deadly affair. If she finds out he's been unfaithful again, it might destroy her this time.

Worse than that, he might leave Catherine for Maisa.

"Tell you what," he says, as if he's feeling generous. "Once we've seen this, we can go."

Her stomach lurches. She breathes through her mouth, and after a while, the sick feeling subsides. All marriages involve compromise, a little voice inside her says. But you're doing all the compromising, another one points out. And she begins to wonder, why is she so afraid of him leaving her anyway? Once the initial pain is over, she'll be free of his moods, his sulks, his cold silences, his erectile dysfunction.

Finally, here they are, standing before another chilly, irreverent tableau. Two more presumably willing donors are captured mid-rut on the dais, 'The Lovers', the plaque sardonically proclaims, the smaller print expounding upon the health benefits (and risks) of sexual intercourse. It must be uncomfortable, Catherine thinks, all those exposed, fleshless nerve endings rubbing against the hard, white plastic of this altar. Robert, pulling his wedding band back and forth over his knuckle, is carefully examining the point of entry—the wound, Catherine finds herself thinking, and she remembers their own abortive attempt at intercourse in the cramped hotel bedroom. For a terrible moment, she clutches her own wedding ring and wishes upon it that he could be as utterly naked as this before her, that he could actually feel something for once. With no scrotal skin sac, the testes hang suspended, joined only by flimsy tubular vas deferens to the erect penis. Denuded of skin, the rod of plastinated muscle rests against one side of the vaginal wall, the other side peeled away to allow inspection of the nerves and muscles inside. It looks to Catherine like the female figure has been sitting too long on the Spanish Horse. She wonders why pale, bristling pubic hairs still line the female genitals despite the heads of both participants in the frozen sex act, like all the other figures in the exhibition, lacking so much as a single strand of hair. This thought draws her eyes to the couple's faces, set in lipless grimaces of pleasure, presumably, the woman on all fours as the man grips her pelvis with sinewy fingers and fucks her from behind. It's then that she notices the eyes of the couple, which, unlike those of every single other inhabitant of Body Worlds, are not a bright, cerulean blue.

The man's are grey, the woman's dark brown.

"Right, you've seen it now," she snaps. "Let's get out of here."

He looks crestfallen but nods, presumably by way of reply to Catherine; yet as he does so, he's staring into the dead dark eyes of the corpse crouching sphinxlike to receive her lover's cock. He falls into step with her as she marches toward the exit.

"What's the matter?" he asks. "I don't see what the problem—"

"I know," she cuts him off. "Like mummies—Egyptian mummies in the British Museum or whatever."

"Catherine," he says, a warning plea in his voice in his response to the withering scorn in hers.

"What? I never agreed not to speak about it. Are you ashamed? You can't be embarrassed. There's no one here!"

He takes her hand. Angrily, she shakes it off. He blinks as if expecting a blow to the face. The look in his eyes is precisely the one that makes her want to hit him.

"I just don't want you upsetting yourself, Catherine."

"Me upsetting myself? Bit late for that, Robert…"

And she's about to storm out of the exit when she realises what's missing from his hand.

They retrace their steps through the museum.

She avoids looking at any of the human exhibits, keeping her eyes fixed upon the black-painted floor, where anything shiny should easily show up. Robert, too, is studiously staring straight at the ground. Nevertheless, it's hard not to look up occasionally and catch a pair of unblinking blue eyes staring at you from a face naked but for taut, pink muscle, unclothed with flesh and skin.

"It should be easy enough to find a dropped ring in an empty museum, shouldn't it?" she says.

He just nods.

The search seems to take hours, going right back through the exhibition in contravention of the floor arrows prescribing a single direction of travel, a relic of the Covid era that seems rather redundant now, especially given the absence of any other punters. Eventually, they go back along their original route. A cavernous voice booms out something in Flemish. She barely notices it, but Robert doesn't bother to translate it for her—it's obviously warning them it's almost closing time, and in any case, its repetition in English confirms that this is the case. Finally, they end up back at the copulating corpses, which she definitely doesn't want to see again, so pays exaggerated attention to a floor devoid of marital jewellery.

"Catherine," Robert calls. "It's here."

She looks over, sees the wedding ring on one of the sinewy fingers gripping the pelvis. She gapes at it. Has the museum curator played some kind of sick prank on them?

"I don't want to touch it," she says. "Are we allowed to touch it?"

Robert sighs.

"I think, under the circumstances…"

Catherine hears him grunt and gasp, presumably with the effort and unpleasantness of forcing the ring off the dead finger, but she doesn't want to see him, averting her eyes so she doesn't have to watch him do it.

But then the risk of her seeing it dims with the lights, abruptly extinguished.

"They must have locked us in," Catherine says, her voice brittle with suppressed panic.

"Don't be stupid," Robert snaps, scrabbling for the torch app on his smartphone. "Who would do a thing like that?"

But they both look at the finger slightly bent out of place by his efforts to remove the ring. Someone who would put a wedding ring on a cadaver is quite capable of shutting them in a museum full of them for the night. Robert uses his phone torch to guide himself towards the exit, finds it shut, rattles the door handle impotently.

He brushes past Catherine.

"I'll go and see if the other door is open."

"Don't leave me here," she pleads, and her voice sounds to her like a petulant child's.

But he's gone without another word.

Now that her eyes have adapted somewhat to the dark and having found the torch app on her own phone, she feels confident enough to go after him, but it isn't only fear of the dark that has held her back for the last few minutes. Admittedly, she doesn't exactly relish finding her way back through the exhibition, her phone torch picking out staring eyes and skeletal faces in the gloom. Her pride, too, has made her unwilling to go running after him straight away. As if the humiliation of her taking him back after the affair wasn't enough, now he leaves her alone in the dark in a room full of cadavers, giving her the choice of waiting around until he gets back or running after him like a pathetic, frightened lapdog.

Neither of those options are particularly attractive. But after he hasn't returned for minutes that feel like much longer, she decides to look for him, not in a blind panic of terror, but coolly and calmly, taking long, deep breaths, the kind she knows hold off the panic attacks that restarted for the first time in years after she found out about him and her.

"Robert," she calls, forcing the tremor out of her voice.

There is no reply, but she hears a hiss of movement in one of the adjoining chambers of the exhibition, and a kind of high, whimpering ululation. She shines her torch towards the source of the sounds and sees a door in the wall. Moving closer, she hesitates. There is a sign on it, marking it as 'private'. Usually, such a threshold would be taboo, and the unnerving nature of the vaguely human keening is an added deterrent. Yet, her instincts tell her Robert might have gone in here to find a way out, or to remonstrate with the staff who may have maliciously incarcerated them in here.

She opens the door slowly, hesitantly, half-expecting it to set off an alarm or something. Even under these extreme circumstances, breaching such a boundary feels beyond the pale.

All it triggers is a kind of soggy shuffling. Catherine has a ghastly intuition that whoever is beyond the door flinches at the possibility of contact. In the darkness, she can just about make out Robert's form, with what appears to be a long pale garment draped over his quivering arm. It could be a coat, except that it has trouser legs as well as sleeves, and a hood. An overall, then? It must be soaking wet, because she can hear a steady dripping to the wooden floor. And there is a metallic odour about him. His breathing comes in pained shudders.

"Robert…?"

"You wanted me to feel again," he gasps. "They said so when I slid the ring off." He pauses to take a few sobbing breaths. "They're alive, Catherine!" Despite her horror, Catherine must admit she has rarely heard him so energized, so alive.

"They spoke to me. Guided me. Showed me how!" He raises his free hand, shambling closer, and she notices something glinting in his grasp.

She remembers the torch on her phone.

Instinctively, she presses it—and instantly wishes she had not.

"Robert," she screams, furious and terrified, "what have you done?"

Usually, her anger would make him blink in that infuriating way of his, but not this time. By the light of her torch, Catherine sees him standing, darkly naked, lidless eyes wide, birthday suit draped over a skinless arm, dust and air searing his exposed nerves. His footsteps squelch, sticking and unsticking to the floor as he shuffles past her, carelessly discarding a scalpel and his own skin. She recoils from these things and doesn't follow him. She doesn't want to see what will happen next. She knows where he is going, a man possessed, inexorably drawn by an invisible thread seemingly attached from the red-raw cock jutting out perpendicular from the red-raw rest of him to the sphinx-like figure waiting to receive it.

THE SUNBATHER

Gary Smith

Award-winning poet and short story writer **Gary Smith** holds a Ph.D. in Creative Writing and taught creative writing subjects at Holmesglen Institute and Deakin University. Gary has performed at the Melbourne Writers Festival, Montsalvat Poetry Festival, and on Melbourne and regional radio stations. His writing has been published in a variety of national newspapers, journals, and magazines. Gary is a past Secretary of Melbourne Poets Union. You can find him on Facebook @garycleverwords.

Since his light bulb blew out nine weeks ago, when Thumper Dave moved in, Luke's room seemed as small as a coffin at night. His mother kept forgetting to pick up a new one, though she passed them in the aisle at Safeway every week. She had other things on her mind, she said.

Luke looked up at the ceiling as the wall adjoining his mother's room gave out small thuds like arrhythmic heartbeats. Every now and then, he heard her low moans sifting through thick summer air, and then his neck tightened, his teeth clenched, and his brow furled deep into the pillow as he imagined Dave and her in all the twisted positions he'd seen on the porn pages of the laptop he and Thommo stole from the Japanese kid last June.

Luke rolled onto his stomach, wedged the doona up over both ears, and fell asleep after a short while. Within that state, Luke conjured his dream. The one where he swaggers past a naked sunbather, beautiful with skin as white as his own. In the dream, she always pretends to be asleep, but he knows she is watching him out of one eye as the shore break propels him up toward the sun and forward to the warmth of waiting sand. In the dream, he is never dumped by the cresting whitewater, but always emerges tall and clean and tanned, with the naked woman smiling as he stretches his immaculately dreamt self onto the sand beside her. She passes her suntan lotion, and his fifteen-year-old hands explore the imagined flesh like a blind man learning a new room. Finally, he lowers his mouth; it widens over her warm nipple, and in the dream, he falls asleep—an easy little darkness nurtured in full sun.

Awaking from this dream always brought Luke to loneliness, layered and multiplied.

But this night, he awoke and resolved to chase it off. Tomorrow, he thought, I'll go to Bondi Beach tomorrow.

Luke was small, just five-four, and so light his mother could lift him off his feet with a good hit. His usual attire—a black tee shirt with Kurt Cobain written boldly across the front, his black and blue checked woolen jacket, and the wide-legged denim jeans that crumpled up at the laces of his K-Mart specials—all worked hard to conceal rather than dress him. If anyone were ever to hug Luke, they would feel his ribs. Shoulder blades. Spine.

But like his father, Ted, the boy had beautiful full lips and oval brown eyes that could save the worst of faces. Teddy Billings was a dealer in hash, speed, the big H, cocaine, and other assorted mind-benders. His mother always said that Teddy was soft on the boy, and a clingy adulation—a childhood leftover—had nurtured the bond they shared. But Luke cursed his father for a lack of height that ran like a cruel joke down the Billing's sperm line, and, because he was doing five to seven in Long Bay jail, Ted had left a vacant hole into which Thumper Dave had moved, and sat around, and ate and drank huge slabs of grog by day and shagged Luke's mother senseless into the night.

"Ya kid's like a pretty bloody ferret," Dave slurred and laughed the first night his mother, drunk herself, had brought him back to their dogbox Ministry of Housing weatherboard. "An them bloody lubra lips of is—dead-set looks like eez been suckin eggs all is life, eh!"

She had looked from Thumper to Luke then, with a slow swivel and tilt of her head, teetered a little, slapped the wiry man across singlet-clad shoulders in mock admonishment before giggling through a cupped hand and joining Thumper in pulling the boy down.

Thumper Dave was twenty-three years old and in his short career he'd done over at least one house in every other street within fifteen Ks of his favourite haunt, the Bricklayer's Arms. The Bricky's was a clapped-out corner pub smoke-thick with stolen goods, cash deals, and SP bookies that oozed sly winks and nods and mutual distrust. The other drinkers there were petty thieves and thugs like Dave himself, a thousand years of done time between them; close-knit through need though chronically resentful and suspicious each of the other. They had nicknamed him Thumper after he'd successfully cleaned up three cops who came to the Bricky's to nab him on what eventually became his second twelvemonth stretch for break and enter, plus another six for tearing off one copper's ear and jagging a broken glass across the cheek of another. Back at the watch house, six truncheons whirled and laboured into Dave—he earned his new tag in the hardest twenty minutes of his ugly life. He acquired a slight limp in his left leg from this and an extra layer of hate that loomed up quick at irregular times and surprised the Christ out of everyone with its crudeness.

Luke's mother worked bar at the Bricky's—sometimes behind it and at others, off-duty rousing with a rabble of grogged-up blokes and their women at the tables. The pub was only two blocks from where she and Luke lived, and that's where Thumper Dave chatted her up just six weeks after getting out that second time and four weeks after Luke's father had gone back in, having been lagged in and lumbered with a kilo of H. She was older than Thumper by ten years and well past her prime, which had been ordinary at its best, but Thumper's social skills endeared him to no one better, and he needed somewhere to root down for a bit and tool up for another run on Bondi's glittering assets.

A couple of losers bound ankle and wrist in folly was how everyone at the Bricky's thought about them.

"Put a fuckin bag over er ed, Thumper, you'll be right," one of his mates had suggested just before Thumper sent him cartwheeling across the beer-slopped tiles with his top lip split to the snot-line of his left nostril. And as he laid into the bloke with his boots, it was plain, even to this mob, that they did have something, Dave and her. It was brittle, and it was tense—and Christ knows the kid didn't like him—and maybe the something they had was so small it amounted only to a warm spine to belly into on a winter night between stretches in the slam. But Dave was smart enough to know everybody needed at least that.

The next morning Luke came into the kitchen to find Thumper in red jocks and toes hanging an inch over a pair of his father's thongs. He was slouched over a bowl of cereal; half a fag drooped, burning itself out in an ashtray; nine empty beer stubbies and a half bottle of scotch scattered across the sixties-green laminate. The stench of stale beer, after-smoke, and his mother's dried sex coming up off Dave turned Luke's stomach.

"Eh, champ," said Dave, "race up an gemme the paper wi ya. Wanna see wot gee-gees is goin roun this arvo." Just then, the mother appeared in the kitchen and sat at the table, her lightweight dressing gown falling open to expose her thighs, blotched and rashy. Before she could straighten it, Dave had pushed a hand up to her crotch. She grabbed and pulled it away, catching Luke's glance—contemptuous, then gone in a blink—at the same moment. Dave snaked the hand back, smirking up at her. "Go gemme that paper wi ya champ," he repeated to Luke.

"Can't, I'm going to the beach."

"Come on cob, ere's two bucks, keep the change, eh?"

"Get it yourself."

"Luke!" said the mother. "You watch your mouth or I'll clip your bloody ears."

"Can't he get it? I'll miss me bus."

"Will you please get the paper for Dave?"

"He's not a cripple."

"Do I have to beg, Luke?"

"Do I have to beg for a light in me room?"

As he tried to continue his breakfast and let her handle the kid, Dave's teeth met and forced the muscles at the side of his jaw taut as piano wire. The mother ran her left hand through straggled hair and looked to one side, eyelids lifting before turning back to Luke. Her eyes squeezed into a narrow slant, and there were bluestone chips in her voice. "I told you, I got things on my mind—I forgot. Now can you just bloody well go and get the paper?"

He returned her hardness. "He's rootin you, not me. You go and get it."

Dave's look of surprise came slowly, but with intent, up out of the cornflakes. He and Luke both stared at her then. Her face froze over, and her lungs filled involuntarily with air as she clasped both hands up and over her mouth in disbelief. And then Luke saw her eyes collapse into silence, and his gut dropped, knowing he'd gone a mouthful, a step too far, just like with the Japanese kid.

Out of respect for her, Thumper had stayed calm well beyond his normal span—she'd told him never to touch Luke—but the kid had overstepped. "Eh, come ere ya little prick an ol teach ya some effin manners." Luke reached for the back door, but in a flash, Dave was up and had him firmly by the left arm. His fingers and thumb wrapped around it and met. He brought his other hand up and pinned Luke to the porch wall. He squeezed both thumbs into Luke's tiny biceps, increasing the pressure as he spoke and searching for a sign of pain on Luke's face. "Now, ya gunna pologise to ya mum an then ya gunna get the paper, eh cobber?" Thumper's fingernails dug in deep.

"Let him go, Dave," she said.

"Not til the little arse says sorry."

She squared up to Dave. Grappled with the steel that had become his wrists. "I said... let the little bastard... go. I'll get the paper." Dave released his grip. She stared hard into Luke; voice shrill-edged off a lemon-dipped smile. "Are you happy now?" Luke didn't look at her or answer but gazed deep into Dave's face and then beyond, into that fierce zone that enabled him not to cry out or concede. "Well are you?" And she swiped Luke hard across the back of the head. The boy flew down the back steps, thumbnail bruises already beginning to blue out on his arms. "Luke!" the mother yelled. "You bloody well come back here."

He stopped momentarily at the bottom of the steps, face twisting out of shape, and shouted: "Go fuck yourself!" pole-axing her. And then he was gone down the laneway onto Main Street, where he'd catch a bus to the station. From there, Bondi Beach was just a train and another bus ride away.

Inside the house, she slumped onto the nearest chair, picked Dave's half-fag from the ashtray, and drew the smoke lung-deep. Tiny veins webbed the whites of her eyes; bottom lids welled but did not let go.

Thumper stormed in, slamming the door. "Effin little prick... y'okay?"

She looked up at him. "What have I told you?"

"Wot?"

"You know bloody what."

"Juss tryin t put im inta line."

"I told you never, not never, to lay a hand on him."

Dave rolled his head to one side, then back to her. "Eez a cheeky little bastard. Om not gunna let im give us shit."

"He's my kid. I'll deal with it..."

"Well, why don't ya then?" He noticed her left hand straddling the top of the ashtray, knuckles going white.

"If you ever touch him again..."

"Eh, settle! Om not lettin im slag us off, no fuckin way."

She relaxed, let the ashtray go, stood, and looked hard up into his face, coming hard back at her. "The last thing I'm going to say, Dave, is if you do it again you better be packed and gone before I find out about it."

His arms begged to be unstiffened from his sides and allowed to hurl the balled fists. "Or fuckin wot?"

They were nose to nose. "I'll do you, Dave... I will." She was finished then. Dropped back into the chair.

Mistaking this for retreat, he half-laughed and pointed a finger. "Eh, yd only end up on yr arse."

She turned, leaned back, drove a nothing-to-lose glare straight into his face, then glanced off in a deliberate arc that took his eyes with hers to the stay-sharp knife sheathed in its plastic holder on the wall. "You'd have to sleep sometime, Dave," was all she said, and then she went back into the bedroom and lay down, Luke's words circling with cruel intent on an endless loop.

She was rough, and she was loud, and she was not great-looking, he knew—and in anger, she was the cruelest person with words he had ever known. But the bottom line was Thumper couldn't stay sane without her. Shortly, he followed and climbed onto the bed beside her. They lay back to back for an hour, then, out of nowhere, he said: "Won't touch im agen," and released her into tears. "But e better smarten is act or someone's gunna drop a brick shit'ouse on im." Dave rolled and fronted her back then, reached an arm over and cupped her right breast. He just clung to it, not a finger moving to arouse her as they fell asleep. It was their ritual; it was what they did.

Out of the twelve dollars Luke had left, he bought a hamburger and chips, and a box of painkillers from a chemist on the Bondi Esplanade. He swallowed four of the little white pills at once, and after six or seven minutes, the pain in his arms became bearable. As he headed across the road toward the beach he could see a group of surfers performing hi-jinks on the medium swell at the southern break. Luke sat on the sandstone retaining wall and scanned the full arc from the rugged northern point, where rich houses chested their excess at the Pacific, to the congested southern end—cheaply tourist, buzzing with latte and Italian breakfasts.

He moved down onto the sand and sat in the shade of the wall, his back to cold stone. He watched the shore-break crash on three children, their squeals and laughter mixing with the squawk of a dozen gulls greeding for last night's pizza scraps. A bunch of Japanese tourists sauntered and chattered with their cameras click-clicking on the promenade above the wall, and as he drifted into a half-sleep, Luke thought again of how the Japanese student had gripped his laptop in anger when they'd demanded it from him, remembered the look of terror when Thommo slammed him up against the brick wall of the railway underpass at Balmaine.

"We're takin this," Thommo said, and he pulled out his knife and held it to the kid's nose. "Any objections?" Luke stood by, shuffling from one foot to the other, hands in his pockets, not wanting to look at the Japanese boy. But when Thommo turned smiling, Luke was cornered into an awkward, conspiratorial grin. There was fear all over the kid, but he refused to let go of the leather carry case. Thommo brought his right knee up into the boy's balls, and he dropped deadweight onto the bitumen. But still clutching the bag like there was an attempt to tear his heart away.

"Give us a hand, mate," Thommo said, turning to Luke, who reluctantly made his way over and began pulling and twisting at the shoulder strap. The Japanese boy went rigid; there were tears but no sound, and his eyes threw rage at Luke's emerging shame. Thommo then gave him two mighty kicks to the ribcage, and as Luke reached to pull the strap over the kid's face, he grabbed the hand and bit hard into Luke's flesh between thumb and forefinger, breaking open the webbing.

"Ya fuckin prick," Thommo yelled as Luke reeled back with blood running from the hand. Thommo flicked up the blade and jabbed the Japanese boy in the forearm. He let go a piercing scream but still clung to the laptop. Luke walked back over to him, nursing the injured hand, getting red in the face. "Give im a kickin, Lukie," Thommo yelled as he grabbed the screaming Japanese kid by the hair and held his face in Luke's direction. Luke thought of his errant father then, who loved him, he knew, but was never there; all the kids at school who'd taunted and rejected him because he was small and weedy; Mister Ballard, the teacher who'd expelled him. But most of all, as rage and retribution swallowed him whole, he thought of Thumper Dave and his mother, and in an act he knew to be as cowardly as it was pleasurable, he took three quick steps forward and dropped-kicked the Japanese boy's face; felt the cheekbone give back into the face with a queer grind and the nose cave sideways with a spray of red across the white-tiled wall of the underpass. He drew back again and moved his aim to the kid's stomach, where he released his anger again and again and again. He stopped finally, but the Japanese boy had been unconscious from the first kick.

"Me grandad fought them Japs in the war," said Thommo as he backslapped Luke. "He'll be fuckin rapt I done one over." And they walked off into the night, Thommo swaggering along with his prize, and in his shadow, Luke, hand limp and dripping blood, victor of nothing.

When Thommo spotted Luke on the sand, he gave him a sharp kick in the thigh to wake him. The sun was well up over the wall, and the beach flagged and billowed a multiplicity of tossed shirts, shorts, thongs, coloured hats, and towels and umbrellas with sun-doped bodies lolling on top, over or under them. At the ocean's edge, the foam tossed limbs and torsos every which way, and beyond, the sea reflected the sun like scalloped gunmetal. When Luke tried to lift an arm to shield his eyes, the pain was excruciating, and it fell dead at his side.

"Ahh, shit."

"What's up with ya?" Thommo asked.

"Bastard me mum's shacked up with."

"He bashed ya?"

"A bit. Nearly broke me arms I reckon."

"Bastard. Giz a look."

"Yeah, I hope the coppers kill him next time... ah, jeezus!"

Luke grimaced as Thommo rolled up a sleeve to inspect the arm. "Fuck, look what e's done to ya." There was the four-inch, blue-black bruise with a fringe of dull yellow and, above that, four smaller ones, each as dark as the first and topped with four half-moons of broken flesh where Thumper's nails had gone in hard. "Didn ya mum do nuffin?"

There was a small silence. "She weren't home," Luke lied, rolling his head to avert Thommo's gaze.

Thommo reached into his pocket. "Hey, Lukie." He held up his knife, pushed the small ivory button, and the blade snapped out, gleaming in the daylight. "Take this," and he touched the flat of it against Luke's cheek, directing his gaze until it met his own. "If e comes at ya agen, put it into im." And with that, Thommo stood and picked up his skateboard. "Ee's not your ol man, Lukie. Don't take shit from im."

Though Luke knew himself incapable of using it, he accepted the glinting gift, retracted the blade, and slid it into his pocket. Thommo smiled in accomplishment. "Gotta go, mate," he said. "See ya in the park around eight or 'alf past. I pinched some o' me ol man's weed—nough for a cuppla joints, I reckon.... tin o' chrome, too, Lukie. We'll 'ave a ball, mate."

"Yeah, okay." Luke watched as Thommo dropped the skateboard onto the concrete path and glided away.

•

The sunbather comes down onto the beach twenty minutes after Thommo leaves. Thirty-two years old, she has the palest skin, in a bikini two years in the drawer. Though still a little thin in recovery, her figure is fine-boned and curve-hipped with soft, full breasts a little disproportionate to the rest. She has mid-length auburn hair framing a face that remains strong despite the ordeal of the birth and holds its beauty in profile, though not from the front, where anguish has manipulated the corners of her eyes and mouth. As she stands just a metre away, contemplating whether to prop in full heat or shade of the wall, it is the breasts that hold Luke in a fascination that is sensual and then something more.

Standing to one side, awaiting her decision, the husband tries hard against annoyance. "Here?" He points to a spot half-sun, half-not. He is well-tanned and muscular in a subtle way, a true-lined firmness earned from his daily five K run. Anger at the child's death harbours in every cell and hones itself on everything he has to do for her. The man is very tall, Luke notices, looking sideways and up from his squat against the wall. "Here?" the husband says a second time, agitating from left leg to right. "Or do you want to be in the sun…" Shielding her eyes, the woman looks high up into the sky as if in need of some sign to help her decide. "You could burn," the man finishes.

Luke slants his head toward the sand, feigning disinterest. By their body language he can tell they have come down to the beach in the thick of some battle.

Five seconds of silence ensue until she finally turns to the man. Her mouth tries for a smile, but her eyes disown it. "Isn't that what happens to sinners, Rod—they burn in Hell?"

"Don't start."

"I have to burn… every day, don't I, Rod?"

"Should have thought about that while you were pregnant."

"Do you think I wanted to lose it?" Her head cranes forward. Her arms come up a little from her sides, palms facing him, her fingers spreading like a plea.

"Him. It was him, not it," the man snarls.

She reaches for his hand, but he recoils just enough for hers to miss and fall brick-heavy. "For once, will you just listen…"

"You never wanted a kid, admit it."

"Not at the start, but…"

"Murphy told you to drop back, take it easier." Luke looks up from under his cap and into her face, then to the husband's unrelenting glare. "It wasn't like we needed the money." Luke wishes they would move ten meters down the beach.

"I know, Rod, I made a mistake…"

"A mistake. Jesus, just plain selfish. Nine to seven every day of the week… Saturdays."

"I worked six months to get the Kyoshi contract."

"Someone else could have handled it."

Luke sees her eyes blaze. "Oh, yes, sure. I could have handed it over to David, or Peter, or Brad… You just don't know what it's like… having to prove yourself three times over to get the same job a man does simply by being adequate and then blowing a few blue jokes into the manager's ear… Do you think if I'd realized it could hurt the baby—"

"He's not hurt, Sandra, he's dead."

Her arms and shoulders drop. "What I've been through. The stroke. Isn't that punishment enough?"

Luke sees there is nothing coming back from the man's eyes, dull like dead fish. He watches the woman shrink into herself as the man's head swivels away. "Fuck this," he says, more to himself, and then he throws her towel and beach bag down. "I'm going to be late," and her sunglasses spill out to within inches of Luke's feet. Walking off, not even turning, he says. "I'll pick you up at five."

"Don't bother," she replies, "I'll get the bus."

"Suit yourself," his voice trails off, neither fire nor ice. And then, from somewhere unfathomable, he adds: "If you're not back by seven, I'll send an ambulance." The brutality of his words stops him dead, and he flings his face skyward. "I'm sorry, I didn't—"

"No, of course," she cuts in, "you didn't mean it… Look, just go."

She stares at the ocean for a full minute until the man has reached the car park out of sight. She turns and, spotting the glasses, becomes aware of Luke. Before she can bend for them, Luke reaches over and offers them up. His face contorts a little. "Thanks," she says, thin voiced, and her eyes, black-rimmed and immediate, notice the bruises on his arms as they red-flag up at her. "A fall?" she asks, trying for a smile as she reaches to hold up his left arm from underneath. And then, as if the bruises might not really exist, she softly brushes them with her fingers. "They're deep," she says, her brow wrinkling slightly. "And those cuts look really angry."

"I'm okay." But a small grimace gives him up.

"You need to clean them," she says, leaving no room for dissent. "They'll infect, wait here." She lowers Luke's arm, grabs a dozen tissues from her bag, and makes her way in a gait that measures itself out to the ocean's edge. She bends carefully, then dips the tissues in and returns to Luke's side in the same slow fashion. It reminds Luke of how Tibby, their Border Collie cross, had walked home after being hit by a car. When she arrived, she only had a few cuts. She was slow-moving, yeah, but otherwise, she seemed okay. When she collapsed the next day, Luke's father took her to the vet.

He came home alone. "Sorry, Lukie, she was all busted up in the guts, mate. C'mon, we'll bury her out the back." At the end of it, his mother had come out to the yard, and the three of them sat around the edge of the fresh mound, arms over shoulders, and bawled themselves wet-faced.

It was the closest Luke had ever felt to them, to being a family.

As the woman bends down in front of Luke, her cleavage bulges a little, revealing a white vee below the tan line. Luke blushes. "This salt water will do the trick," she says and she runs the liquid across Thumper's nail marks.

"Aahhh, jezzus!"

"It'll hurt at first," she says. But as she begins to bathe the second lot, the pain becomes excruciating. "I'm sorry," she says and, sensing his anguish, places a hand on his face. "You alright?"

Refusing to cry, he pulls away, retreating from the pain, the unexpectedness of touch.

"They'll be okay," he says.

"Are you sure?" Her arms are outstretched, wet tissues still on offer.

"Yeah… thanks."

As the pain begins to subside, he rests back against the wall. The woman comes off her knees slowly, palms pushing against the sand to gain a lift. When she rises, Luke sees the left side of her face tic strangely. He thinks about asking, *Are you okay?* But then she has turned. She stands before her towel now, and after two or three seconds, she reaches with her right hand to feel her left bicep. Then she bends, kneels, and finally lengthens along the towel, stomach down, her whiteness stark against the red material. Luke can only see one wet eye and moistening cheekbone because of the awkward angle her folded arms make across her face, hemming her in as she lies there regretting way beyond what Luke can ever know.

Luke pops two more aspirins and lies back against the stone, feeling warmer. He makes short, languid sweeps of the human panorama on sand and sea. Drawn back to the woman, he becomes aware of the short curls of hair in the pit of her left arm. Answering the adolescent mind's crude vocabulary, slow electricity syringes up from shaft to the head of his penis. She is no one to him, and he can find no rational reason to dismiss the urge to gaze at the laid-out flesh. Below the short curls he sees the white side of the breast bloom under the weight of her. In the middle of the breast, he knows, is the small brownish circle with a nipple—he remembers masturbating to nipples he saw in the Penthouse mags at Thommo's. Fantasizing, he imagines removing the bikini bottom of the sunbathing woman so she would be fully naked beside him. For a full hour he watches the exposed hills and plateaus of her white body pink-up in the sun. His eyes run the curve of shoulder, spine, and buttock, of legs splayed with indecent possibility.

Suddenly, she lifts her head and looks at Luke as if she's been thinking hard about it: "You really should get those cuts seen to. Do you live far?"

"Bout an hour… They're not hurtin now."

"I've got a mobile if you want to call your mother and father to pick you up."

"Me dad's, um, away. And me mum works. I have to go there soon."

She eases herself down onto her towel. "Good," she says, "you're lucky to have someone to look after you."

"Yeah…" But his tone betrays the lie. "You been fighting with your husband?"

Before answering, she looks hard at Luke for two, three seconds, deciding whether she will go this notch with him, then: "Yes." She does.

"He's real tall. Bet you feel safe with him, nobody'd try nothing."

"Yes, I feel safe with him."

"And he's never hit you, has he?"

"No, he'd never do that."

"Then I reckon you're the lucky one. Will y make it up with him, when you get home."

"Maybe."

"Jeez, you'd be able to go anywhere with someone that big. Nobody'd say boo."

She looks at him, wishing his logic could rule her world. "I'm a bit tired, I'm going to have a sleep now. If the cuts start to hurt I'll take you up to the surgery on the Esplanade. Wake me if they do."

For nearly an hour, Luke watches her lie there, still. At the end of that hour, she makes just one movement when the whole of her upper body gives an involuntary shudder. It startles and slightly shames him, as if her unconscious had suddenly become aware of his unsavoury thoughts. Had shelled them and was registering its disgust. But when her body finally slumps back, he relaxes once again and is drawn back to the breast swelling out of the red of her towel. He thinks how it would feel to place his whole mouth over the sunbather's nipple, to fall asleep there, stretched like a warm god in full sun. He no longer has an erection as his thoughts lull him into a serenity where the whole world has disappeared and there are only the two of them—no tall husband, no Thumper Dave, no need for dogs or fathers, mothers or light bulbs…

Two-thirty and Luke wakes to find the back of the woman has burnt. She has fallen into a dead sleep, and he has an urge to reach over and wake her or put his own towel across her body. He knows too that he must go soon, find his mother—she'd be doing her twelve to four shift at the Bricky's—and make things right from this morning. She would slow-burn for weeks otherwise. But the thought of confronting her frightens Luke—and what if Thumper is there? He wishes instead that he could wait here, watch over the sunbathing woman, not leave until she leaves. He wishes he could lie down in the shade of her until his life becomes more clear. Less painful.

Luke stands up. "I'm goin now. See y later." Nothing from the sunbather; she doesn't stir. He looks at her, then up to the sun, and, removing his towel from his backpack, drapes it gently over her. Small towel for a small boy, it cannot cover everything. Still, she doesn't move. Luke wants to wake her up and thank her—he will probably never see her again. A small black wave breaks in his gut as he walks off toward the bus stop. His mother won't like the towel not coming home, but he doesn't care.

Down at the Bricky's Arms Luke's mother is lazily pulling the last few beers of her shift. Thumper Dave, already eight schooners and two pies into the afternoon, has crammed himself into a corner with four blokes in a foul-mouthed gaggle of footy talk; the races; and the usual talk of women—seen one fanny, you've seen em all, eh Thumper… only two sizes, mate, big and bigger… And in each corner, the same conversations circle and drip septic from fur-white tongues to be trodden into the beer-stained grout.

The mother catches Luke's eyes the moment he slinks in. She is still bull-ant angry at what he'd said this morning, but she keeps her gaze neutral, summing up the mood and the possibilities as Luke walks up to the bar. Is he going to apologise? No, it has never been in his or Teddy's repertoire to say sorry—rather, it was done through the backdoor—the way their bodies spoke, the slump of shoulders, a dog-down tilt of the head, averted eyes. But always with defiance hidden in their pockets. But this time, only words will mend her. She knows, too, because of what he'd said, that the moment of power is all hers. When she looks at him now, she sees Teddy: elf-small, useless and in jail while she pumped grog six days a week and washed the clothes and cooked the meals and woke without a glimpse of hope for better things—and only Thumper's feral slag between her thighs; his three-day bristle scratching at her neck. She looks at

Luke and knows that she is owed something more from somebody—and at this moment, it doesn't really matter who.

"Got anythin to say to me?" She is halfway through pouring a whisky and Coke. Luke's upper body swivels slightly away from her as if trying to make off without permission from the legs. His face points to the ceiling in search of the words that, for him, were barely possible. "Well... have you?" This time it is a demand.

"Ya servin me or not?" the customer scowls.

She turns on him, flint and spittle. "I'll serve you when I'm good and fuckin ready." Then she returns to Luke, who is surprised to find himself on the precipice of saying what he knows is her due.

"About this morning, I'm..." he hesitates for just a second.

"You're what, Luke?" Then, thoughtlessly, without letting him finish, she raises the bar. "Your useless bloody father could never say sorry neither." Now, slagging Teddy off to Luke was a big blue, she realizes, just a millisecond too late. It was true; Teddy was useless, but he was all the father the boy had; it was a thin thread of identity that stretched from Teddy's cell at Long Bay straight to Luke's heart. Her trying to break it pushes remorse to pain, pain to anger, and gives Luke the out he is grateful to be offered.

"I don't remember," he says, chin jutting a little, "ever hearing you say sorry to no one."

"Oh?" she replies, her eyes rounding out; hands readied on hips, "and why would I need to do that, Luke?"

"The lightbulb in me room for one thing." And then Luke begins to scan the room. The mother's eyes follow his—she has taught him this game—until both sets find Thumper. Then Luke looks her square in the face. "You tell me," he says, and that is bad enough—but then the start of his smirk curls up at her.

A battle has been lost, but she is not prepared to lose the war. Her arm stretches back, her eyes just whites. "You little bastard," and the flat of her hand collides with his face. Leaves a shock-red tattoo there. "You're just like him... just like your father." She is bawling now. The commotion reaches Thumper, and he stumbles his way to the bar. As Luke recoils, holding his stinging cheek, Dave grabs him by one arm, reinventing the bruises and their pain.

"Dave," she screams, "let him go and piss off back to your corner!"

"Wot've ya fuckin done t'upset er this time, eh?" he slurs, shaking the Christ out of Luke, whose whole face scrunches up. As Luke struggles for release, his mother sees Thommo's knife fall from his pocket. She races to the other side of the bar, picks it up, and then, as if a knife knew why knives are honed, the thing is into her right hand; the button is pushed, and the blade is out searching for muscle and sinew before she has any say in it.

The buzz in every corner of the Bricky's falls dead as the three of them stand, a wide-eyed trinity staring at the thing buried hilt-deep into Thumper's seeping gut.

"I told you, Dave," she whispers.

"Jeezus," he cries, "y've fuckin done me." As she lets go of the handle, Thumper collapses against the bar, eyes scattering for a place without pain.

She holds him up and looks across to Luke, her face dissembling. "Are you happy now?" Luke looks to where the life-red drools from Thumper's gut to drench the denim purple as it spreads all over his jeans and the mother's dress.

Then Luke runs. And he keeps running—until he is on the bus, then the train, and on to where the second bus will take him back to Bondi Beach—will wind back the hour.

Luke came down onto the beach and the horizon was a clean black arc on vibrant orange. The sunbather—though without the sun, we can no longer call her that—was the only one left on the sand. Luke drew the hood of his coat up over his head and huddled back against the sandstone. She was still asleep, Luke saw, and he thought how foolish she was, how vulnerable, and how cold she must be, with only his small towel for cover. The lights atop the esplanade threw a warm blanket of color over the ridge of her shoulders, and Luke could see the fine hairs outlined on them. He remembered the contempt the man had shown when he left, the animosity. Like Luke, perhaps she simply did not want to go home. Perhaps she was just lying there in her own fierce space, thinking, and because of her sunburn she hadn't felt the darkness envelop her. She was dreaming, perhaps, trying to work out a way to patch things up with the man just as Luke was trying to think of what he might ever again say to his mother.

Luke watched the woman—for something—a slight rise of the shoulder blades brought on by breath, the sign of goosebumps on chilled flesh. Nothing. A black seed took root in the centre of his brain and froze him to the wall.

"Hey," he whispered, then louder: "Miss." He released himself from the cold stone of the wall, crabbed his way over and touched her back, almost not touching it. He ran his hand along her spine, then placed it on the back of her head. He went to wake but not frighten her because there were just the two of them on the beach now and he wanted her to rise up again and be surprised, even embarrassed, at how long she'd been asleep. "Hey, miss," his voice squealed as his hand softly prodded cold skin. Only stillness. He moved to one side and looked into her face. The exposed eye was half open. It was finished with all looking, and sand had blown up to trace the journey of her last tear in grit.

Luke began to rock backwards and forwards. "Oh fuck, no. Oh fuck." He whispered it over and over, his bottom lip quivering, his face curling acid-dipped, his head lolling from ocean to sky to woman and across the horizon from north to south, then up the sand and back to her.

With knees dug into the sand, Luke gently rolled the sunbather onto her back. He wedged himself in behind to cradle her head, and his arms went around, the fingers reaching to fuse themselves below her breasts. He settled them both in against the tomb-cold stone, covered them with his towel, inhaled, and a great sob let go from his lungs like the release of all life.

D = LOG N/LOG S

Bryan Miller

The fiction of **Bryan Miller** has previously appeared in *The Bombay Literary Review*, *Shadowy Natures*, *The Monsters We Forgot*, and several other literary journals and anthologies. He is also a standup comedian, and in that capacity has performed on *The Late Late Show with Craig Ferguson*, Sirius/XM Radio, and featured in numerous magazines and newspapers. For more of his jokes and scary stories, you can follow him @realbryanmiller on X/Twitter or @funnybryanmiller on Instagram.

Mama said I can't hang around with Dirt Pete no more on account of he's the cause of all my badness and the way I've turned out, which she cannot control. Of course I told that to Dirt Pete right away when I saw him the next day on the school bus. You can say that sort of thing to Dirt Pete. You can say anything to him really because Dirt Pete never talks, not one single word.

Mama is suspicious about Dirt Pete because he never talks but also because he's so dirty. That's how he got his name. Obviously. The older kids in Lavender Court had all sorts of nicknames for him. Dumpster Diver, Pete-ing Soil, Pete-ing Zoo. Pete-ing Tom, on account of he likes to look in people's trailer windows when they don't know. But sometimes the meanest thing you can say has no cleverness to it at all, just direct, like Dirt Pete.

When I told him what Mama said he didn't shrug or make no face or anything, I guess because we both knew I wasn't going to listen to her anyway. I told him it's mostly not the dirt thing, it's the no-talking because people get suspicious when they can't understand the inside of something from looking at the outside, that's what I think. Dirt Pete reached down and grabbed a handful of gray soil and poured it all over his own head then, and he rubbed the dirt into his short red hair and laughed at himself inside the dusty cloud. He don't make a sound when he laughs either, just smiles his open-mouthed smile and shakes his shoulders and slaps his knee. I laughed too.

It wasn't just the rubbing dirt on his head. Dirt Pete really was dirty all the time. He was always smudged around his cheeks and eyes and his skinny arms were streaked like he'd been working on an old car that didn't make it. He smelled like soft vegetables. His Mama took pills she bought from his older brother Cody so she was too sleepy all the time to see that he ever washed, not that she'd been real on top of it when she used to be awake more. He was shorter'n me and had narrow, dark eyes that was beady as all hell. I suppose they looked pretty suspicious if you didn't know what Dirt Pete meant, unless you was someone like me.

What we'd got in trouble for this time was this possum on the frontage road somewhere had got turned inside out with a stick up its a—hole and out through its long mouth. The complainer lived in Lot #34, the lady who dries her big old flower-print bras out on the clothesline but never her drawers, which makes me wonder, does she not wear any? She's a mean old thing and she always yells about what everybody else is doing in their trailer, whether it's the music or the shouting or whatever she don't approve of. Her trailer faces the frontage road so I would have known it was her even if Mama didn't say that's who when she was hollering at me about how the stick was still in the possum so everybody knew it was some sicko, no doubt that Dirt Pete. You stay away from him, she told me. Even the grownups knew that's what he was called. She said that he gets up to foul, nasty things.

Dirt Pete was never too mad to listen. He didn't do nothing but. You could tell Dirt Pete anything. You could tell him about how Mama gets the blues and says she's going to kill herself and she waves around a bottle of Drain-O or the kitchen scissors. He liked funny jokes about the man born with five things and how his pants fit. You could even tell him about weird stuff too like how you saw numbers in everything and your mind was always counting, which nobody else ever wanted to hear about, not even the math teachers at school.

He even stole me a fancy math book once. Dirt Pete stole a lot of things, which was hard since people always suspected he was going to swipe something on account of him being so dirty. But Dirt Pete was so good he did it right under their noses anyway. His pockets was always full of batteries and candy and whatever he could grab. I still don't know how he got that math book since it was such a big hardback thing it must have been a b—d to sneak out but he brought it to me one day and I look at it a lot because numbers aren't like words, you can read them easy and they all fit together.

Inside my brain every number there is has its own shape and color and when you want to figure out something like what's two-hundred and seventeen two-hundred seventeen times, you just think of the shapes and the colors and how they go together and you know the answer is the lumpy yellow round thing that means forty-seven thousand and eighty-nine. There's way more tricky numbers than that in the math textbook but I like reading it because even if the words are confusing the numbers all make shapes I like to think about. When I told that to the math teacher at school she said to stop talking nonsense. I never get good grades because I don't show my work and she says I cheat.

Everything makes sense if you just follow the numbers. The hardest thing there is to do is make sense with words even though that's what everybody always wants you to do. I'm only even writing all this down because you made me.

Dirt Pete didn't have a Daddy and I don't have a Daddy. That is one thing we had in common, although there was Rick. He was married to Mama for awhile before and was a cop. He came by sometimes still but you never knew when. He was always calling me faggot, that was his word for me. When Rick comes over he parked his squad car with the flashing lights right out front of the trailer and he f—ks Mama. Sometimes he leaves us some money afterward and sometimes he doesn't and sometimes he stays and sometimes he doesn't but when he does I can hear him f—king Mama which is something I don't think no son wants to know about. I don't got any interest in sexy stuff, but Dirt Pete does, and it was because of both of those facts that people think I did something terrible.

How it happened was, we'd all of us got dropped back off at Lavender Court on the school bus. Dirt Pete goes to special ed classes but he rides the same bus as the rest of us. It let a whole bunch of us off out front near the caretaker's office where they have the washers and dryers that don't hardly work. Me, Dirt Pete, Big Robert, Jahnalee, Dreama, Rosita, and Kaylee, who is still just a baby in the first grade but follows us around like a little blonde dog. The other kids on the bus give us s—t and call it Scavenger Court and ask us how we can tell our houses apart since they all look the same, which is not really true. The trim on a lot of the trailers is different colors or sometimes will have come off entirely, which is its very own color, and some of them are older than other ones and have little porches or rust spots or flower boxes. You can tell them apart if you want to.

The kids on the bus give extra s—t to Dirt Pete because he never talks and he smells and also they say he f—ks his brother, which isn't exactly true. His brother does f—k Dirt Pete sometimes, which to me ain't the same thing at all. He sorta explained it to me once in his way, with me asking a bunch of questions. No telling how anybody else found out about it except that the trailers in Lavender Court are close together and the walls are real thin. I told a group of them kids they was all b—hes and b—rds and they wouldn't think it was so funny if somebody was f—king them and the bus driver heard and it was a whole big thing I got in trouble for, which is why I try not to curse no more. I told Mama I wouldn't. She says I got the foulest mouth in all of Kentucky.

After school nobody much usually wants to go back to their trailer right away so we played games and stuff in the courtyard, which has some lawn chairs and a big dusty fire pit filled with cigarette butts. That day we was playing tag down by the little woods there behind Lavender Court along the dry creek where people threw their trash. We'd been playing awhile when Big Robert said he had to pee and pulled it right out and started to pee in front of everybody and Dreama and Jahnalee and Rosita covered their mouths giggling. Robert is two grades ahead of me in seventh but he's been held back a couple times so he's closer to Dirt Pete's brother Cody's age. So then Robert said if you think it's so funny let me see you do it and Jahnalee said I bet you'd like it and Robert said she didn't have the nerve and she said oh yeah and she pulled her jean shorts and underwear right down to her ankles. The other girls started laughing even harder and Jahnalee said to stop giggling, it made her too nervous.

Like I said before, I don't have any interest in sexy stuff so I kinda slipped away down the dry creek bed. Dirt Pete followed along behind me even though I knew he wanted to stay and watch Jahnalee try to pee because unlike me he has a powerful interest in sexy things. We sat down on the rocky edge of the dry creek to enjoy the quiet. Dirt Pete can just be, without making noise all the time. It makes me feel less anxious. But I'm not like him that way. Sometimes stuff just comes bubbling up out of me, and pretty soon I was showing him how if you held a leaf up to the sunlight you could see all these crazy patterns repeating in little squiggles in their skin and they looked like these things I studied over in that math book called fractals. The book says the numbers for that are $D = \log N/\log S$ and I'm not entirely exactly sure what that means but I think it's true because these fractals are like the numbers with their colors and shapes but they're the most special shapes of all. When you look at them real close the shapes inside look the same as the big shape from far away, so these fractals are really exactly the same on the inside as on the outside, which makes them true, unlike people.

You can't always be sure Dirt Pete is following what you're saying but this time his eyes go wide and he jumps up and cocks his head back toward Lavender Court for me to follow. He don't usually get so excited so when he does you just gotta go with it. Off a little ways in the distance we could see Jahnalee sitting on the ground. She had her pants pulled up but she was crying now and Robert was standing there with his arms crossed looking mad so something had went wrong with the peeing but we didn't have no time for that.

Pete was moving quick on those short little legs. He brought me around the back side of Lavender Court and up one of the rows near the side road to one with a little wood porch and a blue plastic baby pool out front filled with brown water and leaves and cigarette butts. He motioned for me to follow him along to a back window that was closed but the blinds was busted up so that there was a dark little slit you could look through into the living room. Dirt Pete knew just about every looking place there was. He pushed me up against the window so I could look inside the trailer.

It was dim inside but you could make out a couch facing a TV on the floor leaned up against the other wall and a table in between them. On the table there was some kind of video game with a whole mess of wires running to the TV and next to that one of them colored glass vases people smoke dope out of. But next to that was this rock that was split open to show this big old crystal inside. What light there was in the room sparkled off all the jagged little tops of the crystal and you could see that part of it was smooth flat and on that flat part there was one of them crazy fractal patterns in all different crystal colors. It was the most beautiful thing I'd ever seen and I knew right then I had to have it.

Me and Dirt Pete come to an agreement that he would steal me that big crystal rock and in return I would help him hide his brother Cody's ninjy sword. Cody had this real ninjy sword like the real Jap ninjys use, with a black handle and a long silver-looking blade that was rounded on one side but sharp as all hell on the other so they could cut off each other's heads like they do. For some time he kept it hanging on two nails up on the wall of his bedroom, which was painted all black and covered in sexy pictures Dirt Pete liked to look at. I only saw inside a couple times on account of Dirt Pete and me both tried to keep clear of his brother, which was easier for me because I didn't live in the same trailer with him. I didn't think he'd try to f—k me, but when somebody would f—k their own brother you can't be too sure just what they'll do to you.

Dirt Pete brought me over to his trailer. I asked if Cody was gone and he nodded. We sneaked past his Mama, which wasn't a hard thing on account of she was so sleepy she barely opened her eyes. We went down the hall, which was all filled with dirty clothes we had to step over, and into Cody's room. It smelled like sweat and dope in there and the walls was all covered in pages torn out of magazines of ladies with their boobs out and their legs spread to show toothless pink mouths down there or else they were playing with some guy's thing. For the life of me I don't know why anybody would want to look at all that. Usually Dirt Pete did but not this time. He took me right over to Cody's closet. Some of

Cody's clothes was hanging from a rod but most of them was on the floor so that you could barely see his black boxy combination safe where I guess he kept all his pills and dope. Behind that, way in the corner, we found that ninjy sword.

Dirt Pete waved for me to go back outside and around to Cody's bedroom window. When I got there Dirt Pete had already opened it up and he passed that ninjy sword out to me inside of its round ninjy sword holder so we wouldn't get cut. I could see what he was up to right away. That ninjy sword was so long it was hard to hide to sneak anywhere, so we went back to my trailer and he carried it this time around to my bedroom window. I opened it up and he passed the ninjy sword through so I could put it way back in my own closet for safekeeping. This way he could visit it whenever he wanted without worrying about Cody. While we was doing all this Mama yelled from the living room what was I doing and I said nothing, just playing in my room, and she said well at least you ain't with that screwy Dirt Pete. I winked at him outside my window there and he smiled. When Dirt Pete smiles his eyes get real narrow like you can't believe he can hardly even see.

I wasn't worried he couldn't get me that crystal. Dirt Pete is a sneaky devil. Sometimes he shows up in my bedroom without me even knowing how he got there. He must jimmy open the window or some such thing. I guess he comes by to wait for me or just to get away from his own trailer. Well, just like Dirt Pete shows up sometime without no warning, so did that crystal. It was just in my closet back by the ninjy sword one day. I was real excited to see it up close. The outside was like regular rock but the inside was smooth as a mirror with a rocky little pit like a cored peach, only this was dark blue with lotsa purples and pinks swirling in those patterns. When you spun it around it looked like a thousand million numbers all coming together to add up and divide and multiply. It was like you could hold $D = \log N/\log S$ right there in your hand. When I knew Mama was asleep and nobody would come into my room I'd take it out and stare into it to see all those shining numbers.

I was looking at the crystal early on a Saturday morning while Mama was over at the office doing the laundry when I heard a tap tap tap at my window and there was Dirt Pete. His left eye was black and his lip was bloody. I opened the window and pulled him through, which was easy on account of he's so small. His hands was shaking and he didn't want to look at me. He didn't have to say his brother had been at him again, not that he could have said. But I knew. I tried to distract him by explaining to him about the patterns in the crystals and the numbers and whatnot but he pushed past me and went into the closet and came out with that ninjy sword. Then he went right back out the window, so I followed along.

We walked down by the dry creek bed where lots of crooked, leafless little trees grew along the trashpiles. Dirt Pete slipped that sword out with a sssssshhink! sound like a metal snake hissing. He looked at the shiny blade for a minute, quiet as ever, and then all the sudden he was swinging the sword at a tree. Thwack! Thwack! Thwack! He sliced off branches like arms and legs, like he's some ninjy warrior. The tree was pale white inside like bone where he'd cut it. After awhile he was panting out of breath with all the little trees he'd cut up and he handed the sword to me and I took a turn. It was fun. That blade sliced clean through the trunks of the littlest trees. I pretended I was a warrior dealing out death to all my enemies. Pretty soon I was out of breath too.

We traded off back and forth. We was having a good time until we heard footsteps and there come Big Robert with Jahnalee. I guess she wasn't sore at him no more. She was walking behind him with a little smile on her freckly face. Big Robert was smiling too but not a happy smile. He asked what us d—ks was doing. I told him it was a private game. His eyes went down to the ninjy sword in Dirt Pete's hand and he said, Ain't that your brother's, I seen that before.

Then Big Robert said, Didja blow him for it?

Dirt Pete's shoulders hunched up and his eyes clinched shut and his whole face got dark red. Jahnalee giggled. Then real fast Big Robert stepped forward and shoved Dirt Pete hard down to the ground and said I'm talking to you, faggot. That made my stomach go all hot inside.

The sword laid there in the grass. Big Robert kept moving forward while Dirt Pete tried to crawl backwards. Robert kicked at him a couple and Dirt Pete tried to block it with his own feet and Robert kicked one of his shoes plum off. It rolled down into a pile of empty bottles and potato chip bags.

Then Jahnalee said Um, Robert? because I was standing right behind him with the ninjy sword in my own hands. I didn't even know I'd picked it up but there it was. The sun was shining off the blade and when Robert turned the tip of it was right up against his nose and he got real still. He told me, Devin, you better put that down now before I hurt you both. I let the blade slide down his chin until the edge of it pressed into the skin of his neck. Blood dripped into his shirt and one fat drop of it ran down the blade like a tear.

I told Big Robert I'll cut your f—king head off, even though I promised not to curse no more. Behind me I heard Jahnalee squeal and run back toward Lavender Court. Big Robert stood still as them little trees. I said So help me Jesus I will cut off your god—n stupid head and he believed I would. After a minute he took a slow step back and then one more. He must have felt that blood on his neck but he didn't look down or grab at it or nothing. Instead he ran faster than Jahnalee. Back to his trailer I guess.

When he was gone I turned back to Dirt Pete and said we sure did show him, huh? Dirt Pete was on his knees next to the trash pile trying to fish out his old shoe. He hopped on one foot while he was getting it back on. The filth around his cheeks was smeared where he'd been crying. I told him, don't you worry. It made my stomach hurt to see Dirt Pete all shook up like that. It wasn't fair. He'd stole me the math book and the crystal. He'd got blamed for the thing with the possum too even though he wasn't there. That was me. I hadn't meant no harm. The possum was already dead. I just wanted to know what it looked like on the inside, to see if all the shapes and colors inside made sense. But I'd let him take the fall for that one even though I knew it wasn't right. Sometimes I wondered if what was inside me added up to anything either.

The police come to get me that next week at school. I was in Social Studies class where Miss Powell was telling us about Antarctica, which was a whole big country made out of nothing but ice crystals, which I actually thought was pretty interesting, but then two cops in their uniform walked in and said we want to talk to Devin. All the other kids started giggling and whispering. I could hear Miss Powell trying to calm everybody down while them officers marched me right out of class out to their squad car, which didn't have door handles in the back. There was a wire cage between the front seat and the back seat like for chickens. Neither one of them said nothing except to tell me I was under arrest.

I'd never been inside the police station downtown. They walked me inside to a room that was empty except for a table and chairs and I sat there awhile. Pretty soon a cop came in to tell me Mama was on her way and I told him I knew why they wanted me but I hadn't hurt Big Robert that bad. Big Robert hurt people all the time and never got guff for it. I hadn't even really used that ninjy sword except to scare him. The cop just kept nodding. I told him about the possum thing too. I guess I was pretty scared.

Then Mama came in and she was crying and they let me talk to her for a bit. She kept saying this can't be true it can't be true and I apologized for the possum and for Big Robert but that just made her cry harder. Then some lawyer fella came in and told me to keep quiet.

It wasn't until later that day I found out Cody was dead. His own Mama had found him in his bedroom all sliced up. I guess there was blood on his windowsill and blood in the grass going back to our trailer. They found the ninjy sword in my closet with blood on it and a bag of pills from Cody's safe too. I kept asking did they find the crystal too but nobody knew what I meant.

Next day they brought me into another room with Rick of all people. He wasn't in uniform like the other cops and the guards, just his same suit he always wore when he came to see Mama. But he had a gun and a walkie-talkie thing on his belt like the other cops. Right before he came in I saw him talking to Mama through the little window in the door but I couldn't hear what they was saying. He came in with the lawyer fella and told me things would be easier on me and Mama and everybody if I just told them why I did it. He brought me a Coke, which he never did at home. I tried to tell him the blood was just Big Robert's and that I only took the ninjy sword so Dirt Pete could play with it. They said if Big Robert lost that much blood he'd be dead too like Cody. I told them I didn't take no pills, either. Rick shook his head and said so you admit you broke into his room and you admit you stole the sword and people saw you threaten this boy Robert with the sword, plus we found the pills and the blood in your room, but you didn't do it? I kept telling him I didn't know nothing about any pills, but why would Rick believe me? If I was gone he could come over and f—k Mama whenever and not have to deal with me.

I guess they brought Dirt Pete down to the police station too. But he didn't say a word, not one single thing. That's what Rick told me later. They let him loose.

I know this ain't what you want to hear. When you told me to write out what happened I figure you thought I'd see the errors of my ways and I'd say yes, yes it was me all along, I cut up Cody and stole his pills and his ninjy sword and I'm sorry about it to Jesus and everybody. But it didn't happen that way. It was Dirt Pete. But he don't say anything, so what's he gonna tell you?

I only told the judge I was guilty because the lawyer said to. He said that way they might try me as a juvenile rather than as a adult. And they did. That means when I turn eighteen I can maybe get out of here and go home. Not to Lavender Court though. Mama moved to a different place on the other side of town. She said she couldn't stand it there no more.

It's not so bad here. We don't have regular school exactly, but we take lessons during the day when we're not in our little rooms. You and the other teachers here was real interested when I talked about how numbers have shapes and colors. Not like at my old school. Here they give me all kinds of problems to work on. Some of them are pretty hard. It's fun, though, like solving a puzzle. They even started bringing in Mr. Federman from the college so we can work on the problems together. People are interested in my answers, which I guess is what Mama would call a real change of pace.

I could tell why I did everything I ever done but I don't think it would matter. I guess what I think is that you could like to study someone their whole life but you could never get the numbers to add up correct. There are things that are the same on the inside as on the outside. Those are the most perfect and beautiful things, like my crystal. But that ain't how people are. You could look and look but you'd never know.

I guess Dirt Pete was right. Sometimes there ain't nothing to say at all.

BRIDGETTE'S BABY BUMP

Leon Peter Blanda

Leon Peter Blanda is a New Orleans-born writer, standup comedian, ever-evolving human being, and proud dad. His nonfiction, essays, and reviews have appeared in *Out All Day: New Orleans*, *Raised By Whoops*, and *Story Unlikely*. His novel *High Moon*, a genre splicing debut, is available now. For more info visit LeonBlanda.com.

Edna Louise Dean, the trusted secretary for the First Assembly of God church in Pearl River, Louisiana, was cooking the Lord's books on a rainy afternoon when three loud knocks made her sit up straight in her highbacked chair and mutter a prayer of protection over herself and the building. It was a weekday, and she was alone; the sanctuary was closed to the public. At first, she thought it might have been a tree limb smacking the side of the building. Then came three more heart-stopping knocks.

Quiet as, well, a church mouse, Edna tiptoed across the ceramic tile in the foyer when an angry hammer of thunder broke open the sky. She gasped!

Summer storms in southern Louisiana grow from puppies to pit bulls in seconds. Most are more-bark-than-bite. The puffed-up thunderstorms move quickly, giving credence to the adage, "If you don't like the weather in Louisiana, wait five minutes." Though, they can just as easily stick around all afternoon, causing flash flooding and mass destruction. When the sudden storms eventually move along or dissipate, what's left behind is an oppressive humidity that has more in common with a simmering pot of gumbo than breathable oxygen.

The storm in our story has only just arrived.

Two solid oak doors stood between Edna and God's wrath outside. She quietly checked to ensure the lock was bolted, then spoke in her singsong, country drawl, "Who is it?"

"Hello?" A tiny, quivering voice on the other side was all but drowned out by the storm. "Is someone there? Can you hear me? Help me, please."

That's all you have to say to most God-fearing, southern women: help me. Edna Louise Dean did what she believed the traveling Samaritan from the gospel would've done in the same predicament; she opened the door.

Black mascara tears streaked the hollow cheeks of a soaking wet, pregnant woman. Abandoned on the side of the road in upside-down rain by her son-of-a-bitch husband, Bridgette, as she'd introduce herself, hiked over a mile down the busy highway, and not a soul stopped to help. Addict thin, other than a pumpkin-sized belly, without money or a phone (this was the early nineties, only Dick Tracy had a watch-phone)—Bridgette sought shelter and found it at the First Assembly of God in Pearl River, Louisiana. Edna looked at the wretched, shivering thing and thought of the blessed mother, Mary, seeking a room at the Inn and being turned away.

"Oh dear," Edna studied the rain-soaked creature. "Come in, come in. Please. You must be freezin' solid, sweet'art."

Ominous torrents of rain and screaming wind followed the sobbing woman into the house of the Lord.

"I won't stay long," Bridgette said. "May I use your telephone?"

"Of course." Edna handed Bridgette a box of tissues and led the shivering woman upstairs to Edna's office.

Edna invited Bridgette to cross the threshold. To step on holy ground. Knowing what I now know—and what you will soon learn if you continue reading—I often wonder if, like Dracula, Bridgette would not have been able to enter the sacred sanctum of God's house had she not been invited. Similar to the swarthy Count, Bridgette did not outwardly appear to be a monster, but as wiser scribes have written far more eloquently: looks is deceivin', y'all.

Bridgette quickly entangled herself in the church like a briar patch. She became a fixture, doted on by the kindly, southern ladies, politely ignored by the men: classic, southern gospel manners. Not only did she attend every service, of which there were three per week—Sunday a.m., Sunday p.m., and Wednesday p.m.—Bridgette also popped up at Bible studies, ladies' luncheons, youth group lock-ins, Royal Ranger powwows (the Royal Rangers are the Assemblies of God's answer to Satan's Boy Scouts of America). I know this because my family followed the same schedule. When we weren't at church, we were at some church-related function.

Most found Bridgette's newfound faith inspiring, but some thought she just didn't want to go home to her terrible husband. Why she stayed with him is the same reason any woman stays with an awful, no good, rotten man: lack of escape options. It was assumed the church had become Bridgette's sanctuary.

When the church's nursery needed a new attendant, Bridgette threw her name in the hat for the open shifts and got the unpaid job. During church service, the very young children—those whose cries of boredom would disrupt the preacher's sermon—were kept in a nursery/playroom upstairs so the Holy Spirit could move freely and without interruption.

Holy Communion was offered at every service: a plastic shot glass of grape juice and a round wafer that looked and tasted to be made from the same Styrofoam as packing peanuts. Unlike Catholics, who must complete Communion classes to partake of Christ's flesh and blood, Protestants don't check IDs. Pentecostals don't care who gets in line for sacred hors d'oeuvres. (Do you accept Jesus Christ as your personal Lord and Savior? You do? You don't? You should. Have a stale cracker and a splash of cheap grape juice.) Everyone is offered Communion; even people not in the room, like the nursery attendant, were sent a holy snackrifice.

The delivery job would sometimes fall to me, just a boy, and no hero in this story.

Bridgette never accepted Holy Communion, and I chalked it up to her having her hands full with the crying infants and screaming toddlers. No big deal: Sunday morning service usually ran long and cut a little too close to lunchtime. I was always starving before the sermon started, famished by Communion, and would gladly scarf the extra sacramental Styrofoam and drain the thimbleful of sugary Lord's blood as lustily insatiable as the vampire Lestat.

So, I didn't really care that she never took Communion. That wasn't what was weird about her to me.

What I found most peculiar about Bridgette was her smelly car. Kids don't lie, and this air-conditioner-less rust bucket reeked. It reminded me of sour gym socks and molded tighty-whiteys. My frame of reference came from earlier in the school year during Physical Education class; a disgusting pair of once-white Fruit of the Looms was purposely jammed into a urinal in the boys' locker room, where it stayed for a month. Every day, all the boys would pee on the trapped Underoos, which would dry over the weekend and be remoistened at first period on Monday. Unlike the sweet smells that wafted from the hallway to the girls' locker room, the boys' locker room was a petri dish of filth and foul stench. Young boys are the most despicable creatures God has ever chosen not to smite. That is what Ms. Bridgette's car smelled like, the rancid piss of sweaty little assholes, curdling in the Louisiana summer sun.

I was nine or ten at the time, and we were a one-car family. If my dad wasn't using it to commute to work, he was making repairs, as our vehicles were always old, used, and forever breaking down. Unluckily, Bridgette was always willing to offer up her Nissan Jockstrap if we needed a ride to church, or even to school on several occasions. On those days, I worried that I smelled like her car while in class, as the odor seemed to linger in my nostrils all day. Maybe I did, and nobody said anything. Though I doubt that's true, because if I was the smelly kid, someone would've spoken up, said something, made fun of me. Kids are, as stated above, little assholes.

Bridgette became a fixture in our home, one my dad wished would go away. Not that he didn't like her; he just didn't like company. His brother, my Uncle Mike (God rest his soul), did give an ominous warning to my mother, I only recently remembered.

After spending an afternoon at our house, hanging out with his best bud (my dad) his favorite nephews (my brother and me), and my mom's new friend Ms.

Bridgette, my Uncle Mike pulled my mom aside before he left for the day, and said, "Watch out for her. There's something… not right about her."

My mom laughed it off, as my Uncle Mike was a funny, creative guy who loved to joke around. Little did we know, our sweet, perceptive, sensitive artist Uncle was right.

Bridgette made herself comfortable at our home, and her other new home, the church. The kindly, simple folks who comprised the Holy Ghosting, speaking-in-tongues, slain-in-the-spirit, non-denominational—but mostly Pentecostal—congregation took her in and showered her with baby gifts. Every lady at our church could have been a cast member in a stage production of Steel Magnolias, and they threw together a beautiful baby shower on the fly that'd make your average church potluck look like a porta-potty at a Pantera concert.

Maybe it was because Bridgette's story was so dreadfully sad—an abusive husband who abandoned her on the side of the road at eight months pregnant, but she can't find the strength to leave, even with all this new support—or maybe it was because the church folks really believed in being in the service of others, but nobody ever questioned why Bridgette looked more like a middle-aged glue-sniffer than the twenty-something expectant mother she claimed to be.

To a child, all adults seem ancient. But even at nine years old, I could tell this woman was not in her late twenties, the same age as my young mother. Bridgette's skin reminded me of my mom's mother, a chain-smoking sunbather whose skin became as brown and wrinkled as a weather-beaten saddlebag. Although Bridgette's pallid complexion looked as though it had never seen a sunny day and couldn't absorb Vitamin D if it tried, it was creased with deep lines like my Marlboro-loving Maw-maw.

Most days, Bridgette's pregnant belly looked like it was about to pop. Other days, it appeared half-deflated, like a tire with low air pressure. Seeing her every Sunday morning, Sunday evening, and Wednesday night, on top of her being at our house all the time—and me being a hyper-aware, overly observant nine-year-old—I noticed the inconsistency, but it didn't register as odd. Bridgette was already weird; why wouldn't her pregnancy be odd as well?

One afternoon, my mother picked me and my brother up from school in the family car, my father having fixed whatever major issue last befell the humble family sedan. As soon as we climbed into the back seat, my mom whipped her attention to us with an urgency that only meant trouble.

My brother and I froze mid-buckle, the chrome of our safety belts hot as crucibles pressed against our tender flesh.

A grave expression clung to my mother's face. It was the same look she gave me and my brother when she found a hole in the sheetrock covered by a Spider-man poster. It was her "fuck around and find out" face, but my mom didn't swear. It was the same face she gave me years later when she found a pack of Marlboro Lights in my underwear drawer.

"Boys!" she shouted after a long silence startling us.

My brother and I exchanged looks of perplexed innocence, both silently imploring the other to confess to whatever crime committed before the hammer falls and we're both crushed.

"Boys," she repeated, softer this time but remaining as serious as a traffic cop at a search and seizure. "Listen to me. Look me in the eyes. If Miss Bridgette ever tries to pick you up from school, or from the house when I'm not home, or you see her near the church, DO NOT go with her. DO NOT get into her car. Even if she tells you I sent her to get you. DON'T go with her. Do you understand me?"

My brother and I exchanged side-eyes. While my mother could be dramatic and overprotective, something about how she stopped carline traffic to give us this intense warning made it feel like there was a real threat to our lives.

"Do. You. Understand?" my mother repeated, annunciating each syllable.

What I wanted to say was, "So, you're saying DON'T get into the weird lady's smelly car? No problem."

What I did say was, "Yes, ma'am," in unison with my brother, who was equally perplexed by my mother's Oscar-caliber line delivery.

After a long silence, as curiosity boiled my brain to mush, I asked, "Why, Mom?"

My mother looked up prayerfully, staring past the sagging ceiling upholstery in our little, beat-up car, as if prodding God for an answer to my curiosity, and after a bated breath, she calmly said, "She's just… not a good person."

My mind raced. Does Ms. Bridgette want to kidnap us? Is she a child molester?? Did she kill somebody??? Was it her asshole husband???? I bet that's it. She killed her husband. Now she's on the run and she's got to tie up loose ends—like my family. Well, that ain't happening on my watch, Sister Creepy.

"Just… don't go near her if you see her. Okay, boys?" my mom said solemnly, snapping me out of my revenge fantasy.

"Yes, ma'am," my brother and I again answered in unison, but exchanged silent glances full of unasked questions.

My mother returned her attention to the windshield after the car behind us in the carline honked their horn. "I'm goin'. I'm goin'," she said, and that was it. My mother never spoke about Bridgette again.

Obviously, that was not the answer I was looking for: "She's not a good person." The ambiguity of it almost made me insane. I mean, what kind of weirdo was this lady? She never touched me or my brother, and we were cute kids. So, maybe she was just waiting for the right time to make her move. But she had had opportunities. Not long stretches of time, but I was definitely left alone with her in our living room once or twice.

Did she rob a bank? No, she was much too frail and strange to plan a successful heist.

Maybe she did kill her abusive husband.

Whatever happened, Bridgette stopped attending church, and she never came to our house again. She disappeared from our small town altogether, and I forgot about her for many years. All told, she was only in our lives for about three months, and that was over thirty years ago.

I stopped going to church when I was eighteen. Trust me, I've been to enough church services to praise ten Jesuses. Every Sunday morning, Sunday night, and Wednesday night sermon, plus Royal Rangers on Tuesdays, youth group meetings on Saturdays, Bible studies sprinkled throughout the week, and every other extracurricular activity offered by the church—I was there, whether I wanted to be or not.

One day, many years after I'd turned from God's path, I remembered that odd, gangly, pregnant lady who had frightened my mother so much and decided to find out the truth. You know how, when you're a kid, your parents will say things like, "I'll tell you when you're older." Well, I was older, and I wanted to know what happened to Bridgette. Only I couldn't remember her name.

"Hey, Ma," I inquired in my nonchalant, New Orleans-Italian broken English. "D'you 'member that pregnant lady from church back in the day?"

"You're going to have to be more specific than that, Leon," she said, removing a pan of something delicious smelling from the oven.

"I can't remember her name... Maybe Cathy, or Bonnie?"

"I don't know who you're talking about," she said.

"You remember," I implored. "The weird, pregnant lady, with the crazy hair, and the stinky car. You warned me and Dominick not to go with her if she—"

"Bridgette." My mother whispered, a breathless gasp, and her body froze, face drained of all joy. I thought she might drop the pan, but she got it to the countertop before stating bluntly, "Bridgette. Her name was Bridgette. Or, at least, that's what she said her name was."

My mother unfroze, and she pretended to be as cheerful as she was the moment prior to me bringing up the subject. But something had changed in the room. A shift had occurred. Her mind was not with me, or with the pan of food she'd just removed from the oven, but swimming in some forgotten memory.

"Why are you asking about her?" she asked, trying to sound normal and not doing a very good job.

I attempted to retain an air of casual disinterest. "Oh, I don't know. I never hear you talk about her. Weren't you friends? I remember her being around the house all the time. Then one day, she was just gone. Did she have the baby? Was it a boy or a girl? Why'd you two stop hanging out?"

An uncomfortable amount of silence passed before my mom said, "She just... She was not a good person."

Dammit. It was the same deadpan warning she'd given me as a child all those decades earlier. I should've eased into the questions.

"Yeah, you said that back then. What did she do?" I persisted anyway.

A heaviness fell onto my mother's shoulders, the weight of old memories; it's the same way she looked when we got the phone call that my Uncle Mike had a heart attack roughly a year after his warning about Bridgette.

Bridgette was not who she claimed to be, my mother explained in so many words. She wasn't a Christian by any stretch of the imagination, and she wasn't pregnant! She faked it. To fool everyone, she sometimes carried a balloon, various melons, or a basketball (I knew it!) interchangeably beneath her maternity clothing.

Not only was Bridgette not pregnant, and not a Christian, she was, in fact— Are you ready for this?—a card-carrying member of the Church of Satan! (Cue the dramatic opening orchestra strikes from Beethoven's Fifth Symphony. That's the scary one, with the big intro.)

Through a trustworthy network of gossipy church ladies, my mother discovered Bridgette was part of an elite crew of Satanists, given a special task by their leader, who I suppose was ordained by the Devil himself.

Bridgette's mission was a "neighborhood outreach" of sorts, but, you know, evil. It wasn't a "get to know your local Satanists" outreach. It was clandestine. Secretive. Bad guy stuff. She and several of her "sisters in Satan" were ordered to infiltrate local Christian churches, Bible study groups, and religious organizations within the drivable distance from their own dark church (of Satan). Wolves in sheep's clothing.

Once a "wolf" was accepted amongst the sheep, the next move was to cause chaos, breed strife, make mischief, sow distrust, and plant seeds of contempt throughout the flock. You know, devilry.

The diabolical plan worked like a bad luck charm at the First Assembly of God, Pearl River chapter. Her dastardly plan all but destroyed our little church. After Bridgette's arrival, rumors began circling about infidelities and other sordid untruths and half-truths.

Shortly after Bridgette's abrupt disappearance from the church, and perhaps due to completely unrelated circumstances, the pastor left his wife and children and filed for divorce.

I was too young to connect all the dots, but I remember Bridgette always gossiping about the other ladies when she was over at our house. My mom kind of shrugged it off, but Bridgette was relentless, telling my mom things like, the other ladies at church hated my mother because she was so young. (My mom was nineteen when she had me, but that's a whole different can of pinto beans to open for another time.)

Bridgette always had an unkind word to pass along. Often it was a juicy bit of gossip dripping with poison.

What tipped everyone off about Bridgette's nefarious plans came during an after-church picnic. Sometimes, after church in small towns, there is a potluck for no reason whatsoever. There are games for the kids, and fellowship for the adults. A box of Popeye's chicken goes fast, but there's three folding tables of food, with no space between all the crockpots, chafing dishes, and Tupperware containers full of every family's easiest to prepare bulk dish.

It was during one of these innocuous potluck picnics that a kindly old lady, the mother of one of my mom's friends, outed the wolf.

My mother's friend's mother—I'll call her Ula since describing her takes too long—was not a member of our church. Ula was a member of the nearby Baptist establishment and was attending our church's service with her daughter on this fateful Sunday, probably for the free post-service Popeye's. Before the picnic, in the middle of service, when it came time to "give peace" (shake hands with/hug other churchgoers), Ula saw Bridgette and gasped. Horror stole the Lord's joy from Ula's wrinkled smile. Icicles filled her veins, and she shivered. Ula's daughter apologized to Bridgette for her mother's reaction. And Ula could not place from where she recognized Bridgette.

Then it struck her just as David's stone struck Goliath.

According to Ula, Bridgette (who went by Margarette back then) had tried a similar con with the Baptists; though she wasn't pregnant, she claimed to have an abusive boyfriend (which may have been true) and was taken in by the Baptists.

Well, I don't need to tell you the rest; she tried the same strategy and got found out.

A plan was hatched by the Baptists. Bridgette was invited to a Bible study, a ruse for what was to be a spiritual intervention. Ula was there, as well as the pastor, the deacons, and several board members of the Baptist church.

When Bridgette arrived, she quickly realized it was not a Bible study, became agitated, and tried to leave. When a deacon blocked her exit, she Hulked out, exhibiting otherworldly strength far beyond that of her frail frame.

Bridgette lashed out with clawed fingers and tore at the deacon's face. The deacon was a hefty man, and Bridgette barely broke a hundred soaking wet and fake pregnant, but she managed to overpower the sturdy man. That's when the other men in the group rushed forward.

Screaming and biting at those closest to her, Bridgette fought like a Spartan, keeping them at bay, snarling and growling like an animal.

I was told, it took seven God-fearing men to seize her, and she still broke free, kicking and clawing at anyone unlucky enough to get within reach.

My imagination took over as I heard the story, and I pictured Bridgette crying out with several voices—her own and two or three others of lower octaves, like a movie possession. Cursing all things Judeo-Christian, she dashed out the sanctuary of the Baptist church, ran through the foyer, and crashed out the front door, knocking it off its hinges, disappearing in the lush woods behind the Baptist church, never to be seen again. That is, until Ula spotted her at our church, eating potato salad and rubbing her regulation-sized basket-belly.

When my mother finished her story, I was silent for a moment.

"What happened then?" I asked, eager to hear a first-hand account of a real demon possession. "After Ula spotted her."

"I guess someone talked to her, and she left," my mother said. The least dramatic ending I could have hoped for.

"That's it?" I asked, confounded.

"That's it," she said, and went back to the stove to turn off the heat.

"You sure?" I nudged a little harder. "Nothing else happened? No spinning head? No pea soup projectile vomit?"

"Nope. Not to my knowledge," she smiled, lying. My mother never lied, but I didn't believe her.

If I was in Bridgette's maternity shoes, possessed by a demon, and confronted about it, backed into a corner like a wild beast—I would surely use those dark powers to silence my accusers. There would be blood running through my fingers and teeth.

After my mother finished telling me the elaborate story with the anticlimactic ending, I felt a little empty inside. Growing up in a semi-Pentecostal church will do that to any normal person.

From the time before I was making solid memories, I listened to crazy testimonials from seemingly well-rounded adults about angel sightings and hearing the Lord's voice audibly. One man at our church claimed his legs were different lengths from birth, right up until the Lord healed him, and one grew to match the other after a revivalist minister "laid hands" on him. Since I was five years old, I've witnessed—with a skepticism that would rival Doubting Thomas—as grownups spoke in tongues and convulsed in the aisles, stricken with the "Holy Spirit."

But I never saw anything supernatural. I never saw anything crazier than regular, 9-to-five-job-having adults mumbling gibberish (they claimed to be "the language of the angels") and faking seizures. I never believed they were possessed by the Holy Ghost. I assumed they were just showing off for one another.

Shortly after Bridgette disappeared, I discovered masturbation and forgot all about the weird, creepy lady with the smelly car, who may or may not have been a card-carrying member of the Church of Satan. My greatest fear evolved from that of eternal damnation into something far more corporeal; I was scared my parents would figure out my new hobby.

I became deathly afraid of going to the doctor, fearing my pediatrician might notice a change down there. The reason I believed this fallacy: I'd once seen a TV show where a doctor could tell a young lady had lost her virginity after looking between her legs. This was a scene in a gynecologist's office, obvious to me now, but back then, I didn't know that and assumed if my pediatrician got a peek at my "bathing suit area," they'd know something funny was going on during those long showers I'd been taking recently.

That's why sex education is so important, and it isn't taught at Sunday school or during Mass. So, if you can't explain it to your kids or are unwilling to, have a teacher or educator talk to your child about sex. It's weird, and they have questions.

I wonder what Bridgette's gynecologist saw during her prenatal visits, then remember: Bridgette was never pregnant.

THE SOMEWHERE MAN

Sarah Liddle

She thought she was dreaming, but that silhouette at the end of the bed could only have been her husband's. Mike stood, facing her, with his arms at his side and his features hidden by shadows. She stared for some time, maybe longer than she knew. At one point, he leaned forward and turned his gaze to the ground.

Only then did Carmen realize she was awake; she had been for some time. Maybe he had woken her without her fully realizing it. Left her to slowly inch herself out of the dreamlike state. But back into the dream.

Her eyes grew more adjusted to the dark. The moonlight was bright through her window, and she could see his hair—the way it stuck up on his head—and the spaces between the strands. His head shifted up again to look at her, and he shook his head. The motion was slow, and at first, she thought he might be telling her no. No, Carmen, don't.

But it wasn't that. Not quite.

It was more that he was telling her another kind of no. A don't-make-me-do-this kind of no.

"Mike?" It was supposed to be a whisper, but her voice cracked to life. He stood up straight again, back as he was when she first awoke, but he didn't say anything.

She was so aware of her breaths and the pauses between.

Who was this man really? For twenty years, she'd felt so certain. Sure, their marriage wasn't perfect—Whose is?—but he had her, and she had him, and wasn't that supposed to be what it was all about?

But at that moment, with his looming silhouette at the foot of her bed, she felt the strangest sensation, like it could have been anyone standing there, that the man before her had no specific shape or form. That, maybe, she had no idea who Mike really was.

It occurred to her then that perhaps having and knowing weren't the same thing, and maybe that was something obvious, something she always should have understood. And Carmen supposed she had, only she hadn't realized it yet—and not in the same way she would soon.

A hollow and damp boom pulsed through the air. Carmen jolted back, her hands slamming into the mattress. It was a gunshot maybe. No. It *was* a gunshot.

Far away though. Not in the house at least.

She stood up, ready to race to the kids' rooms anyway, not because she thought they were hurt, but because she needed to see them not hurt, not scared.

Mike's eyes were wide, watching the window—the direction where the sound seemed to come from.

"Should we call the police?" Carmen said.

Mike nodded, then turned, walking to the dresser and reaching for his phone. She opened her bedroom door and entered the hallway, examining the other bedroom doors. Luca's was already open. She could hear him snoring, undisturbed.

Jamie came out of her room then, eyes squinting in the light. She was the oldest—a senior in high school, ready to get out.

"What was that?" she asked.

"I don't know, Sweetie." It wasn't a lie because she didn't know it was a gunshot. Not really. After all, what would a gunshot be doing in this neighborhood? "Dad's calling the police," she said anyway, knowing that her feigned ignorance hadn't done enough to stifle Jamie's concerns.

Jamie's face curled. Twisted.

"It's probably nothing," Carmen added.

"Should I get Luca?"

Carmen hesitated. She feared waking him would only create more chaos, something she didn't need right then.

In hindsight, she was so glad she hadn't woken him, so glad he remained unconscious during the events that would transpire. That already had.

That couldn't be changed.

Carmen told Jamie to go back to bed; she pretended to believe that Jamie would do as she was told instead of lying awake in her room and staring out the window or listening for anything unusual. Something to indicate that everything wasn't okay.

Something besides the gunshot, anyway.

Carmen returned to her room to talk to Mike, but when she entered, he wasn't there. The room was dim, the only light from the grey sky outside indicating the sunrise yet to come. His phone was on the nightstand.

She grabbed for it and tried to unlock it without really being able to explain to herself why. To see if Mike had called the police?

But why wouldn't he?

But even then, she knew that wasn't true, that there was some other reason she was so desperately trying to get into his phone. She didn't know what it was, but she could feel the way the need pressed against her skull as her fingers tapped away at the screen, unrelenting in its insistence on keeping her on the outside.

She slammed the phone down on the nightstand and turned to face the empty room.

"Mike?" she said but kept her voice quiet so Jamie wouldn't hear. There was no answer, and she peered out the window, knowing that he wouldn't have been able to get outside without her seeing but checking anyway.

The house across the street had lights on in all the upstairs bedrooms, and in the house next to that one, her neighbor was standing on his driveway in a bathrobe, looking back and forth to each end of the street. He was probably wondering what it was he had heard exactly.

Weren't they all?

Carmen tiptoed downstairs, walking slowly so Jamie would have no cause for alarm.

"Mike?" she called again. She heard the words drift through the empty house, the dark walls. She became so aware of how still the house was.

How still.

She shook her head, not letting it last more than the second it took from her, and marched across the first floor, looking adamantly for a husband who was not there. She made her way to his study because *maybe he's working, got up early to do some work, and now he's just going to be sitting there; he's working*, but she swung the door open to another empty room.

"Where the hell are you?" She jumped at the sound of her own voice; she hadn't intended to say it out loud. It was then she processed the state of his study—papers strewn about the floor, the desk chair on its side, a dent in the wall with his pencil mug on the floor beneath.

She stepped inside, turning around and around, and she felt like she might never stop. There were too many details to absorb. The trash can upended, the pens scattered on the carpet just a few inches from the mug. The blinds were closed; the keyboard askew. The glass desktop was smudged with handprints. And there was a sticky note on the computer monitor.

She walked to it in slow motion, feeling it resist as she peeled it from the screen.

I love you all.

His handwriting. She heard his voice in her head, repeating it. *I love you all I love you all I love—*

She accidentally rammed into the desk, and the screen blinked awake. The computer didn't ask for a password, as it usually did, but instead led her straight to the desktop image: a picture of the family from their last camping trip. Mike was in a camping chair, a fishing pole hanging over the lake. Jamie was helping Luca make some sort of village out of the sticks and rocks by the water. Carmen's face was at the front of the image, her arm at the side as she held it up to take the picture. All had looked up from their activities and gave their glowing smiles. She remembered that day—how quiet everything was, how warm the sunlight felt on their cheeks.

At the bottom of the screen on the taskbar, there was nothing open but a single document, untitled.

She glanced at the sticky note and placed it on the desk, then turned again to the computer and opened the document. She scrolled through pages of lists, all containing websites, usernames, and passwords. Many were insignificant, but some Carmen had never even known existed, including various bank and email accounts.

And at the end of the list, it said it again.

I love you all.

She stepped back from the computer and backed away until she was out of the room, backed away until she was in the living room. Until the back of her ankles hit the stairs. Jamie was standing at the top—Carmen hadn't turned around to see this, but she heard her breathing, the restrained panic.

"Mike?" she shouted it. She heard it everywhere. She heard it inside her body. Between the air. Across the earth. "Mike!"

"What's wrong?" Jamie asked. Carmen shook her head. Luca's door opened. She could hear him sobbing and the shuffling steps of Jamie reaching over to rub his head.

But Carmen couldn't speak. There—her children, behind her, their voices scared and lonely, and she couldn't say anything to them. She fell to the ground and closed her eyes, hoping that this was nothing, that this would all make sense. Maybe she just couldn't see it yet. She just couldn't see it.

"Mike!"

She wasn't quite sure what happened in the thirty minutes that followed. She felt the hands of her children on her skin. Luca was wailing. Carmen could only point Jamie to the study and tell her that something was wrong, but she didn't know what. Jamie tried to call Mike, but no, Carmen remembered the image of his phone on the top of the dresser, and Mike nowhere to be found. His car was still in the garage. His wallet was in the kitchen. Jamie found them both. It was as if everything was fine, and Mike was here, but he wasn't was the only thing.

He wasn't.

The police sirens were so much louder up close, but they never made it to Carmen's house even though Jamie had finally made the 911 call that Mike never did. Carmen found out later, weird as it was, that when Jamie had called to report the noise and that her dad was missing, at the exact same time someone else— some motivated person on a hike at five-something in the morning—had made a 911 call to report a body on some of the boulders beside the trail. The trailhead was near the end of Carmen's street, and the body had a bullet in its head.

It wasn't Mike.

That's what Carmen told herself.

But it was. It was. The gun was still in his hand; his legs dangled from the boulder, body pointed towards the view of the valley where they lived, but now slumped over on its side, blood spreading across the rock like melting snow.

They already had the crime scene tape out. Investigators snapping pictures. Officers surrounding the area when Carmen got there. They'd closed the trailhead, but after Jamie called to report her father missing, a few minutes later they got a callback saying they needed Carmen to identify the body as Mike or not Mike. And it wasn't.

But it was.

And it always was.

There wasn't a lot to say about the days that followed. They didn't quite exist. People came and went, giving Carmen various gifts and premade dinners so she wouldn't have to cook. Her parents and sister flew in from Pennsylvania. Jamie and Luca weren't in school. No one was sure if Luca knew what had happened or not, but no one had bothered to tell him. No one had wanted to tell him. How could they?

But Carmen didn't really put these details together at the time. Or didn't care to. These were pieces that filled in after the fact, while the present stayed walled off from despair by disbelief, all of that magnified by the funeral, a week later.

They were in a dark auditorium at one of the local churches. A portrait of Mike and a bouquet of flowers were in front of the stage, and in the background, there was an enlarged slideshow of pictures of him and the family. Each picture was a happy memory because these things were supposed to be a "celebration of life." Or at least that's what people try to make you believe about funerals.

"Mike was always the happiest little kid." His older sister, Tess, gave the first eulogy. She was in tears by the second word but pushed her way through to the end. "He always wanted people to smile. We would put on plays for people. I was always trying to create serious screenplays and every time, he would 'ruin' them with his antics..." She went on about their childhood, and Carmen held herself together. She hadn't known Mike as a child; this could have been anyone that Tess was describing, not necessarily him.

But then Tess talked about his later years, in adulthood, when they lived far away but stayed in touch by phone. "He was scared, at first, about Luca. He told me, 'I don't know how I'm going to raise a kid with special needs. I don't think I'm good enough.' But I'll never forget, two months later he called me again. It was late at night and he was in tears. He was sobbing actually, through the phone. And he—" She choked on a sob herself, then wiped her nose. "—he said, 'I'm so happy. I'm so happy.' He just kept repeating it, over and over like that. He couldn't comprehend it. Just sat there, dumbstruck with Luca and how..." She surveyed the room. "...happy he was."

Jamie spoke after Tess. Her long blonde hair shielded most of her face, and she kept her eyes lowered to the paper trembling in her hands.

Mike made everyone feel worthy. That's what she said. He talked to you, and it was like you were a person again, not just a face in the crowd. He made you feel like you meant something. Carmen nodded along, keeping her face still. She didn't let the words sink in too much, but that was easy nowadays. Her breathing was focused, and the tears of everyone in the room around her did not phase her.

Jamie continued to talk about his death. "It's clear that my dad was not himself on the day he died. The man who killed my father did not know how much he was loved. The man who killed my father did not know how much we needed him. The man who killed my father..."

And the crowd nodded along encouragingly as if it was all true. As if Mike's death could be attributed to some faceless killer that roamed the streets. But it was him all along, didn't they see? It was Mike who killed himself. Not in his right mind maybe, but in some part of his mind that existed then and existed long before that night.

The eulogies continued. Carmen wrapped her arm around Jamie as she sat back down. They sang Amazing Grace and parroted a few Bible verses. All those clichés. Then the crowd broke free; snacks and beverages were served while Carmen entertained a long line of people, one by one, who wanted to tell her how sorry they were. She felt like she'd been treading water all day, but now, she just wanted to let herself drown. Only dozens of people wouldn't let her.

Those fuckers.

At the end of the day, Tess came over to Carmen's house. They shared a glass of wine and sat in front of the fireplace while the kids "slept" or whatever they did after the doors closed. They'd adopted a system of believing each other's lies.

"Wanna know something?" Tess murmured, holding her glass in the air. The fire crackled, and the wind outside squealed against the walls.

"Sure," Carmen said, not looking away from the embers.

"It's kind of weird," Tess said. She wasn't looking at Carmen either. She took another swig of wine and continued. "This silent Mike comes into my room at night. Not as he was, but as a kid, you know?" She laughed a little. Looked down. "Dressed all up in mismatched costume pieces like when we were young. And I try to tell him I'm sorry, see? I'm sorry. That maybe something went wrong we could have fixed, that maybe there was a way to save this little boy. But he doesn't say anything. Just puts his finger to my mouth, like be quiet, Tessy, be quiet. And he doesn't say a word, not a word, but I can tell what he's thinking then. It's that what is there to say? And what is there really?"

"Silent Mike?" Carmen knew that wasn't the point of the story, not what Tess wanted her to hear or what needed to be heard. But it was all Carmen could say at this point, the only part she could respond to.

Tess shrugged. "I see him sometimes. At night usually. He never talks. And it's not the real him anyway, just some puppet."

Then who's the hand?

I see him too.

Neither thought quite made it to the surface. But Carmen didn't think either was important enough anyway—not in a way that could change anything.

His touch rustled her awake. But when she did, he wasn't moving. He lay on his back with his eyes on the ceiling. Carmen couldn't tell if they were open or closed. She supposed it didn't matter.

She curled over to him, moving his arm away from his side so that she could lay beside him and pull it around her body. She leaned into him and burrowed her head into the side of his chest. He wasn't breathing as far as she could tell, and she supposed that didn't surprise her.

He brushed her hair with his fingers. Began rubbing her scalp. She pulled her head up to his and kissed his cheek. It was lukewarm, like bathwater that had been sitting out for some time now. She left her forehead on his cheek and felt tears forming in her eyes. They spilled onto him, and she brushed them off his skin.

Do you want me to go?

She heard the words in her head. His mouth didn't move, but it was his voice nonetheless. She would have known it anywhere.

"No," she whispered and shook her head. "No."

She sat up suddenly and stared straight ahead. She felt Mike's hand slip off of her, thud against the mattress.

"I want you to stay."

Wasn't it obvious? She wanted to scream at him, shake him. *I wanted you to stay.*

He laughed at that. Not in Carmen's head, this time, but out loud. She jumped at the sudden movement in his body, at how harshly the sound hit the air. He didn't stop but kept laughing and laughing until she crawled away from him and lay back down on the bed. She fell asleep sometime, but not before he stopped.

This poor old woman, a neighbor of Carmen's, came to their front door a few days after the funeral, crying madly. Carmen didn't want to answer the doorbell; she didn't know who it would be, but it didn't matter. Another person she'd have to thank for being there to support her. Thank you for your condolences. Thank you.

It all felt so stupid.

But she kept hitting the doorbell, knowing that Carmen was always home nowadays. So regretfully, she emerged from her bed and dragged herself to the door.

When she opened it, the lady, whose name was Marge, put her hand over her mouth. She was already crying, Carmen could tell, but somehow managed to burst even further into tears.

"Oh!" She fell into Carmen, hugging her, and kept repeating that nonsensical word without following it with anything. "Oh." A desperate cry to someone who certainly couldn't help her.

Carmen invited her inside, and they sat down in the living room. Marge put her hand on Carmen's leg and stifled her sobs enough to be able to speak.

"I'm so sorry."

It's what they all say. Carmen had perfected the solemn nod. The appreciative nod. "Thank you."

"He was a wonderful man," she said. Carmen could feel her cheeks heating. She kept nodding, afraid that, if she stopped, she'd be sent into mirroring the woman's sobs. And once it started, it would continue. On and on.

"I know it must be so hard for you," she continued. Carmen couldn't see anything but the woman's pursed and wrinkled lips. "I never would have imagined he would do something like this. He always seemed so happy. You always seemed so happy. You have such a beautiful family, such a wonderful… You always seemed so happy."

Carmen could feel her stare softening, the edges around Marge's lips growing fuzzy, and the blurred background starting to swirl inside of itself. She blinked, nodded more, to keep everything from slipping away entirely.

And all she could think was: *Yes, yes lady. Tell me more about how happy I must have been.*

The stupid, horrible, obvious thing that Carmen learned weeks later? Life carried on, and the world grew indifferent. Soon, people every now and then would ask her when she was going back to work, in an off-hand sort of way. But Mike still came in the night, even long after the pitying visitors thinned.

This needed to stop.

She had a plan—one that might finally make him leave.

He came in the night, same as always. This time, she could see the outlines of his face from the streetlights pouring through the window from far away. He stood at the foot of the bed, and there was that way his face was always pointed downward so that when he was looking at you, he was looking upwards with the flesh on his face drooping towards the ground. His lips were constantly pursed, always looking like he was about to tell you something terrible but never quite made it.

He put both hands on the wooden railing lining the edge of the bed. When he stared, Carmen stared back, unflinching.

She could picture it in her mind—her hands around his cold neck, squeezing tight to stop already stationary blood from pumping. How she would feel the skin on his face inches from hers—the cool and silky texture seeping through the air into her flesh. How remarkably dead he was. And she would kill him again. Again.

Because how could he come back after all of this? How dare he slip into her bed. Shake her from what little sleep she could sink in, feel her skin, and pretend it was all the same. She was the one with a dead husband, with a husband who hated it here so much he'd rather be nowhere. So many implications, so many ways in which going on felt like a thousand things tugging at her skin from different directions.

But him? He was just dead. And nothing went with that. No implications, no grief.

An idea struck her. An obvious one.

There was a knife on her bedside table, one she'd been saving for him. She wanted to know how it would feel to press it through the heavy and yielding flesh of a corpse—or of a ghost, she wasn't sure. But maybe she wanted to know how it felt to press it through a living one too. Of either.

She grabbed the knife and held it up to her throat, parallel to the bed. Mike didn't shift from his position. Just kept leaning over the bedframe. In the dim lighting, Carmen could swear she saw him raise an eyebrow. A challenge maybe.

He climbed over the wooden railing and crawled to his space beside her. He turned so that his chest was to the ceiling, eyes to the faraway wall. He folded his hands together, intertwining his fingers over his waist, and didn't turn to look at her.

Minutes passed. Carmen was briefly conscious of a car slowly rolling down the road, a garage door opening and closing a few houses down. A dog barking.

She looked over again, saw he hadn't moved his gaze from the wall, and suddenly became so aware of the knife in her hand, the weight of it in her fist. She tossed it to the ground. It hit the carpet with an unremarkable thud.

Carmen reached over to him, pressing her hand against his chest. The stillness of it was unrelenting. She never thought that she would even notice a heartbeat within a body as she touched it, but in its absence, the difference was tangible. It hit her in her chest, beneath the ribs, how empty this thing was beside her.

She could feel tears slipping down her face, and she pulled his far hand over his body and hers so that it wrapped them together. Perhaps like some sort of fucked up present wrapped in dead skin. His arm fell limp, and his hand draped over her, increasing the distance between the graze of her flesh. She pulled him back. Pressed his hand against her chest.

"Mike," she said. She could feel tears slipping off the side of her face and hear the soft sound of them hitting the bed. "Mike."

Please.

She curled to her side, into him. She clenched his skin in her fingers—his lack of reaction, lack of pain, verifying that this was nothing and that he was nothing.

She pulled his arm again, reaffirming its position on top of her, and she jumped when he yanked it away. He threw it back to the other side of his body and placed it firmly against the mattress.

Carmen looked up at him, at this strange man, and he had not moved his stare from the wall. No, never. But the skin of his forehead was scrunched together, and his eyes began welling with moisture. Not spilling. Never.

She had never thought about it before, but she realized it then. How much he didn't need this: seeing her face, feeling her in bed beside them as if he could feel it back. As if he could.

She wondered why he kept doing this. Why he kept coming back to torture himself. Why any of them did.

She pulled his hand back again, defiant, and wrapped it around the two of them once more.

"Mike."

She looked up. The veins of his forehead were protruding, but he wouldn't move his hand this time. She immediately regretted her actions and lifted his arm, placing it back on his side, out of contact, where it belonged. Still, his face didn't change; his muscles didn't seem to relax.

"What do you want?" she asked, unsure what she meant by the question— whether the answer she sought had to deal more with this moment or the rest of eternity. Though she supposed it didn't matter.

A tear fell from his left eye. The first time since time stopped.

But there was nothing. Was there? Nothing she could do. Everything she wanted would hurt him more—these touches only for her, these shadowed pillow talks, these midnight indulgences. Maybe there wasn't a reason he was here. Maybe there was no message. Maybe he just couldn't figure out how to leave. And she couldn't figure out how to do a god damned thing that wouldn't hurt him further.

But wasn't that how it goes?

She emerged from bed, found a suitcase in her closet, and filled it with mismatched clothes and belongings she didn't consider. She tiptoed into her kids' rooms, woke them from their sleep, and told them to do the same.

All the while, Mike watched her. He didn't move, but his eyes followed her in perfect unison, even when they couldn't see.

An hour later, they were driving, and he was gone. The kids hadn't pushed past their initial inquiries after she denied answering the first; Luca probably didn't understand anyway.

They would suffer for this. This decision would hurt them. Carmen hadn't thought about where they would go or for how long.

But they would suffer.

Mike would leave that house eventually. She was sure of it. He would leave.

And he would be lonely.

The sun rose somewhere. Though between mountains, the view was hidden. But the pink sky and grey trees told that somewhere morning was rising. Carmen looked to the passenger seat: Jamie was asleep now, her head leaned against the window, her body curled beneath her comforter from home. Luca was in the back, asleep as well. Carmen looked at the sky. A few stars—planets maybe— remained. The world was empty, and she had found a road where no cars would pass anyway. Deep enough into the mountains so that five in the morning would have no visitors.

Somehow, within the haze and delirium of the sleepless drive to nowhere, she'd figured it out. Or at least, before the moment passed, that's what it had felt like.

The moon was still present in the colored sky, and she got it now. Finally.

She married a ghost.

But so had he.

So had all of them.

And they would wake up soon. They would find out, too.

TREASURE CHEST

Sean Kilpatrick

Known for his unique and often provocative style, poet and author **Sean Kilpatrick** has numerous writings published or forthcoming, including in *The Boston Review*, *Fence*, *Bomb*, *Vice*, *Evergreen Review*, *Columbia Poetry Review*, *Forever Mag*, and *The Malahat Review*. His novels include the acclaimed *Gil the Nihilist*; *Sucker June*; and, with Blake Butler, *Anatomy Courses*. You can check linktr.ee/seankilpatrick to find him on the Internet venue of your choice.

1.

A former friend tried my trust and locked me in a trunk. Vertebrae hunched against the brim till either element almost split. My whipped bunch of skull fought wood, directed by a panicking spine. The dark became a bigger body inside mine, landscape of bangs wrenched through a keyhole. Oxygen stayed encased, stuffed aloof, clenching along the pulse of this constriction. My skeleton, abridged around an unending dread congealed into thought, lost and grew its skin many times again. At some juncture, a series of kicks began, inviting me to piss a path to freedom. Jostled numb, I could still feel universes bobble in diminishment, an ongoing bruxism. Bottoming electrolytes aged me stiff beyond the use of creams. I searched my many crimes against others for his possible motivation and returned lacking. Perhaps existing was provocation enough. Through the kernmantle key breach I stuck a portion of eye. His beautiful sister was scribbling on herself. I'd only ever confessed affection with stolen glances, skimmed defilements. Bent letters abbreviated her skin. She stirred, dusk till dawn, pupils mowing to and fro in their lids, rows of sight between dreams, picking which one to ride back to her body. No clue from the sheets she graffitied.

All my game overs went with me, crunched in the trunk. History blinked present behind the eyes, a thirteenth tense reedited, baroque composites confined by whomsoever. I placed myself as bait to earn a different life and was left with this one. Mocked by a towering clock on my walk to lunch, every day the same set of integers stood, looming. The computer lab ran on floppy discs and DOS launched button-slugs, neon green digits. Agonadal bunnies shuttled diagonally. We were babies of the strike pattern Sega, sperm count Genesis, debased brains of our brand, surrealist pitch reverberating techno bleeps, colors stroking the wall, trained by strobes to fuck well. We killed sprites, living forever in a scrolling poink of despair on spikes, the boop of hopping left to right, alive inside drugs, chromatic whiffs rubberized within. The controllers sat heavier in your hand, a decayed crustacean. You felt the weight of each numeric hit, the heavy thunk. Dolphins rode their own fluids through the air. A generation bedizened under tinny Engrish, digitized chalk outlines, trippy clog dances, high off undercarriage, noosed on nipple, wept here by static.

The half-finished basement bathrooms of Detroit felt like shitting through the construction of the world, stranded at the abandoned site of it, relief in matching your surroundings out the back. One's imagination had space to let the muscles activate. You felt your movement occur free of chronology, after matter, post heat-death in some zombie galaxy bubbling, interlocked, between dimensions. Then you could flush that happy thought and return to wiping a voluminous while. I only enjoyed the aftermath of food for these reasons. We went on a fieldtrip to some farm up north. Through the fair exchange of smog for manure, a sow lay nursing. I moved to pet its piglet and, having studied a mini-mall version of karate, was able to withdraw my hand before the offended protector smashed me with her snout. She missed and hit her kid, a thick strike marrying fractured jaw to flesh. Her baby fed through death throes. She waddled with it dangling there, caught and mangled worse between her hindquarters, each hoof erasing the remainder. Her nipples became gnashed apart pork, bloody half-moons, red lactate spurting everywhere. The body hung an hour, reflexively suckling, bobbing as she trotted—like a teen climbing some caryatid with its throat slit, millennial iconography. The wrenched tit sagged to mud, still sprinkling blood-laced milk on her litter. The farmer tried to pull it off. No give, wouldn't budge. He returned with shears and, little by little, snipped away whatever he could grab: a tiny hoof unclad and flew, haunch scythed asunder, chest autopsied, spurting metallic dentition. Even the tail potched gone. Just a fetal mouth stayed there, clutched: wretchedly decorative nipple ring abortion. Ain't how you supposed to chew bacon, kids, the farmer muttered. She in a rodeo panic... ham got one greedy suck left, class. Girls cried with the litter. I retrieved its severed tail and yanked it straight. That shit will uncork your butt, the farmer almost sang. Whiplashed by her child's carcass, clogged into multi-axle constipation, she caressed her long-compiled fertilizer instead, the bedded playground strewn with her own private outhouse to miscarry in. I whipped the side dish ear on high and bid her suffer more. That summer, allowed in a slimy, polluted lake outside the city, I bumped into someone, turned to apologize, and was met with a floating turd a quarter of my size. I decided to go through with the apology, thinking fondly of a piece of hardtack the school fed me that continues to obstruct.

The word friend meant whoever interchangeably loitered nearby for an unusual length of time. This friend owned different bodies. I sought people who saw the enormity of our system's flaw and buzzed around it, drunk off the mosquito afterglow. Parasites allowed to organize ourselves outside an organization, we shared leakages, pointing our pointers inward, through to the circular suck from which we'd absconded, and vice versa—teenage observations extending no further than an elaborate game of the dozens, where I discovered how my mother had rolled a flower in her butt till I came out the other side, smoking a ranch dressing cigarette. That bitch held a vacuum over her panties to beat off, scarfing thrush while the engine snagged, throwing off cheeseburger smoke in a halo above the sin. She went blat in her britches, combing peachfuzz areolas. She threw her tampon at the ceiling and I hang-glided alive, rappelling public toilets at the beach, my lifelong grammar in one stench. There was more how to the hustle of speech back then. Style surpassed intent. The strength of a thing said could carry you far beyond the weaker message. I decided whatever shunted art into the holster of a person, that person was less the exception, and pursued the connection of this mysterious end result: the product above the human being designing it, so the phone could rot on its hook. During recess, our lopsided pride lined lunch up and batted it with a binder into the teacher's desk. She was a morbidly obese nun who tore up what I wrote. Every weekend I'd see her holding a sign outside women's clinics. Demanding snacks, we speculated. Stem cell feedbag runny with silent, vacuumed screams and mashed apples we gave the Ty Cobb treatment. Food fireworked from its bag, deep in every crevice the class had. After she fit three knuckles down a girl's throat and was let go, squat tyrant incubated by her own harsh lesson, I posted satirical fliers over school windows, loogieing on the sidewalk as a cop followed me.

Orbiting the abandoned lots of youth, seeking absolution for an unserviceably bereft life, every nightmare petted the same strip of ghetto where I biked myself lost. Nostrums tossed syndromes into trivial remission, health syrups strained a little better than the other joint poisons. To feel different kinds of sick, I drank a drink omnifariously bred to titivate the gut biome and spat scoby on the cement outside my former place of education, eyeing the façade. Peppering demolished jigsaw pieces in my brain, configurations occurred and reoccurred, an attempt to fix how foul things were, why I was turning forty, with no more Mulligans, inside a box. The handyman next door once removed my pants and put me upside down in a trashcan, but no further steps were taken, no real horrors to compare with the isolation tank lifestyle, buoyant in my blood and waste. Not since our first-grade teacher refused trips to the bathroom, unless we demonstrated the many ways in which we loved her more than any parent, could I conjure such warm displacement. The grifter diocese that taught me mediocrities repatriated into a charter school. Down to the coterminous church switching denominations, nothing of these forgone skids had been allowed to persist, proof everything I endured came to repudiate itself before further analysis could reveal the hoax. Their parish drifted, plight to plight, auctioning the security of a like kind, a safety-in-numbers spiel proven close enough correct to buttress wafer-thin curriculums.

We felt like a sleazy sketch of the scene we left, blotted memories of bruises matched and mastered. The band had reached glorious crescendos, halting shy of homicide, staking the life of its crowd, teetering on consequences we were ambivalent to survive. A strobilus of limbs demolished into one serving, swirled over a bloody cone, the rubies in our veins chasing drainward, the residency ripped through our flesh for the length of a generation, garbage disposal kids, jolly slab of an organism smashed together, rioting against the placement of its own cells, going on to cultivate scores of disorders. It was the kind of mosh pit your grandchildren would end up paying for, if you hadn't already decided against ever having any. We planned to inhabit the entire human dynasty of PTSD by the concert's close. Thrashed through opium smoke, lyrics bubbled with tinnitus, the screech outlasting its echo. Afterwards, we remained standing in an empty arena, cursing every unbroken bone. All our worst thoughts born out of one another in a chain, a can-can timed by urination as each leg lifted. There weren't enough victims to go around, wasn't enough rape for the rest of the class. Girls stopped by to spit on our drugs for us, lacing them with their glands' glamour. One had spent detention with us, using a pointer to strip off her uniform. Collared for violating inch-above-the-knee skirt regulations, she took revenge, standing in panties, clapping erasers, drawing dirty drawings on her tummy with the dust. Since age six, I requested to couple with everyone and everything: railings, clothes hampers, pillows put in therapy. Then the copious arraignment of a living girl pranced by and we both shrugged at my zipper as if to apologize. Tumbled door-to-door for Halloween, I went as treasure. They canvassed a rich neighborhood to up our treats. Three men in tuxedos urinated into a grand piano. We left, afraid, because there was another sister my friend's unidentified family had lost down a rain-pooled crack in the street. I requested she turn her first pube in the keyhole. Become extinct, she moaned.

I was stuffed in a tux and sent outdoors because my parents hoped the ghetto would resolve me. Bike-jackers stomped off my training wheels, smashed me babbling, shoes caught between spokes, blood netted into a chain link fence, punched unconscious, then conscious again. Bladder control was an even worse issue. My nose reset twice as oblong. I refused to snitch without teeth. A girl groupie of the gang followed, yanking my waistband, trying to check if fresh laundry might be required. A friend handed over padlocks for brass knuckles, goading me back outdoors. Men in purple work uniforms threw a used condom at us. The trunk was some kind of antique, but they rolled me home from show-and-tell with a pink slip in the hole. No one could piece together why I'd been stored away. Smeared somewhere over the years, a stove door was shut on a swathe of my hair while the homeowners went boating, but this was an unrelated event.

I had a posture that supported anything prochoice. Some girl who personified the perfection of her gender, who I never stopped thinking about, came over to the getting-toward our-twenties-full-of-passive-aggressive-chore-list-notes-because-low-IQ-girls-also-lived-there in-an-unsanitary-party-hole, talking herself into it out of some kind of ironically intrigued politeness, after our date failed. She left insulin in the fridge. I fucked my neck with it, came the material back into an ovoid cove I could crawl into, sketching pictures of her in the slime. For four months, we took long walks across town while she explained my already-acknowledged flaws to me, capping it off with drawn-out erection-inducing hugs she was curious to tease further, with enthusiastic elaboration, so she could press charges. Girls tended to join the larger borg of the culture right after I met them, scraping their aspect across every medium. Too late, I matured proper. Uncountable chill, hate-free adult interactions ensued. Nothing they did mattered, post-coital or otherwise, and they tended to fall in love with me because of that fact, thinking they alone could change us into a gooey myth. I was kind enough to break contact when I sensed that transition, but if anybody had been shitty, even once, I would let her linger a short while, in accordance with her shittiness, not for many excruciating years, as had been done to me, but long enough to be stung for ten minutes, before she went on, always, ultimately, annoyingly, unharmed, informed by formal indifference, to corral herself a sucker. I often stood before the fridge, slapping my own ass in reward, yelling slurs at a week's worth of prepackaged, organic meals.

Sorting through boxes in the garage, I broke skin on a dead possum's jaw, hooked by the scream it made passing. The wound turned worse as I aged around the festering rest. Bosky soffits bled beneath each vessel where the keloid went devoid of value and kept me sick without receipts. Tendril apparitions darkened the opening. Grown gray inside and out, eyesight retained out of spite, shaking to remain continent, a rig of veins skinned just above the surface, I missed awaiting the decades-long jump scare of waking next to a dead loved one, seeing them thumbed off a corner of the world, scraped hollow by god, a noxious thrush you once cuddled, a rind drawn to abjectly resemble the person you had just interacted with, all their individuality cosigned to adjoined graves. Every day was autopsy day, the single happy occurrence, life-wide: touring morgues. Soldier of the blank slate, blind to one's pulse, mute inside pussy walls, recalled by momentum, sheets of fleas with Lyme disease toppings, living a nonstop itch. Whichever repo arm of government recycled my friend's house was kind enough to plop me in the lot where our school used to exist. Hooded men rose from rubble, juggling trikes and rusty craniums that switched species on cue as they regurgitated each other—the recipe for an amenable inferno, my final, most blessed peep show. I didn't have room to clap.

2.

All Ski Mask Summer long I ran into commercial businesses, circumspectly selected a purchase, and paid, grinning. An astonishing lack of vision from the frozen patrons—yet, it was a better time: no handheld intercoms for summoning cops. They only arrived if we walked at night, asking, in a rage, if we were okay. They got out of their cars and felt us up. We strolled on, hours above the idea of a destination. They cuffed us, transported us hood to hood, uncuffed us, drove away, came back, inquired after our status, fined us once more, uselessly. We kept walking. They were anxious about 9/11. We were disappointed it hadn't continued forever. The boots wore off our feet. We left toenails behind in their tongues.

I sat, ambiguously overcharged, threatened with inexplicable FBI investigations and inquiries about prom, posing in a corner of the jail, refusing to blink for eight hours. A trustee stole my blanket during arraignment. Still want it, he asked, menacingly, upon return. I snatched the scratchy, diseased thing, then handed it back. Now we were religiously perplexed. The cell had two climates: freezing and boiling. Ten of the incarcerated encircled us, examining my blanket. Someone unfolded a corner with his sandal, as if testing a dead animal. Don't do that, whispered the trustee. Yeah, I whispered. Sorry, the man replied, after an unknowable amount of silence. The food was okay.

A four-foot-eleven therapist spent the afternoon dropping rocks on my lap. Bopped into a water closet, fingering herself to the pain recited in her honor— advanced astrology tucked into a behavior in the name of some relief wasn't cutting it for most anyone, unless meds could step them into suicide—I talked about movies with her for a year. She learned a lot. Therapists were always a she, even if she wasn't.

'What have you done this summer' was her first assignment. I puked a block of yeast at the beach, shed my back and grew it back, thinned and mole sick. Aimless wandering before useless products between diners murdering us with grease-inspired epic fatigue and synthetic enhancement. We stripped the shit from shrimp dumped on tabletops. A rat slinked down my collar, as if from an immeasurable height, before I could complete a bout of piss. It was found drowned in the toilet, wearing my girlfriend's makeup. The head was staked next to the roach bodies as a warning—to my girlfriend.

You're in possession of a D plus psychology, the therapist interrupted. But a girl with a coat hanger driven through her braids entered the house and curled around me in my crib, whisper-singing hymns, I explained. My first thought formed on the end of them—never too late for a home-skewered termination. I longed to revisit our tryst, escorting her through ghetto glitz locales, including the heavenly Club 500: gunplay video games mean as the pizza, honeymoon incineration, an entombed circuit. Any balloons handed to us would pop on contact.

An entrepreneurially sound single babysitter mom left my diapers brimming. She questioned the validity of a hemorrhage after the slide was misused. Inspecting a two-dollar bill I owned, she handed back ratty singles. Marge Simpson comparisons were made during a bad haircut. You hail from your grandfather's gangrenous lap, untreated due to Christian Science. Last confirmed kill the Nazis notched, ten years overdue, she reminded. Too busy beating off to hear me? And the other side's chromosomally defunct. Roasted through a majority of the community waterslide, I admitted board and card games were for high IQ assholes no one stoned with errant rocks mid-contemplation— triggering the subsequent abandonment of that process. We were taken on trips to the country, fed soda for hours, never allowed a stop to urinate. The mutt traveling with us bit my hand, unprovoked. I began methodically sneaking punches to its hindquarters. As we piled forth, wetting our shorts, the bitch had to assist her disabled pet from the van.

There was a treehouse on stilts built by a drunken ex-husband hoping to cash in on a death. Thirty feet straight up with no rope, steps, or ladder. Exposed as a pussy if unable to climb each wobbly, termite-ridden pillar trammeling the structure half in place, against physics, saddling clouds, I shimmied the topmast, almost dropping out a hole inside the center. We clung to the plywood room, spitting through rain-damaged floorboards. My bottle of Crystal Pepsi circled the opening.

Family dentists couldn't afford Novocaine then. Mine put a boot on the clinking chair and steadied needles between gum line and tooth. I perched, knees risen, defensively postured. Saltwater darted into my head. He smacked me flat and kibbled his drill along the enamel. I ate most of my own ground-down material. Shut up, he echoed, blood round the mouth. Metal seared a third inner ear, staying mid-brain, soaring always near, grown wider than sound (a frequency I can, to this day, eavesdrop on at will). Count to ten while you can, he advised.

I upgraded babysitters to a beatboxer who accidently shattered the chewing end of my front teeth trying to help me dunk a basketball. He organized an accomplished Def Comedy Jam with my action figures to apologize. I dreamt of being bearded, shaving holes in baby fat till pubes sprouted. The principal, scared of a barbate ten-year-old, held his beard whenever he told me to shave mine. Mentally aged next to the Columbine school shooting, I donated every remaining thought, sporting twice the deranged glare of its perpetrators. Their holy plot would prove a red carpet for my kind. One last piece of trash, I implored, spitting in the therapist's eyes, before the police arrived again. She poked me as if launching a barge of shit downriver.

Carlos followed anyone who agreed to play bloody knuckles down the hall, refusing to quit unless the opponent became hospitalized. He'd hurdle from classroom closets, slamming hands. The lenses of my glasses were wrenched from their screws. "These mugs thick…" he repeated, fixing them wrong. His family took us to a fifties-style restaurant with an obese teen for their logo. We popped creamer loosies on the rump of that quaffed gay, flung smoke bombs under a parked car. Many brigades and departments and agencies arrived to wipe us up. Other poor authorities failed at tough love.

A senile woman had been given control over a peripheral quarter of the curriculum. She was little more than the outline of her diaper and resembled Faye Dunaway if that skeleton had been born in a microwave. Her urine could only present itself incrementally, a daylong trickle, till death took the rest, mid-mumble, during an incoherent classroom lecture—years of built-up bladder released, crinkling the adult undergarment past full, twin streams cuffing out her pants, down a swiftly scooting row of desks, students kicking away in protest from the unending fountain our school board voted to instate. They propped her head up with a ruler so the eyes were fixed on the cross. She was completing a treasure hunt for the dead husband who established and abandoned her pelvic distress. We embezzled a bibelot with her title at the top and scribbled sexual horrors.

In one of her many anarchic, unscholarly, wayward classes, students barked assorted discourse. Carlos and I abandoned our incompetent teacher to visit the store, drink a drink, and return, unnoticed, save for my stopping at a window to make the slit-throat gesture at some freshman who owed me five dollars. The freshman, Boaz, had asked to examine the bill—weed trick excuse—and strolled away, as expected. I meant to purchase a crash test dummy for my hatred. Now he had acted as an informant, earning us our first puerile detention for playing hooky from the woman whose arbitrary grading and inability to remain coherent had nudged me out of, gratefully enough, any secure entry to a college.

A black girl named Swastika wheeled her arms at a friend who refused to hump her anymore. He calculated the windmill, introducing a single, well-placed punch. Her father went door to door looking for the perpetrator. A swollen deformation cried behind him, head a whole process unto itself. I recommended ice, claimed not to know my friend, nor his whereabouts. The gang haunting our block pointed my way every time I left the house because random busybody witnesses called the police when they beat me. My first girlfriend's father was of a kind to send industry pals, sirens tooting, past my place every five minutes because I made burlesques about his whore and the downstairs wreck she possessed. The first millennial false accuser regularly begged I film her fermenting with the rest of the lettuce those panties could not obscure.

I got called to the principal's office for turning sideways in my seat during Morning Prayer. The teensy suite had lost a light fixture. Murmuring gloom below a panel gave way to… Carlos! He bounded from the ceiling, jeering bloody knuckles, and broke my wrist in three places. Inspired by such strict guidelines, trained further during a visit to white trash suburbs, returning with a limp, ten pounds lighter, dressed like Lord of the Flies after a negligent week of drugs in an expansive backyard, I envisioned Boazian pronunciamentos. His landline was obtained and called night and day, every imaginable invective recited feverishly. I fired caps against his dog's barking head, permanently disequilibrating it. We tore his lawn apart with a friend's truck, but the grounds were already rotten. A favor had, in fact, been granted.

We assembled into the death squad we were meant to be. Chaplin moustaches painted on our faces—fingers held up in quotes while calling them Chaplin moustaches—we turned desks to face Boaz at every opportunity, followed him home, goose-stepping all over our minority neighborhood. He was too stupid to place a reference or notice much. We fried pennies in a pan and flipped them onto our forearms. Whoever caught one and kept it sizzling in place the longest won, Lincoln's beard branded on. I had ten beards. For freedom. Inside Boaz's bedroom, infiltrating his dreams, fearing no law, no reprisal for my sublime comeuppance (five dollars!) owed and instigated by the inexcusable acts of others,

I emitted a whistling, fricative shriek that lugged us right to hell (where we remain).

My therapist came, belatedly.

3.

The idiot kid who puttered about on a go-cart died at last. Twin hit-and-run drivers rolled him up and down the block like a cartoon recycling its own celluloid. Gravitationally flayed on an abrasive machine of concrete, shoulder and back avulsed intact, he sat upright, in shock, smudged by his anatomy, an order of broken incapable of being graphed, or grafted, arms distending as if adumbrated by god. I pinned a flap of skin with a stick and hid it behind a parked car, to collect later, saving up for Detroit's famous festival of the disinterred. The city disbursed corpses down the hills of its freeway every autumn, a festive type of speedbump, spun floppy, right up to your car, like a petting farm. You could lean out the window and chop down the bodies hanging from the overpass with your hand.

We strapped into elaborate commando costumes and pretend-shot one another. I hid deep in a pine tree till blood blinded me, burrowing under the foxhole, vanishing way past our battle. My friends went indoors and continued living. I laid in wait, preparing an ambush far preponderant to whatever ambitions they'd pursue, a snowballing violence my stillness underscored, all our futures about to be blasted into television static, victims the earth sold back. The backyard scrolled longer than possible that night, ingested by the meter. Crenatures linked fence rust landscapes onward to a state fair where child rappers wore backwards jeans, serenading what we screamed across a patch of bats.

Before Satan went corporate, what little of his fans remained hoped to resurrect the Satanic Panic, sorry to have just missed it. We scooped fish flies, thin-winged pests coating lakeside buildings, minikin pogo sticks with antennae, plucked their tongue-fucked wings, collecting the sediment in baggies, and inserted sparklers so they'd lace a plastic blast together. Stiff clumps of these were tickets for entering underground churches we happened upon. Government-built bunkers meant to house animal mutations stippled the hood, stations for dosing classmates we loved with pheromones, dug visible by bums for space to masturbate in peace. The moldy hunk of human gak I stored in Masonic tabernacles shriveled to next to nothing.

A friend's young mother tanned too much, bra unlatched. I considered decapitating her to further the visual privilege. After pilfering used lingerie during a sleepover, I would avoid the entire toilet bowl, too hard to follow through on a symbol. Satan was yet to flop on the charts and hadn't lost my indoctrination. Led by sibilant, night-voiced specters toward a secret room walled-off under the basement staircase of their house, tunnels revealing other basements, pentagram thoroughfares, I was shown a dog skeleton with a toolbox between its ribs and prayed to these blades at midnight.

11:55

Rob Grafrath

Babe,

Words cannot describe the torture I'll be experiencing in my hospital bed tonight. The dreaded terror awaiting me goes by the innocuous name: *time.*

I have little left before I will have an unimaginable amount of it—time, that is. You think you've got it figured out—how it moves, how it ticks by in its plodding way.

You don't know shit. Nobody does.

I didn't explain my situation very clearly when you visited earlier. I'm better at writing than talking, so I'm putting it all down for you here. Thankfully, they let me have this pad and pen. They have to be careful about what they give to people on suicide watch, but they aren't too worried about me now.

I'm sure you'll read this and maintain that I'm psychotic or schizophrenic or whatever. That's what I'd do in your position. It's genetic, after all. Or maybe you'll assume I'm trying to justify my dramatic shift in behavior with a wild story that nobody would ever believe instead of confessing to some darker truth. Drugs, maybe?

Nope, there's nothing more to it than this: Time… it's *not* on my side. No, it isn't!

Let's start at the beginning. I worked all weekend on that disastrous system restore I complained to you about. It's laughable to think that was the worst of my concerns. My sleep schedule had been thrown completely out of whack after pulling all-nighters with only a couple of power naps to keep me going. I nodded off during our status update call yesterday evening. Jeff insisted I needed a good night's sleep and that we'd reconvene in the morning.

I wonder if they got that piece of shit system online without me today.

I got ready for bed, laid by your side, and stared at the ceiling for a while before I looked at the green-glowing digital clock on the dresser.

The time: 11:55.

I closed my eyes and tried to get to sleep. I knew that energy drink was a bad idea. My pulse throbbed in my neck and my heart hammered in my chest. How long would it take to get to sleep? On one hand, it should've been easy since I'd barely slept the prior two days. On the other, it seems like the more I know I need to get to sleep, the harder it is. I get "in my head" about it or something.

Time passed—half an hour, at least. But when I looked at the clock…

11:55.

Wasn't that what it said before? Or was it 11:35 before? Whatever the case, I was nowhere near Sleepy Town. I rolled over and faced your back. You'd been looking at your phone earlier, but now you were breathing steadily with your eyes closed.

I decided against bothering you to complain about needing *help* to get to sleep. It was my own fault for drinking all that caffeine and messing up my sleep schedule all weekend.

The problems with the system restore started bouncing around in my head. I shouldn't have changed that config file without making a backup. I should've left the database online when I cycled the Windows services. The damn vendor had been zero help—worse than zero, really, since they wasted my whole day making me gather logs before they'd escalate the ticket. Even then, all their engineer would say was they were still investigating.

After at least an hour of mental wheel-spinning, I looked at the clock.

11:55

What the fuck? I was certain that's what it said the last time I looked. I started counting.

One, two, three, four… sixty.

And it was still 11:55. Maybe I was counting too fast?

Sixty-one, sixty-two, sixty-three…

Nice and slow, all the way up to one hundred and twenty—definitely over two minutes. What was wrong with my clock? It was old, but it had done nothing wonky like this before. It might not wake me up in the morning if it was broken. I decided to set a backup alarm on my phone.

Deciding is one thing; doing is another. I couldn't muster the will to pick up the phone and set the alarm. I supposed that I subconsciously wanted to sleep in. Jeff would understand after that marathon weekend. Maybe it was for the best.

I lay there a while longer, alternating between staring at the ceiling, rolling to one side, and rolling to the other. I got up to use the bathroom and considered looking at the clock on my phone. When I got back to bed, the idea slipped my mind.

This wouldn't be the last time something like that happened.

What felt like another two hours went by. By this time, I'd given up all hope of getting to sleep. I stared at the ceiling and waited for morning to come. Maybe some new ideas for the system restore would come to mind.

I found I could count the seconds or do any other mental exercises I wanted, but whenever I got the notion to pick up my phone, go out to the kitchen, or (lord save me) go back to work on the server, I'd never follow through with the action.

With nothing to go by other than my skewed perception of time, I couldn't say how long I lay there waiting for a dim blue glow on the shades to herald sunrise. But after what felt like a full twenty-four hours of waiting, it was still nighttime.

After another bathroom break and another missed opportunity to look at my phone, panic set in. What the hell was going on with me? I wanted to nudge you awake, but I couldn't do it. I wanted to say something if only to hear myself talk, but I couldn't fucking do it!

I've had plenty of time to dream up analogies for this not-quite-paralyzed paralysis, and my best one is this: imagine you're playing The Sims but with your own body. You can only command your sim self to do things in the sleep routine menu. You also can't make it do anything more frequently than you normally would.

For example, you can issue the "roll over" command, and you'll roll over. But then there's a cooldown period before you can do it again. There is no option in the menu for you to look at your phone because you're not in the habit of picking your phone back up after you've decided to go to sleep. Okay, well, *you* are, but I'm not.

The "check the time" command only makes me look at my digital alarm clock, and the time on that clock refuses to change from the increasingly maddening time of 11:55.

My system was frozen. There was no reboot button.

Why 11:55? Wouldn't midnight have been a more appropriate time for me to get stuck in some sort of time vortex? I started trying to get to sleep at 11:55, so that's the time I was stuck on. At least it's a nice symmetric number with the double ones and the double fives.

I waited.

I waited and waited and waited some more. This is where we start to get into horror territory, babe. I laid there, losing my mind for what must have been a month. That's when I got serious about counting.

Sure, I'd counted down minutes and even a full hour at one point, but I needed a firmer grip on time. And so… I counted.

There are eighty-six thousand, four hundred seconds in a day. My first attempt to count that high ended at around one thousand, two hundred. That's when I realized it took longer than a second to mentally recite a number like "one thousand, two hundred, twenty-one."

I switched my approach. I'd count up to sixty and keep a tally of the imagined hour and minute I was on. Starting over again, I counted up to sixty, then told myself it's 11:56. Then I counted to sixty again and declared it to be 11:57. I did this until I had counted for twenty-four hours, refusing to count down the last minute to bring me from my mental clock of 11:54 to the digital demon mocking me with its intransigent 11:55.

Still no sun.

Still 11:55.

But you were still by my side. I'd use the "snuggle" command from my Sim Sleep menu from time to time. Sometimes, you'd wake up and look at your phone to pick a new podcast to listen to. I was happier when you were awake, but a part of me was haunted by the idea that you might be caught in the same time trap.

You'd have no way to signal that you were stuck, too! What if everyone in the world was experiencing this?! Or what if I get stuck in time every night but forget about it the following day? That was an intriguing new nightmare I was reluctant to entertain. There was no way to tell.

The theories that ran through my head about what could've caused this time standstill were wild and varied. You know I've got a lively imagination, and I've had ample time to cultivate ideas. It'd take too long to go through the full details of all my prominent theories, so here's a summary of my top five.

<u>Idea number one</u>: I was imagining the whole thing. My sleep deprivation and hopped-up caffeine-addled mind were fooling me into believing that time wasn't moving. This spat in the face of all the counting I'd done. Time, memory, and perception are strange things, babe. They're simple enough if you take them for granted and don't think too hard about them, but I was thinking *really* hard about them.

How would I know if my current mind was hallucinating memories of having time stand still for what felt like months on end? There's a thought experiment that some philosopher dude came up with where they conjecture that the universe popped into existence five minutes ago. The creating force implanted all of your memories from before that moment into your brain. It fabricated all evidence of all past events. Ancient redwoods were plopped down into the soil. Reminders supposedly written yesterday were forged and stuck to the side of the refrigerator. Dust was meticulously arranged on the dresser. YouTube videos of cats tucking themselves into fish bowls were doctored up for our viewing pleasure. It's a stupid idea, but there's no way to disprove it.

What's a memory? The only moment you can be (somewhat) sure about is the present. When you think back, you have a good idea of what has happened in the past, especially the very recent past, but it's not the same as experiencing that time again. If I can imagine being stuck in time, could I have fabricated a memory of having counted for a full day?

Fuck philosophy, what about science?

Idea number two: probabilistic quantum field infinite multiverse entropy-defying bullshit. You know I'm into sci-fi stuff, so this was a fruitful idea. It's pretty technical, so bear with me.

Here's how it works: I was moving *sideways* through time.

Some magical combination of things going on at 11:55 kicked my consciousness out of our linear time. There are weird relationships between space, time, and entropy. I've heard some interesting pseudoscientific theories about how the human brain interacts with quantum fields. This was all fodder for my imagination.

The position and state of subatomic particles don't exist as fixed and discrete attributes; they're probability fields extending infinitely in every direction. But at the macro level, the probability field resolves to meaninglessness as probabilistic quantum fields give way to classical physics. You're most likely to be where you were in the previous moment, adjusted for your velocity. You don't have to worry about teleporting halfway across the universe at random.

The constant collapse of probabilistic quantum states to precise particle positions as they interact with other particles produces an infinitely branching multiverse (citation: my imagination). Every "tick" of time at the smallest possible measure spawns another infinity of multiverses containing every possible subsequent state of every subatomic particle in the current universe. The only difference between this universe and the one adjacent to it was that one subatomic particle in one location somewhere in that universe is positioned one Planck length away from the same subatomic particle in our universe. Everything else is identical in every way.

"But that's too many universes!" you decry.

"Infinity doesn't care if it can't fit in your puny human brain," the multiverse says. "Infinity plus one equals infinity. Infinity to the power of infinity equals infinity. How many numbers exist between zero and one? Infinity. Deal with it."

Now, imagine laying snapshots of the same moment in time across the infinite universes side-by-side and traveling between them. You'll be able to find a universe where I was in almost the same position as this universe, but my left arm is imperceptibly higher. That's because, in *that* universe, I had gotten the idea to roll over one zeptosecond before the same thought occurred to me in this universe.

Instead of progressing *forward* through the branching trees of infinite possibilities, I was traveling *sideways* through the multiverse, experiencing a seamless reality without time moving on to the next moment.

The neural activity of my parallel universe selves was synchronized with my own, but only for that fraction of a second when I was passing through them. Those versions of me were having typical nights, thinking typical thoughts. I was nothing more than a fleeting half-thought to them—never sticking around in one universe long enough to affect that Rob's behavior. My sideways timeline had one train of thought, and my multiverse of forward-moving timelines had another. At the infinitesimal sliver of time when I skipped through the mind of my forward-moving alternate self, our neural patterns matched. They'd diverge a moment later as I moved on to the next parallel universe. I was on one axis; they were on another.

The idea reminds me of those sculptures made up of suspended shapes you can view from one angle to see one image and then move to another angle to see another image. Maybe the first one says, "Black Lives Matter," then you walk around to the side, and the shapes resolve into a portrait of George Floyd. Both images exist simultaneously yet independently in the same medium.

Confused yet? You should be, because it makes no sense. And although this was an engaging mental exercise, it still didn't give me any ideas on how to escape.

Fuck [pseudo]science! It was time for some goddamn religion!

<u>Idea number three</u>: I was either in purgatory or hell. I died in bed of a stroke or heart attack at 11:55. I would now spend the rest of eternity stuck in the moment just before my death. Maybe I'd be released if I repented for my sins… or some such nonsense.

So, I cast my atheism aside and dedicated myself to prayer. I was sincere too! I probably spent an entire month as a True Believer. I said The Lord's Prayer three hundred times in a row.

Nobody answered.

Maybe I had the wrong number. I tried God, Jesus, Mary, Allah, Buddha, Vishnu, God (again), Zeus, Jupiter, Cronos (god of time), Satan (hoping for a fiddle-related bargain), and Superman (just for kicks). No luck. I even prayed to the goddamn clock.

I'm sorry to prove the "no atheists in foxholes" crowd right, but dammit, this was an extraordinary situation! If supernatural anomalies like this happened more often, there'd be more justification for holding religious beliefs.

So, I quit religion (again). If there was a God, I'd thoroughly pissed Him off by now by praying to all those other gods. They say He's a jealous bitch like that, so fuck Him. Back to sci-fi.

<u>Idea number four</u>: It's a glitch in The Matrix.

"Whoa."

Maybe I've watched that classic too many times, but I kept going back to the idea that such an odd experience could only happen if Elon and Neil were right and we were living in a simulation. My character was glitching out. I got stuck in an infinite loop while executing the "going-to-bed" routine.

This idea never hooked me, though it may be the most reasonable one of the lot. I still prefer the multiverse bullshit over the simulation bullshit.

<u>Idea number five</u>: Shit happens. This takes the prize for my best theory yet. It's the easiest to explain and requires no mental or philosophical gymnastics. The only drawback is that it still doesn't leave me with anything actionable.

There's beauty in its simplicity, though. There's peace in complacency. Shit happens! Fuck it! Breathe in, breathe out. Take a piss or the occasional shit (it happens). Blow your nose. Take a sip of water from a bottomless cup. Sigh. Yawn. Listen for the repeating patterns in the noisemaker app's crickets and peepers. Snuggle.

A few times, you woke up, we kissed, then kissed some more, then had a romp. Those were beacons of light in my unending darkness. It reassured me that at least I wasn't in hell. We even talked a bit, though I could never drive the conversation away from the Sim Sleep script.

I figure about a year of perceived time went by before the next mind-blowing thing happened. I had engaged the familiar "look-at-the-clock" maneuver and faced an unfamiliar sight.

11:56

Holy shit, right?! It changed!

A mix of emotions flooded my mind, while my outward self couldn't react with anything stronger than a sigh. Time moved?! What does that mean?!

I was overjoyed at the prospect of time inching toward dawn, but horrified by the amount of time I'd have to experience before my alarm went off at 7:15. Seven hours and nineteen minutes experienced at something feeling like a year for every minute? That'd be like laying in bed for 439 years! What if time kept moving like this even after I got out of bed and showered? If I'm limited to my usual actions, I'd hit the snooze button!

I waited to see if it would switch to 11:57 within a normal amount of time. After a few counts of sixty, I gave up on the idea that there was something about the particular minute, 11:55, that had me stuck.

I vacillated between feeling defeated and elated. What was once a bottomless temporal pit that I'd be falling down for an eternity had resolved into an unfathomably deep pit that I might actually escape. But I still didn't know what would happen in the morning.

I went back and revised my pseudoscientific theory. I wasn't slipping straight sideways through time but inching forward ever-so-slightly.

Let's cut to the next interesting thing that happened. It was still 11:56. I went to the bathroom and got a drink of water, but I found my cup was empty. That had never happened before. I walked to the kitchen.

Can you imagine how exciting that was? It was like being locked in a cell for a year and a half and then walking out one day.

I tried to break the sim spell—tried to do *anything* other than walk to the fridge. I tried to grab the wall and stop myself. I tried to shout. Instead, I got some ice, filled my cup with water, scratched my ass, and headed back to the bathroom to leave the cup beside the sink.

Fuck.

Well, that was fun.

A year later, the clock flipped over to 11:57. Happy New Minute! Should auld acquaintance be forgot…

Sometimes, the weather would change. At 11:58, a storm blew through. Tornado sirens started going off. We woke up the kids and went to the closet beneath the stairs. After sitting there for maybe a week, we all went back to bed.

And it was still 11:58.

By 12:05, I had a good feel for how long a minute took and mentally mapped each passing minute to a calendar. I'd celebrate holidays and birthdays with vividly imagined parties.

At 12:07, I finished another novel. I call it *Dreams of Rainbow Unicorns and Crushing Skulls*. It's about a teen girl who daydreams about fantasy lands. She gets plunged into the mind and body of a barbarous warrior-king every time she goes to sleep. And when he goes to sleep, he inhabits her body. Imagine the hijinks as they swap back and forth, fighting for control and trying to grasp each other's disparate worlds. I've had a lot of time to outline the scenes and look forward to hammering it out in Scrivener.

At 12:28, we had an unwelcome visitor. The Ring doorbell person detection chimes went off on our phones. There was a loud thump, the sound of breaking glass, and the solid beeping sound of the ADT alarm panel registering an open door or window. My heart raced as I grabbed the bat from under the bed and rushed to the living room, finding a man standing inside our open front door. He pointed a gun at me and told me to drop my bat.

I obeyed.

Part of me hoped that the man was planning to kill me. Please forgive me, but after thirty-three year-long minutes, I was already thinking of ending things.

All he wanted was money or something he could sell. I gave him the cash in my wallet and your purse, and he disappeared into the night. The police arrived. We filed a report. I downloaded the video from the security cameras and emailed it to the officer. After they left, we sat in the living room and comforted each other and the kids for at least a month. Eventually, everybody forgot about it and went back to bed.

And it was still 12:28.

In the following year/minute, after I nudged you awake for some help getting to sleep, we talked about inane topics. This version of us obviously hadn't experienced the burglary, or we wouldn't have had such a carefree conversation. I also found, upon my next trip to the kitchen for some water, that there was no damage to the doorframe or the glass panel next to the front door.

I revised my pseudoscientific theory again. My starting point is the baseline from which all other sideways-slipping was anchored. My personal perceived experience was seamless, but anything occurring outside of my frame of reference was fungible. If I drifted into a universe too different from my origin, the multiverse conspired to nudge me back to my baseline.

This works under the Matrix idea, too, but I still don't like that theory. It's almost too easy. "Welp, the Matrix did it."

My "return-to-baseline" theory was reinforced many years later, at 1:45. Sirens woke you and the kids. This time, it was not accompanied by a tornado-producing storm but by the roaring sound of fighter jets taking off from the nearby airbase.

We tried looking online for breaking news, but our searches timed out. Next, our phones blared with an Emergency Alert System message I'll never forget.

> **The United States is under a nuclear attack. Nuclear explosions have occurred across numerous US cities, with more expected in the coming minutes. All citizens are advised to seek immediate shelter in the sturdiest building available in the basement, if possible. Stay clear of windows. Do not go outside or attempt to flee in a vehicle. If you are in a vehicle, head to the nearest structure and take shelter inside.**

My heart pounded as we clambered into the closet under the stairs. You and the kids were crying out with primal panic. My eyes were wide with shock as my forward-moving mind raced, scrambling for any way to increase our odds of survival.

My sideways-moving mind, however, welcomed the quick and painless death that a direct nuclear strike would bring. Please forgive me.

Panic in the stuffy closet was my life for three entire months. The power went out, then came back on, then went out again. At one point, a bright white light illuminated the gap below the door, but no explosion followed it.

How could my Sim Sleep self return to a normal baseline after that?

Well, unimaginably, we tired of sitting in the closet. The kids whined about needing to go to the bathroom. I looked down at my phone, and the weather app was open.

"It must've been a false alarm," I said. "The storm's passing north of us."

Without further ado, we went back to bed.

Somehow, the multiverse (or simulation) had found a thread that would lead me back into a reality closer to my original universe. Whether this was a blessing or a curse, I couldn't say.

I wish I could say that the nuclear scare was the worst thing I experienced, but it was not. I shared it to give you an idea of the terrors that punctuated my years of boredom. I won't tell you the two worst things that happened. There's no reason to put those images in your mind, and I wish they weren't branded into mine.

By 2:55, I had some very solid plans for what I would do if I ever regained control of my body. I had laid in bed for 180 years…

I needed to end it.

Up to this point, I have been trying to convey the unconveyable. I want you to understand why I would do such a thing. I could not risk putting myself through another night like that.

The shotgun hidden in the closet would be the fastest solution, but I couldn't put you and the kids through the experience of finding my body. I also wanted to make sure you got the life insurance payout, and I wasn't sure if the policy would pay if I committed suicide. On top of that, I wanted to leave you with as clean of a conscience as possible. It needed to look like an accident.

Hundreds of ideas came and went, but I kept returning to one. It'd been a tough weekend, with no end in sight for the system restore. It seemed feasible that I'd have a mental breakdown. I hadn't had a sip of alcohol in seven years, but if I cracked under the pressure, it's not a stretch to imagine that I'd hit the bottle. I'd get my hands on some rum and chug enough of it to get alcohol poisoning. But for good measure, I'd also drive my car off the bridge over Lake Worth. I'd be too intoxicated to suffer much.

The major drawback of this plan was that I couldn't say goodbye to you or the kids or explain what was really going on. It tore at my heart to imagine what my passing would do to the family. But your life would go on.

I was trudging through the 4:47 AM year when the most wonderful thing happened: my alarm clock went off!

I woke up and instinctively hit the snooze button before I realized what was going on. It wasn't 4:47 anymore—it was 7:15?! I fell asleep, babe! Time moved!

I *did not* lay back down, as was my morning habit. I stood there, gape-jawed, looking around and grinning like I had just won the lottery.

"I slept!" I shouted. "I can talk! I have control!"

"What?" you asked, squinting at me and sitting up. "Why are you—"

"I have control! I can move! I'm not a sim!"

You might have asked what I was talking about or whether I had a nightmare or something, but all I could do was press my hands onto the dresser, staring down the clock and counting aloud.

"One, two, three…"

Before I even hit sixty, the clock changed to 7:16.

"Yes!" I cried, tears welling in my eyes. "Oh my god, I'm free!"

I grabbed that green-eyed digital demon that had taunted me for centuries in both hands and slammed it down on the dresser. I lifted and slammed again. The damn thing wouldn't break!

I ducked down and grabbed my trusty old baseball bat, then smashed that plastic piece of shit to smithereens. This diverged from my well-laid morning plans, but it felt *marvelous*.

"Rob, what's going on?" you asked.

I looked over at you, panting. The confused expression on your face paled with fear. You grabbed your phone and retreated into the bathroom, locking yourself in the toilet closet.

I'm sorry about that. I must've looked homicidal—you've never looked at me like that before.

The clock was ticking now. Literally. I knew I had to act fast since you were probably calling 911.

I rushed to the closet and threw on some clothes. They wouldn't sell liquor to a guy in pajama shorts. Next, I needed to see what time Specs opens. I returned to the bed and checked my phone, turning off the god-forsaken noisemaker. 10:00 AM. Okay, that wasn't too long. But there was no way I could stick around at home for three hours after that clock-smashing ordeal, so I pulled open the side drawer and grabbed my keys and wallet.

The dogs barked as I stepped into the hall, turned off the alarm, and rushed to the door.

"Rob?" you called out from behind me with a wavering voice.

I paused with my hand squeezing the cool metal of the doorknob. If I stopped now, I might not go through with it.

"I'll be back," I said without turning around. "I just need to clear my head."

This was a line I had mentally rehearsed a hundred times. I needed to make you believe I didn't mean to leave you.

The one thing I *didn't* say was, "I love you, babe." If I had said that, you'd have looked back on it and taken it to mean that my death wasn't an accident.

Tears stung my eyes. My throat tightened. My lip trembled. I had to outrun the emotion. Keep moving. Don't think. Follow the plan.

I turned the knob. It felt like pulling a trigger. I slammed the door behind me on the way out.

I choked on a sob as I jogged to my car. There was no time for that!

I started the engine, released the parking brake, and backed out of the driveway. As I switched from reverse to drive, I looked back at the house. I regretted it immediately—you were standing in the doorway with your phone pressed against your ear, your face red, your tears glistening in the morning light.

Christ, that's the last time I'd see you after all those years laying by your side. It wasn't right.

I swallowed my sorrow, put the car in gear, and escaped.

By the time I reached the stop sign at the end of the street, I remembered a vital part of the plan. I put the car in park, leaned over, and pulled open the glove box. Out came the driver's manual and maintenance log. Rattling around at the bottom of the box alongside the old ketchup packets and crumpled napkins was an Airtag. I rolled down my window and threw it across the street. Next, I tried to unlock my phone. Face ID didn't work—it wasn't used to seeing my face contorted with repressed ugly-crying. It took three tries for my trembling fingers to type the damn password. I navigated to the settings, found the "Find My" section, and turned off Find My iPhone.

I switched over to the Maps app and searched for Specs. I picked the one closest to Lake Worth, on the northwest side of town.

As I drove, I kept checking the time.

It kept moving.

7:18.

7:19.

It was like a miracle. It was moving *so* fast!

After pulling into the Specs parking lot and finding an inconspicuous spot at the back, I picked up my phone and squeezed it. It had been flashing and vibrating with text messages. If I read what you wrote, I'd lose my nerve.

This was the fucking plan, babe. I couldn't read your texts.

But you already know I did.

> **Rob, whatever is going on, I want to help you. I've never seen you like that.**
>
> •
>
> **You're scaring me and I'm afraid you're going to hurt yourself or someone else.**
>
> •
>
> **The police are here. They say they can get you help if you'll come back. They won't arrest you. You haven't done anything illegal.**
>
> •
>
> **Please come home! I'm so scared! I love you so much, Rob! Please, I love you!**

I pounded both fists against the steering wheel as my throat closed up with a restrained sob.

"Fuck! Fuck, fuck, fuck!" I screamed, then doubled over as my abs and diaphragm clenched in an uncontrollable sob.

You were the weak point in my plan. I always knew I'd back down if I talked to you before I left or if you figured out something was wrong. Why'd I have to smash that fucking clock?

I typed my reply with shaking hands, squinting at the screen through a blur of tears.

> **I'm at Specs on Lake Worth Blvd. I had a suicide plan, but I'm not going through with it. I'm a mess. I can't drive like this. Please send help. I love you, babe.**

I screamed at myself as I hit send. How the ever-loving *fuck* could I throw away my only chance to escape that tortured existence? You already know how— I love you and the kids too much to let you go. Christ, I'd even miss the fucking dogs (even Eleanor).

I slumped over the steering wheel and sobbed until the flashing lights on my dashboard told me that the police had arrived. I got out and put my hands up. My temples throbbed and my chest ached.

They had me put my hands on the car and patted me down, but they didn't handcuff me. A brusque, stocky little woman of an officer talked to me for a bit. I can't remember what I said, but I'm sure I made no sense. I'm pretty sure I told her my master plan because the next thing I knew, I was being checked into the JPS Psychiatric Emergency Center.

Was I a danger to myself or others?

Yes to the former, no to the latter.

Did I have a plan?

Yes, and a damn good one, thank you very much.

These doctors and nurses have so many questions. It's enough to drive you insane if you aren't there already. Job security, I suppose.

So I got a room, and they let you come in and see me. You looked about as ragged as I felt. I held you and cried and apologized for putting you through that shit and promised never to do anything like that again.

I tried telling you I had spent literal lifetimes trying to get to sleep, that it wasn't hyperbole, that I couldn't imagine going through it again. It was nonsense, so you did the reasonable thing and concluded that the pressure from work had made me crack.

The clock by the door said it was 1:35 PM. The sands of time were slipping between my fingers. I needed a new plan. After time had moved at a glacial pace for so long, watching the clock's second hand spin made me panic.

"I need some time to think, babe," I told you.

"Okay, you want me to go?"

"I *want* you to stay," I said, "but I *need* you to go. They won't let you sleep in here with me, and I don't have much time to figure out what I'm going to do tonight."

In hindsight, this was a poor choice of words. You started crying again, incorrectly assuming I was talking about new suicide plans. I tried consoling you, but it didn't work. We kissed. You left.

Time to think.

My plan should've changed when I woke up to the alarm. Trying to fall asleep is when time slips sideways, and successfully falling asleep reverts time to normal. God (or the Architect) only knows if I'm right. Maybe it'll never happen again. Maybe it'll happen one day when I'm eating dinner. All I can do is assume it'll follow the same pattern every night for the rest of my life.

As strange as it seems, I think I can live with that.

People always wish for extra-long lives, and I've essentially been given one. It's an odd, useless, dull sort of life extension, but it's something. It's time I can use to think up stories or solve problems.

Now for the new plan. I should be able to avoid sideways-slipping if I zonk out immediately upon hitting the pillow. They had to have something that could do that in this place.

If psychiatric hospitals served drugs à la carte, I'd have self-prescribed and been on my merry way. I told the doctor that my sleep schedule was bananas and that insomnia had to be the root cause of my suicidality. It was pretty close to the truth, too. I avoided the topic of sideways time—I didn't want antipsychotics interfering with my sleepy time meds.

My two goals:

1) Minimize sideways time by going to sleep quickly

2) Don't make (or enact) suicide plans

A less astute planner may have tried avoiding sleep altogether. I know better. It'd be a short-term fix and would further ruin my sleep schedule. As a long-term plan, it ran counter to goal #2. Sleep deprivation will eventually kill you, though you're more likely just to fall asleep by accident.

They gave me some literature on insomnia and sleep hygiene, which I was grateful for. But not as grateful as I was for the Ambien prescription.

At around 4:00 PM, I talked them into giving me this pad and pen, and I started writing.

At around 5:00 PM, they served a shitty dinner in a tiny cafeteria. I ate quickly (which you know is challenging for me) and got back to writing.

Now it's 9:20, and my hand is cramping up. I'm going to brush my teeth, lower the lights, and glare at the bed. Quiet time prepares your brain for sleep.

At 10:30 PM, I'll ask the nurse for my Ambien.

At 11:00 PM, I'll lie down, close my eyes, and hope for the best.

I can't begin to express my regret for how today turned out. I put you through hell and got myself committed to a mental hospital. This was my first day in 292 years, and I've completely wasted it.

I'm *never* going to let that happen again.

I love you, babe. See you tomorrow (five to ten years from now if I'm lucky).

- Rob

P.S. —

I've decided I should destroy this letter, so they don't read it and find out I've been lying to them. I'm also having second thoughts about telling you these strange truths—nothing good can come of it.

I'll give it a few months of thought tonight.

Enjoy Body Shots? Then check out…

…*Moieties*, the critically acclaimed ergodic occult epic from Elytron Frass, one of the most exciting and powerful voices in outsider literature. *The Book Beat* calls *Moieties* "a formally innovative and dense novel combining science fantasy and occultism." Says Logan Barry, author of *Ultratheater*: "[*Moieties is*] an ero guro dark fantasia set in a sprawling gnostic open world… a relentless, visionary work… And, once it has you gripped, it won't be read; it will be activated." *The Aither* concurs, "For those who appreciate genre-bending literature emphasizing personal reflection through mysticism, spirituality, and violence, [*Moieties*] demands to be experienced."

AVAILABLE NOW EVERYWHERE BOOKS ARE SOLD

Follow the QR code and use Discount Code **BCCM6D7** for an additional 25% off your purchase of *Moieties* direct from Subtle Body Press—while supplies last.

9 7989 85437041